The Pleasant Light of Day

The Pleasant Light of Day

PHILIP Ó CEALLAIGH

PENGUIN
IRELAND

PENGUIN IRELAND

Published by the Penguin Group
Penguin Ireland, 25 St Stephen's Green, Dublin 2, Ireland
(a division of Penguin Books Ltd)
Penguin Books Ltd, 80 Strand, London WC2R ORL, England
Penguin Group (USA) Inc., 375 Hudson Street, New York, New York 10014, USA
Penguin Group (Australia), 250 Camberwell Road,
Camberwell, Victoria 3124, Australia (a division of Pearson Australia Group Pty Ltd)
Penguin Group (Canada), 90 Eglinton Avenue East, Suite 700, Toronto, Ontario, Canada M4P 2Y3
(a division of Pearson Penguin Canada Inc.)
Penguin Books India Pvt Ltd, 11 Community Centre,
Panchsheel Park, New Delhi – 110 017, India
Penguin Group (NZ), 67 Apollo Drive, Rosedale, North Shore 0632, New Zealand
(a division of Pearson New Zealand Ltd)
Penguin Books (South Africa) (Pty) Ltd, 24 Sturdee Avenue,
Rosebank, Johannesburg 2196, South Africa

Penguin Books Ltd, Registered Offices: 80 Strand, London WC2R ORL, England

www.penguin.com

First published 2009
2

Some of these stories have appeared previously in English in *The Dublin Review*, *The Stinging Fly*,
Southword, *Short Fiction*, *Vivid*, the anthology *These Are Our Lives* (ed. Declan Meade), on RTÉ Radio 1,
and in Romanian in *Tabu*, *Noua Literatura* and *Esquire*

The lines of verse in 'Uprooted' are from 'Stoite' by Máirtín Ó Direáin and are quoted by
kind permission of the author's estate. Thanks to Niamh Ó Dhireáin Sheridan

Set in 12/14.75 pt Monotype Dante
Typeset by Palimpsest Book Production Limited, Grangemouth, Stirlingshire
Printed in Great Britain by Clays Ltd, St Ives plc

A CIP catalogue record for this book is available from the British Library

ISBN: 978-1-844-88186-4

www.greenpenguin.co.uk

Penguin Books is committed to a sustainable future
for our business, our readers and our planet.
The book in your hands is made from paper
certified by the Forest Stewardship Council.

Contents

A Very Unsettled Summer

It was a very unsettled summer. The hot weather had come and you tried in the day to walk in the shade and at night slept without even a sheet to cover you. But there were also far too many days of atmospheric disturbance – electricity in the sky and a strange metallic taste in the mouth – when it was oppressively humid and heavy clouds massed very slowly through the long afternoons. People complained of headaches. And as the night came the clouds made final sense and broke, and you felt you had been holding your breath all day and could breathe again, and you went out onto your balcony, if you had a view, and looked across the city at the spectacle of inundation, and you nearly wanted to laugh at the cat scuttling across the road, caught in the white lightning flash, the city lit up and trembling with thunder and wetness, the horizon crackling with electricity. It was quite beautiful.

Unfortunately, coming home one of those humid afternoons, his clothes a damp weight, wishing it would happen, whatever it was, he found a bulky brown envelope in the postbox. He got in the lift, pressed the button for his floor and opened the envelope. On the first of several typed pages was written, in very large letters:

HOW I BECAME A WHORE

He read the first few lines. It was a story, it seemed. He looked at the envelope again and recognized the handwriting. They had been together for several years and he had left her the previous summer. So, now she was writing stories. Well, many people did. And poems. To get their feelings down. He smiled. He did not expect much of the story. But at least it was short, and she had chosen a good title. There was no accompanying letter. Not even a note. The lift stopped.

He stuffed the pages back into their envelope and entered the apartment. He put the car keys and the envelope on the hall table, took off his tie, went to the bathroom and urinated. He splashed cold water on his face, took off his shoes and left them in the hall. He stripped and took a quick cool shower. He put on shorts and a t-shirt and padded barefoot to the kitchen and took a bottle of beer from the fridge. He uncapped it and immediately drank a third of the contents. Then he picked up the envelope, which he had not forgotten while he was freshening up, and took it to the living room.

He arranged the cushions on the sofa, put his feet up, took a pull of beer and read the story.

It went like this: It described, from the perspective of his ex-girlfriend, one of the several times they had split up and him saying a number of banal things over a bottle of wine in a bar. The girl in the story hides her feelings of anger and humiliation and does some quick thinking. She offers the man sex for money. She plays the whore. The narrator is at this point no longer his ex-girlfriend, strictly speaking. She has become a character in a story, as these things happen in dreams, where forms and identities are shifting and provisional. And, of course, he is no longer entirely himself either.

The female character has decided to gratify a fantasy the man has long had. Or she is pretending to do so. In any case, the man takes the bait. They play the game. He has to show her the money in his wallet. They do the dialogue. He accompanies her to her place and admires it, saying business must not be bad.

He was reading eagerly towards the end, anticipating the sex scene, when things got slightly complicated.

They are in her kitchen ('*with all the knives*') and she has offered him something to drink, and he is drinking the red wine, smoking and engaging in the foreplay of pre-sex talk, and the narrator – her – says:

I once prepared a rabbit. I marinated it well in red wine and herbs, then cooked it slowly.

I looked at him and offered him another glass. He nodded readily and I poured. He was excited and edgy. Like a rabbit scared of being caught. On the wrong foot. He was all shiny-eyed, looking forward to fun.

It's coming, bunny. The fun is coming.

The story ended there. He had no idea what was supposed to happen next.

He masturbated quickly. Afterwards, cleaning up, he was a little surprised at having reacted in such a way to words on a page. He resumed his seat and continued drinking the beer and wondered was it the strange weather that made him want to play a hard game of tennis, or break something. He went and got another beer and sat drinking that, still thinking about what he had read. It seemed a good story. Or possibly it was simply that in reading it he had imagined himself in it, and that was what made it good.

The ending was clever, certainly; the conflation of a sexual fantasy and a dance of revenge. He did not recall ever having any interest in the prostitute thing, but imagining playing the game with her, the author, had aroused his interest. Pure sex. None of the personal and situational complications that compromised desire. And maybe this was her way of extending an invitation. Perhaps they would go on to meet weekly, playing the sex game. He checked inside the envelope, thinking he might have missed the note. No, there was no message. He looked out his window, which had a view, and the world looked interesting. The clouds suggested they were not prepared to procrastinate much longer. But they had been saying that for a very long time.

He considered phoning her, but suspected he was being toyed with, like the character in the story.

The humid air was congealing into high solid banks of raincloud.

He swigged the beer down and burped gently. His present girlfriend was coming over later and he did not want her to see the story. He arose and slid the pages under a pile of old magazines and decided he would get rid of it shortly. It would be wiser to forget it.

In the dream he sees her naked. He is unable to move, unable to reach out. She holds herself proudly, her physical beauty heightened because it is now hers to deny or bestow. Her skin glows. A proud strange smile as she turns and walks from the room, leaves him lying on the bed, not knowing if she will return. He does not know if the smile means that he is being mocked or promised his reward.

He awoke next to the naked sleeping body of his girlfriend. It was very early morning and there was little light. The long, slim body beside him was very beautiful, yet it was not the body he needed.

This is very awkward, he thought, lying on his back, aroused, beside a gently sleeping girl, as the morning light began to grow in the room.

He was in the bar where they had first met. It was the day after the dream and he felt that he would meet her. He was not one for presentiments, because that meant feeling something would happen when there is no way to explain the feeling. Like believing in dreams, or horoscopes. But he was looking at the door when she walked through, and he was not surprised, and the division between dreams and waking reality was disturbed.

He tried to continue the conversation he had been having when she walked in but was distracted by her presence. Perhaps she was pretending not to have noticed him. He felt invisible, like a ghost, observing the scene.

He watched her speaking to men and wondered if she was sleeping with any of them.

The hoofed beast of jealous panic rode through him. It told him to physically interpose himself. It told him to get off the ground and fight. It's because I'm drunk, and I had that dream, he told himself, that I am thinking like this. I should go home and sleep.

But he stayed and drank more and late at night they were sitting at a table together. It was civilized and they spoke of people they both knew and matters unrelated to her fictional life as a whore, and when finally they got on to the story they discussed it rationally, as a piece of workmanship. Workwomanship. He told her he thought it was effective, and she smiled the smile he had seen in the dream.

Speaking to her, in real life and not in dreams or stories, steadied him and he found he was able to leave. Probably I took it all wrong, he thought, walking home. He was not interested in being wrong-footed.

She was more attractive than he had remembered.

Unfortunately, he thought, that is how it goes. Relationships entailing obligation entirely kill the flavour of erotic sport. It is never so attractive when yours for the taking.

In the end it did not involve laying down money, as in the story. It happened as these things do, talking and drinking, and moving on to bed.

He had spoken to her on the phone, and then in the taxi to her place he felt sharp and high and energetic, like on the crest of certain drugs, the anticipation that the good news was about to be made flesh.

In the morning, he felt he had got her out of his system.

The second time that this sequence of events occurred he was also sure that he had resolved something. Walking home after the third time, he admitted to himself that it was not so simple.

Another evening, an electrical storm moving in from the west, he mentioned something to her about his girlfriend. She appeared unimpressed by the disclosure, but he was already drunk on her good red wine and had begun to tell her what was happening to him. 'It's not normal. It's like I have this intense physical pressure in my balls all the time, like when you are afraid or get an adrenalin rush and your scrotum tightens, like amphetamines kicking in, except it's all the time practically, and all I can think about is your body, the next time we'll meet, what way I'll give it to you. Like this massive pressure that just has to burst out.'

'Do you know,' she asked, 'Aristotle's definition of pleasure?'

He shook his head.

'Aristotle defined pleasure as the release from pain.'

She smiled – sweetly, he thought – and tapped her cigarette

in the ashtray. They were sitting on either side of a table.

'Let me suck it out of you,' she said. 'I'll drink it down and you'll feel better.'

He groaned quietly and slid down in his chair. She arose, walked over to him, kneeled down and opened his trousers. She rubbed her face against his thumping erection and smiled at him and continued looking into his eyes for the duration of some playful licking, then took it in her mouth, unhurriedly, as if she had never had anything so tasty in her life, and sucked him off and, as she had indicated, drank it all down. Then she got back on her feet, wiped her mouth with the back of her hand, drank a little water and lit a fresh cigarette. She returned to her place at the other side of the table.

He slouched, undone, like she had sucked the marrow from his backbone. He lit a cigarette too, with trembling hands. A delicious, dizzy cigarette.

'Feel better?' she asked, with that smile he was coming to know. He was starting to recognize that smile, and to distrust it.

'I'm not sure. I think so.'

He thought of a rabbit, marinated in red wine.

'So what's it like?' she asked. 'Having fun with someone who's not your girlfriend?'

The question was barbed, it seemed.

'Less domestic.'

Good reply. He wasn't losing his mind entirely. He inhaled the narcotic smoke deeply. The funny smile on her lips did not involve humour, however.

'Better, you mean? More exciting?'

He nodded, exhaled. Now he felt the less said the better. Anything could and would be used against him.

'Did you ever cheat on me, when I was your girlfriend?'

Now it was a scary smile.

'Come on. History.'

'Well, *did* you?' she pressed.

'Did *you?*'

Attack, the best defence.

'I asked first.'

The fact that she had not said no tripped his curiosity. He found the thought that she had been unfaithful without him guessing vaguely painful, and also pleasant, as the deepening of addiction always is. After all, it was not impossible. She had been jealous, clinging, moralistic and endlessly demanding. She had shown all the signs of obsession and wounded pride. But this did not mean there was never a moment, when she was annoyed with him perhaps, when something could have happened.

'Alright,' he said. 'I was not faithful.'

'How many times?'

Not enough fingers. Or toes.

'I answered. Your turn. Did you cheat on me?'

She nodded. 'I felt really bad about it.'

There was a lamp on the table. For a moment he thought it had begun to shake slightly. A minor seismic event, four or five on the Richter, could produce such jiggles. But it was his heart. His head was rocking to the beat of his heart.

The details came a bit too fast for him to take in. There were extenuating circumstances. She was feeling this, she was feeling that. They had had a fight one time. Another time he was away hiking in the mountains, being the man of nature, and she felt abandoned. With that one she'd never meant it to go on. But with the other it was just the once, they hadn't even talked on the phone afterwards, really just a quick thing, you know, over and done with. And that other time she was drunk, the time

8

her handbag had got stolen and she had no keys, and she went to his place, not planning to do anything and, well, if he hadn't kissed her it would have been fine but you know how one thing leads to another. Then there was her ex. Well, that didn't really count, she didn't feel like she'd cheated on him there; it was complicated, they had their own unresolved emotional business, nothing to do with him.

'But I felt kind of bad about that too.'

While he sat listening to her, with the storm moving in from the west, he just smoked and nodded, like he understood perfectly. Didn't do to look like you were being gutted. And, after all, it was all in the past.

He inquired about several details, then she yawned and said:

'History. Anyway, I have to get up early.'

'Can't I stay?'

Something in his voice that should not have been there had said, Can't I suck your titty, like a good baby?

She smiled a professional smile. 'Not tonight.'

The sky broke when he reached the street and he stood in the shelter of the doorway of her apartment building. Mentioning the girlfriend had been a big mistake. He considered going back up to borrow an umbrella. A taxi swished past in the rain, slowly, waiting for him to hail it, but he did not. An umbrella would be a good idea. But if he went back up there he would beg to be allowed to stay. Fine, he was going to beg. Then he remembered how unpleasant it was when women behaved that way with him and he set off quickly through the downpour. For a moment he saw himself from afar, cinematically, punished by the heavy rain, walking down the boulevard of broken dreams. Then he was just a wet man in bad weather, and he was glad when the next taxi stopped.

*

In the days and weeks that followed he tried to compose, from what he remembered of her words, a plausible mental catalogue of her infidelities. It was an attempt to construct a complete picture. He recalled the visible part of their relationship – what they had been doing, how they had been acting at the time – and spliced in these new characters that had poked their way into the story. He ruthlessly reduced himself to one more character, turning up in the intervals between her erotic episodes.

Since setting such a complicated saga down on paper would be conclusive evidence of obsession, he tried to keep the calendar in his head, and was therefore always struggling to get purchase on his material. But he could not refrain from trying to get a grip, because he was terrified by the idea that the life he had lived as if real bore no relation to reality. His memories, he now realized, had been fiction.

He began, for the very first time, to understand her jealousy. It was not a measure of greater devotion. It was simply that she had used her imagination. He had failed to imagine.

So he drove himself crazy, trying to imagine his way back to reality.

It was during this period, when he had reduced himself to a character, that they played out his fantasies. These were for the most part variations on conventional themes. But he also found a number of ways to get the hit that had not previously occurred to him, and in addition she came up with a few of her own, which both excited and unnerved him, because he had been with her for a long time and had had no indication. It was a bit like watching your wife getting fucked by another man. The edge of pain was the edge of pleasure, because in such moments he was both himself *and* the other man.

This meant, however, that the jealousy never left him. The

only time his existence did not seem to be on shaky ground was when he was inside her. He kept having to return, to subdue the anxiety with his flesh, as if by having her beneath him he could fuck the wildness out of her. As if, by having her ride above him, and come again, he could finally satisfy her. It went on like that through the summer. There were very hot days, and electrical storms, and such insistent precipitation that rivers burst their banks and you could watch on television the houses of the country people being washed away in the floods. God had promised he would never drown the whole world again, but there were no guarantees that you were not going to get it on an individual or municipal level.

One evening, lying in a sweet fog of alcohol and the nearness of her skin and smell, he noticed it dangling from a hook on her bedroom wall. He had just asked her, 'Do you think we're perverts?' and she had said, 'Well, you are. I'm just being helpful.' He was surprised he had not previously paid closer attention. It was a very plain rag doll – too ugly to be a child's toy – sewn together from coarse sackcloth. It had two distinguishing features. It had a couple of funny rabbit ears. And it had a little cock and balls. More attention had gone into the latter equipment than anything else. The penis was a little red stick, in the erect position. The balls were out of scale, but gathered in anticipation.

'What,' he asked, pointing, 'is that?'

'That's my Bunny!'

She said it like Bunny was a special friend of hers.

'You're a bit big for stuffed animals.'

'A Bunny isn't for a little girl. Every girl gets a Bunny when she gets hair on her cunt.'

Bunny, she explained, had been brought to her by a friend

who had visited an island in Indonesia. As a joke. She could not remember the name of the island. There were a lot of islands in Indonesia and Indonesia was a lot of islands. The story was that the women of the tribe each had one of these rabbit-men, which they kept near their beds so as to keep their men in order. The genital equipment was to keep the male inexhaustibly virile, while the ears were to keep them docile and prevent straying. He asked her how the men kept the women under control and she said she did not think it was that kind of tribe. The men had everything they needed and the women resolved their differences in a sisterly fashion. He took a drink of red wine and lit one of her cigarettes.

She got out of bed and took Bunny off his hook and gave him a squeeze. He winced. That is, the man winced, not the rag doll, obviously. The red wine was getting to his guts. She gave Bunny's little wooden pecker a kiss and put him back on his hook. She got back in bed.

'They don't stick needles in it or anything?' he asked.

She laughed and reached out and gathered his balls and gave them a little squeeze.

'Silly!'

A giant crow was settled on his chest, ripping his heart with its beak, and he sat bolt upright and the bird flew away and dissolved in the ceiling and he saw the doll on the nail. He got up, remembering that Christ's path to crucifixion was called his Passion. The word passion meant suffering. That which must be passed through. Something was wrong with his guts. She was sleeping with just the hint of a snore, and in a dry flash of lightning her features, as she lay facing the open window, were silvery-white. He quietly pulled on his clothes and made it to the street. He walked for a little and in the coolness felt better, briefly. Far skies crackled and rumbled, as the storm pressed in slowly from across the western plain beyond the city. A jet of puke exploded from him, neon-orange beneath a streetlight, as the turbulence shook the trees and the sheet of rain hit the street a distance away and accelerated towards him. In seconds he was drenched by warm water. The world went liquid. The sky was liquid and his insides were liquid, sloshing forth as he walked. He barely bothered to lean over, for it was instantly washed from him. He could not count the times he spewed as he pressed homewards through the deserted streets. He was weak and incredulous. He had not eaten or drunk so much in the past week. Impossible waterfalls of puke. Either it was an illusion caused by the rain or he was hallucinating. Finally, as he approached home, there was retching, groaning, heaving and what he supposed was bile. There was battery acid in his mouth, and the sky was shaking and crackling as the centre of the storm came closer. Fireworks were going off by the time he put the key in the door to his building. Lower, a sharp pain pressed his bowels. He got inside and made it to the toilet. More explosions of fluid. He was just a bag of shit and puke, at the mercy of corporeal spasms. He finally fell into bed, weak and fevered. He had very bad dreams involving giant rabbits and tiny men.

To help himself recover, he wrote a story. To be the author rather than a character. He had read something I had done called *Scenes from an Uzbek Bordello* and felt I would be a receptive reader, though he admitted he was disappointed with aspects of the result. The first pancake of the batch always sticks to the pan and must be scraped off, I told him, flicking through the pages. I read it as we drank vodka and grapefruit juice with big clanking ice cubes, sitting in my kitchen on a hot clear afternoon towards the end of summer, and when I had finished I told him

I thought I could use it, if he didn't mind. He told me to go ahead. I got up and fixed us another couple of drinks.

'You know,' I said, 'it reminds me of how Nabokov got the idea for *Lolita*. He heard about this monkey, or ape, in the zoo in Paris. I suppose it was Paris. They gave it a sheet of paper and a crayon, to see what it would come up with. You know the very first thing it drew?'

He shook his head.

'It drew the bars of its cage.'

'Really?' he asked, sitting up straight and taking interest. 'You think this is in the tradition of Nabokov?'

'No,' I said, shaking my head. 'I was thinking more of the monkey.'

His life with his girlfriend, after his period of instability, or fuck-frenzy, whatever you want to call it, returned to normal. They had good times. They liked each other very much and they had interests in common. They went to the cinema together, took walks in the park, cooked new dishes, talked about books and films and made love unhurriedly. The lovemaking was just one more of those good things they did, and was a connected and natural part of those other things, and left him feeling clean and whole. And he was glad he had ridden out the madness and left it behind.

It is the nature of addiction that the craving lies dormant in every cell. Sometimes he would see a woman in the street and the old drug would buzz in his blood and his vision get muddy and mean. Then he would remember Bunny, hanging from his hook. Although it would be an exaggeration to say that this brought him to his proper senses, it did at least give him pause.

The weather cleared. The electricity and precipitation moved on to torment another part of the planet, and the section of sky he lived under enjoyed the clear sunny summer that had long been hoped for. People had their picnics and barbecues, their trips to the beach, their mountain views.

Everything seemed to be going well. Unfortunately, when he was in his car one day, at a set of lights, on his way to take care of one of those trivial matters that must be attended to unless life in an urban metropolis is to unravel, his phone rang. It was his girlfriend. Choking with tears, she demanded to know the truth. Just the truth. She had found something he had written, read it and reached a certain conclusion.

So that was the end of that story also, the walks in the park together, and all the rest of it.

My Secret War

I have kids of my own now and live in the centre of our nation, where its heart beats strong and true, and sometimes it is hard to remember the life I left behind. I am reborn, but the born-again have first to pass away.

I died that summer night, when Intelligence came.

I was just minding my own business, as they say. I had made a couple of house calls, dispensed a batch of raving little Buddhas that let you dance away your cares. My wallet stuffed with cash, I turned right, away from the water, into my own quiet street. My backdrop was the glittering dinosaur-tooth Manhattan skyline, minus the incisors. The cars on the Brooklyn Bridge were moving strings of lighted beads. Two men in black suits, identical in height, as if they had been made in a factory somewhere, walked toward me through the hot night. They both wore shades.

'Mr Robert Culper?' said one, as the second produced his badge. 'What appears to be the problem?' I asked coolly, as if I was in a movie. They even gave me time to examine the badge. 'Take it in,' said the second. 'Yes, and think about it,' said the first. Their faces were completely expressionless. Beneath the yellow streetlight, frowning, I looked at the logo, and read aloud the motto:

ANNUIT CŒPTIS.

And the needle was already in my arm.

*

When I regained consciousness I was blind. A hood was over my head. My throat was parched and my head ached. My hands were cuffed behind the chair I sat on, and my feet were shackled to the ground.

The badge was the last thing I'd seen. Beneath the words ANNUIT CŒPTIS was an eye, enclosed in a triangle, and beneath the triangle was a second motto: NOVUS ORDO SECLORUM. I found this comforting, somehow. It told me these guys were a very special unit.

From time to time someone would pause outside my cell and I would hear the scrape of a slat being pulled open. The first time, I moved a little to let them know I was awake. Then the slat scraped shut and the footsteps receded. The second time, I cleared my throat. And so on. I waited patiently. Eventually I had to wet myself, and later on I fainted, from thirst I think. But I'm not criticizing anybody. They have manuals to follow.

After days of being chained and hooded and marched about I was put on a plane. When we landed the hood was removed. It appeared to be somewhere tropical. An island, perhaps. Or maybe just Texas. Anyway, it was very hot and we were kept in wire cages, outdoors, and all wore orange jumpsuits. There was a roof to keep the sun off and a mat to lie on. A bucket for water and a bucket to go to the bathroom in. The other inmates were mostly Arabs, I think, dirty sonsabitches with beards. Pretty soon I had a beard too. We weren't allowed to speak to each other. I wouldn't have spoken to them anyway, in case my captors got the wrong idea. On the first day I'd shouted out to the guard that I was an American citizen, and they dragged me out of my cage by the heels and worked me over in the sunshine. It was hell, getting the shit beat out of me. But they had a job to do and I respect that. It made me a better man, in the end.

The interrogations were very repetitive. They'd ask lots of normal stuff, then throw in an Arab name, and I'd say I didn't know him, and sometimes it would be a guy at my neighbourhood kebab place, so they'd have to hang me by my arms for a while. Which is a lot worse than it sounds, by the way. It was my own fault, because I had an attitude back in those days, and when they brought me back for another round I told the interrogator where he could find Bin Laden. I told him he could find him on top of his mother.

So they threw me in the hole. A windowless cell that made you nostalgic for your dog cage. Stress positions, heavy-metal music, sleep deprivation, the dogs, the beatings, more interrogations. I'd heard of the water-torture thing, so I told myself, relax, you're in the hands of professionals. Still, there's something about being trussed up and feeling like you're drowning, especially when you're all shaky after a spell in the hole, that makes you shit your pants.

Then they dragged me back to the dog cage and left me there to stew for a couple of months.

Then they threw me in the hole again.

And so on.

It didn't start to add up until the day the regular guys turned me over to ANNUIT CŒPTIS and I was brought before John, my final interrogator. The black suit, the expressionless face behind the shades. He sat behind a massive desk, the ANNUIT CŒPTIS emblem on the wall behind him, and informed me that he was my final stop. John had very short blond hair. Very short, but he had managed to make a parting in it, which is practically impossible with hair that short, and perhaps pointless. But it scared me too, such determination. For the first few moments he said nothing. He looked at me. I shrugged. I shifted in the chair. My chains rattled when I shifted in the chair.

'It can go one way or it can go another. I'm your last stop, Mr Culper. Robert. Can I call you Robert? Please, call me John.'

I thought to ask if I could call him Johnny. But then I had an image of him attaching electrodes to my nipples.

He pointed at the emblem on the wall above his head. The eye in a triangle. 'See that?'

I nodded.

'Know what it means?'

I shook my head.

'Means you better look out.'

This was after an eternity in one of those stress positions. My feet had been chained to the floor, and my hands chained to the floor, behind my feet. You couldn't stand up. You couldn't lie down. Then the satanic music. In the dark.

'It means, just because you can't see us, don't mean we can't see you.'

He rose from his seat and walked around the desk and leaned into my face. 'That's how people used to feel about God. You don't believe in God, do you, Mr Culper?'

Sweat was rolling into my eyes.

'I believe in the possibility of . . . um . . . a cosmic force . . . um . . . an all-transcendent . . . um . . . an entity beyond human . . . ah!'

He bitch-slapped me forehand and back, warned me verbally against trying to put over any 'fruit-cocktail' religion on him, then returned to his side of the desk. He resumed his seat and took a deep breath. He indicated again the emblem above our heads.

'NOVUS ORDO SECLORUM. What about that one?'

I shook my head.

'Means we're moving into a new era. A final battle. With an enemy elusive as smoke, that knows no borders, that cannot be seen or pinned down by conventional means. An enemy as insubstantial and as all-pervasive as evil itself. And how do you fight such an enemy?'

'Bomb the shit out of them, I guess.'

'That's a good start, Robert. We have the toys, and we're going to use them. But what you need to understand, in order to lose your chains, is that munitions are the cruder half of the solution. For what profit us to hammer them with depleted-uranium ordnance abroad, and yet lose the fight at home?'

'John, I dealt some pills and stuff, but I'm as patriotic as the next guy. I'm not a terrorist.'

He paused for a moment, drumming his fingers on the table. Then he leaned forward, the hard stare behind the shades. I was two little dolls, reflected in the lenses. He pressed a button and the lights began to dim. He leaned forward and recited slowly, emphasizing each word:

'The sun will swell up and engulf the earth. But long before that happens the oceans will burn off as steam and the earth, becoming tired of its journey, will be slowing in its orbit. The days will become very long indeed. The whole thing has an expiry date on it, the whole human venture.' He leaned back again. 'Recognize them words?'

I nodded. I felt I had heard them before. At my birth, or tripping out on mescaline, the TV in the background tuned by chance onto one of those religious shows.

'The Bible?'

He shook his head. 'No. These are your words.'

I was busted. An icy tremor passed up my back, tingled across my scalp. It was as if he could read my dreams and tell me what they meant. The pieces of my life floated loose in the sky, and he could pull the pieces down, reassemble them, judge them, label them.

He pointed to the all-seeing eye. 'NOVUS ORDO SECLORUM. Some people are losing faith in our mission, just as it enters its crucial phase. We cannot vanquish the enemy without, if we yield to the enemy within. The job of Intelligence is to locate the rot and excise it before it spreads. You are the rot.'

He pressed another button and a screen rose out of the desk. A porno movie began to play. The production values, the lighting and so on, were very poor. A guy was whipping a girl with a belt. She was blindfolded, kneeling, ass in the air, her hands tied to something on or near the ground. He unties her. There's some fucking, some sucking and so on. Then I saw the guy's face.

He was me!

'Um,' I interjected. 'This puts me in a bad light. It was at the request of this lady, actually. People in stable relationships, they sometimes have trouble expressing their needs to their partners. I'd had two, three pills and a quantity of vodka and Mad Bull, so here we are a long time after the sun went down . . .'

There is a noise, wind in the microphone, ripping, rumbling, and the image shudders. The man gets off the woman, moves out of frame. Light fills the room, overwhelming the image. It becomes a sheet of white. Morning has broken, presumably. You hear the disembodied voices:

MAN: HEY, TAKE A LOOK. ONE OF THE TWIN TOWERS JUST EXPLODED.
WOMAN: OMIGOD!
MAN: NO WAY THE FIRE DEPARTMENT IS PUTTING *THAT* OUT.
WOMAN: WHAT HAPPENED!!??

MAN: DUNNO. LOOKS LIKE IT BLEW UP. MAYBE IT WAS THE WIRING OR SOMETHING.

WOMAN: WHILE WE WERE FUCKING LIKE DOGS!

MAN: WHAT'S THAT GOT TO DO WITH IT?

WOMAN [*begins to sob*]: IT'S JUST . . . ALL THOSE POOR PEOPLE . . .

MAN: HERE, GET AWAY FROM THE WINDOW.

The curtain falls back across the bright morning and the room reappears. The naked man and woman walk back into frame. They sit on a sofa. He has a little pot belly. Her tits sag. They both look grey and bloodless and tired. He passes her a cigarette and lights it for her, then lights his own. They smoke for a while, then the man removes the condom from his reposing member and throws it toward the camera. The man looks straight at us.

MAN: HEY, LOOK, IT LANDED ON THE TV.

WOMAN: AND US, GOING AT IT LIKE PIGS!

MAN: PIGS, DOGS. CAMELS, MAMMALS.

WOMAN: THIS IS THE END. THE END OF SOMETHING. CAN'T YOU FEEL IT?

MAN: WE GOT A BOTTLE OF VODKA LEFT AND TWO PILLS. I SAY WE KEEP ON GOING.

WOMAN: YOU TAKE THEM. I DON'T FEEL VERY WELL . . .

MAN: I FEEL LIKE I'M IN ONE OF THOSE GOD-ZILLA MOVIES, KNOW WHAT I MEAN?

WOMAN: ALL THOSE POOR PEOPLE . . .

The frame shudders to another explosion, the woman screams.

MAN: NOW WHAT THE FUCK?

The naked man gets up and walks to the window. The picture disappears again.

MAN: YOU'RE NOT GOING TO BELIEVE THIS.

The picture resumes, the man enters the frame.

WOMAN : WHAT?
MAN: THE OTHER TOWER JUST EXPLODED TOO!

The woman gets up, covers herself with a blanket, sits down again, sobbing into her hands. The man lights another cigarette, pops a pill and washes it down with a pull from a bottle.

MAN: I GUESS IT WASN'T THE WIRING.
WOMAN: WE'RE BEING PUNISHED.
MAN: WHAT GOES AROUND . . .
WOMAN: STANLEY IS A GOOD MAN . . .
MAN: WHO THE FUCK IS STANLEY?
WOMAN: THE GUY I'M MARRIED TO. STANLEY!
MAN: OH, YEAH, STANLEY.
WOMAN: IT DOESN'T SEEM RIGHT, US HERE, WHILE, YOU KNOW . . .
MAN [*taking a pull from the bottle*]: LOOK, THE WAY I SEE IT, THE WHOLE HUMAN VENTURE HAS AN EXPIRY DATE ON IT ANYWAY. LIKE A CARTON OF YOGURT. I MEAN, IF YOU ARRIVED FROM OUTER SPACE AND LOOKED AT US, WE'D LOOK LIKE A GANG OF MONKEYS SITTING AROUND IN THE ZOO, EATING OUR OWN SHIT.

WOMAN: YOU CAN'T COMPARE HUMAN LIFE TO
A CARTON OF YOGURT.

MAN [*passes her a cigarette, lights it for her*]: THE END OF
THE WORLD IS A SCIENTIFIC FACT. I DON'T MEAN
THE PLAGUES AND WAR AND OPPRESSION. I
MEAN, THE SUN IS SWELLING UP, DID YOU KNOW
THAT? YEAH, SWELLING UP. IT'S GOING TO ENGULF
THE EARTH. BUT LONG BEFORE THAT HAPPENS
THE OCEANS WILL BURN OFF AS STEAM. WE'LL
HAVE OUR INFERNO RIGHT HERE. IT WAS ONCE A
LITTLE COOLER, WHILE WE WERE RUNNING
AROUND GETTING THE HANG OF BEATING EACH
OTHER WITH BONES, LIKE IN THAT ONE MOVIE,
WHAT'S IT CALLED? THE ONE WITH THE MUSIC.
NOW IT'S A BIT BIGGER, ANGRIER. THE EARTH IS
SLOWING DOWN IN ITS ORBIT. IT'S GETTING TIRED
OF THE SAME OLD JOURNEY. THE DAYS ARE
GETTING LONGER. THE DAYS WILL BECOME VERY
LONG INDEED BEFORE IT'S ALL OVER. THIS IS JUST
A FORETASTE. HERE, I KNOW A BREATHING
EXERCISE FOR THIS. IN. OUT. IN. OUT . . .

WOMAN: SOMETHING'S GOT TO CHANGE . . .

MAN: I'M GETTING A SURGE. FUCK, THAT'S
GOOD. STARTING IN MY FINGERTIPS, WASHING
OVER ME. UUUUGGHHHH!!!!

When the screen went dead and the lights were back on, I sat
there in my shackles, exposed, under the blond glare of
ANNUIT CŒPTIS, beneath the all-seeing eye. I didn't even
shrug. I didn't want to hear the clank of my chains. It was
becoming clear. While Stanley was in his firefighter's uniform,
making the ultimate sacrifice, I was rapping on the end of the

world with the help of a pill which cost about thirteen bucks.

'And ANNUIT CŒPTIS was onto me the whole time . . .'

'Intelligence is everywhere.'

To underline the point the guards entered the room and beat the shit out of me. Then they dragged me down to the hole and chained me in a stress position and put on the music. After maybe a day they unchained me and gave me a blanket, and just as I was falling asleep they hosed me down with cold water. I don't know how many times that happened. Stanley visited me that night, in his firefighter's uniform, covered in white dust from head to toe, floating above the ground in a halo of pale light, and to a death-metal soundtrack he revealed to me that the banners of the crusading army were unfurled. It was marching forth to meet the barbarian, to trample out the vintage where the grapes of wrath were stored. He saw the palaces of Babylon burn with phosphorus flame, their rivers run with blood. The defeated soil would be ploughed with salt, the pregnant beasts of the field would bring forth monsters. Village elders would have pages from the book of democracy rammed in their gullets until it arrested respiration, while their volumes of laws were piled high and torched in their holy courtyards. Their refugees would be scattered down burning roads, the survivors dispersed like chaff on a smoking poisoned wind. From the hills of Jerusalem to the mighty Himalayas, their sacred places would be defiled. War all the time, and everywhere, until the final defeat of Terror. 'The people who did this are going to hear from us,' Stanley revealed. 'No way, air power like ours, we take a running kick in the nuts from a bunch of camel jockeys. Their daughters are going to be blowing our sailors for the price of a sandwich!' I started sobbing, at the apparition of Stanley, at my own unworthiness, and the guards came in and began to work me over, and Stanley got a few kicks in too, and I tried to say thank you each time, but I did not have much of a voice left.

We were on the plane, descending, back to earth, back to America, to the beginning of my second life. John was sitting next to me, by the window. I was wondering if I'd get a suit too, and the shades.

For several weeks they had been preparing me. I had moved away from the dirty Arabs and into a kind of apartment more suitable for an American. I had a shave. I was fed pepperoni pizza and allowed to watch CNN. Stanley hadn't been joking. Much had happened in the two years I'd been out of circulation. John said I could get out if I agreed to work for them and I told him I was ready now to fight for Freedom.

John had not spoken since takeoff, but as we banked into our approach path the sun came through the window behind his face and he turned to me and gave me my instructions:

'Listen up, Bob. We're taking you to a suburban location. This will be your home, and in time you'll find yourself suitable employment. You will be dropped at a corner and will proceed to a church yard sale down the street. You will approach a wholesome-looking woman of childbearing years. She will say, "How you doin'?" Got that straight?'

'"How you doin'?", yeah.'

'And you will respond with "Great, thanks, how *you* doin'?" Got it?'

I nodded, repeated it, with the stress in the right place.

'Then she'll say "Real good" and you'll say "Fine day" and she'll say "Mighty fine."'

'Mighty fine,' I repeated.

John went quiet and he turned to the window as the jet took

aim at the runway. We were losing altitude fast and I swallowed hard to bring my hearing back.

'And then what happens?'

He turned and regarded me from behind the shades. 'I can't reveal more than that. Take your cues from the lady.'

The features of my country were reasserting themselves. The highways like mighty rivers, flowing in both directions. The underpasses and overpasses. The endless commerce of vehicles, their metal and glass shells glinting in the sunlight. The shining towers of the financial district of a city. The strips and malls and parking lots of the suburbs, the rows of suburban homes, and a vast brown plain beyond. Some of the houses had pools in their backyards. I was heading for barbecue country. Men in shorts and baseball caps flipping sizzling steaks and burgers with the right hand, holding a bottle of beer in the left, while they shot the shit with other male Americans. Perhaps there were wives in the picture, and children. This was the birthright I had squandered, and I was being offered a second chance.

A limo with tinted windows met us on the tarmac, and within minutes we were cruising through some nice-looking burbs. John handed me an envelope. It contained an address written on a slip of paper, a wallet containing cash and cards, and a Chicago Bears keychain with a set of house and car keys. My mission was to blend in and never mention anything about the orange jumpsuit. If asked, I had been hiking in Alaska.

The car stopped. John threw the door open and I got out and looked around. The sun was shining pleasantly on the houses and their lawns and trees and mailboxes. I could see a gathering further down the street. It was the church yard sale.

'Good luck, Bob,' said John. 'You might not see us. Don't mean we can't see you.'

This was his farewell. He pulled the door closed and the limo drew away, almost silently, and I watched it grow smaller, round a corner and disappear. I was on my own now. I checked the address on the slip. I was standing at the end of my own driveway. *Culper* was written on the mailbox. It was a strange way to come home, but it looked like I had a car too, and I felt good about the future.

I approached the church yard sale, nervous about blending in. People stood in groups talking, kids ran around. The scene was extra bright and colourful, like a Hollywood picture, and everybody was smiling. There was a little billboard. Little black plastic letters spelled out the lesson:

LIFT UP YOUR TIRED HANDS, THEN, AND STRENGTHEN YOUR TREMBLING KNEES! KEEP WALKING ON STRAIGHT PATHS, SO THAT THE LAME FOOT MAY NOT BE DISABLED, BUT INSTEAD BE HEALED.

Heb. 12:12

I got a visual on the operative I was to contact. I admired her cover. You'd never have guessed she was regular Intelligence, never mind ANNUIT CŒPTIS. She stood behind a stall with home-made pies and cookies and muffins and brownies, wearing a tasteful print dress. Maybe it's not polite to call a lady plump, but she certainly filled it. Her hair was straw-coloured. She wasn't wearing make-up. It wouldn't have worked on her. I could see her hauling herself out of a station wagon with big paper bags of groceries.

I gave a kid a quarter for a little plastic cup of lemonade and drank it down, watching her from a distance, getting nervouser. Then I walked up, checked out the pies, normal as could be. She gave me a big smile.

'How you doin'?'

My heart was going like a jackhammer. I managed to smile back.

'Great, thanks. How *you* doin'?'

'Real good.'

'Fine day.'

'Mighty fine.'

I paused, looking at the pies, waiting for a cue. I could feel the sweat coming out on my forehead.

'You new in town?'

'Yeah, well, pretty new. Just got here, in fact.'

'It's a fine community, real good folks.'

I looked around, unsure what she was telling me. I was still pretty suspicious of the set-up, I guess. I decided to just act natural. I pointed out my house. She said she lived a block over. Her name was Martha. I bought a cherry pie.

Her thumb was pointing straight at the symbol on the dollar bill, clear as day, as she handed me my change. I looked up at her, expecting a further signal. She was cool as could be. A real pro.

'Three dollars,' she said. 'Change of ten.'

I put the change in my wallet. My hands were shaking.

'See you around,' I said.

'Have a nice day, now.'

I went back to my place. I checked the mailbox and, sure enough, a letter awaited me. I paused in the driveway. They'd given me a Pontiac Pilgrim, a good sturdy car. I opened the door. It smelled of having been freshly cleaned and there was only a few thousand on the clock. Then I went up to the porch and let myself into my house. I put the cherry pie down on the kitchen table and opened the letter. It was from the bank. I had a mortgage, but the terms were very favourable. I checked out the cupboards. I had what seemed like a lifetime's supply of cans of Bumble Bee Tuna and Betty Crocker Pancake Mix and Gatorade and the freezer was full of meat for the barbecue.

It was a nice three-bedroomed place, big enough for a family. The drawers and closets contained fresh new clothing, in my size, folded and stacked. I went into the backyard. I was a little disappointed not to get the swimming pool. But the basement had a pool table.

When I had reassured myself I had the power appliances to take care of the yard, I sat down at the kitchen table and took out my wallet and examined the dollar bill. I beheld what I had, in the course of a lifetime, failed to see. What Martha had shown me.

On the right-hand side, a pyramid. And the apex of the pyramid was the triangle, containing the eye. Below the pyramid, the words:

NOVUS ORDO SECLORUM

And above it:

ANNUIT CŒPTIS

I put the dollar on the table, sat back in the chair and gazed a long time through the open door into the backyard, at the leaves in the trees, glimmering and trembling in the sunlight of a perfect evening, and I had a revelation of the interconnectedness of all things. I had been blind. But now I could see, and my second life on this earth, as an active operative of ANNUIT CŒPTIS, began.

Two days later Martha and her mother stopped by with a pie to welcome me to the community. It was a real pie-eating town and I was soon putting on the pounds I'd lost in the dog cage. When I met Martha in the supermarket soon thereafter, both our shopping carts loaded with goods, I praised the pie and she invited me to her bowling night. Whenever she gave me a cue, I took it, and shortly we were talking about getting married. She said I was a good steady guy, all any girl could want, as she ran her hands through my thinning hair. She said a lot of nice things about me and I didn't argue, ever.

Years have passed and sometimes it is hard to remember my life was not always like this – the kids on their bicycles on the sidewalk after school, or me in the bleachers on Saturday evening and Bobby Jr dressed up in his first baseball uniform. It makes me proud as hell when he swings that little bat and connects and sends that ball sailing over their heads. Bobby is eight, he's the oldest, then there's Jim, who's five, and Lisa is three.

I belong to a single-cell organism called Bob-and-Martha. We meet other units called Sam-and-Arlene, Roy-and-Sally, Henry-and-Priscilla, and as we play bridge and send each other signals, glancing over the cards, I wonder who is an operative and who is not. I have my suspicions, but say nothing. The cameras are everywhere these days. There's one behind most mirrors. I'm pretty sure the televisions do not just give us information, but are monitoring our living rooms. Cables go everywhere and every phone call, every purchase with a card, is information into the central database at ANNUIT CŒPTIS. You fill up for gas, the card tells them who and where, and how far you expect to go. Our cell phones have GPS. We manoeuvre around a coloured map, monitored by satellite.

I occasionally glimpse an operative – the suit and shades – turning a corner, or in a car passing in the opposite direction. One night I was watching basketball on TV and I saw John there, as the camera panned swiftly across the spectators. He sat there coolly, while around him the unsuspecting crowd went wild.

Sometimes the woman who lives next door washes her car,

in her shorts, gets lots of foam going on the windshield. But there's no point jacking off behind the curtain, even if I was still that kind of man, because Martha has her channels. Arlene doesn't know the score or else it was a set-up, but I believe last week she gave me a come-on. We'd had a few whisky-sodas and I had slipped out onto the porch to join her while she had a smoke. She complained about Sam, said he was 'absent', and leaned close and put her hand on my leg. And I just said, 'Arlene, I think we better go in now, it's getting cold out here.'

In the evenings, after the kids are in bed, me and Martha might drink a bottle of beer on the porch, listening to the crickets. A flag flies over our tranquil lawn, for our brave men and women in the service. Beyond our island of peace, far beyond, a crusade is being waged, and I know that terror bides its time, just out of sight, beyond our borders. And I know, equally, that evil lies in every human heart, awaiting the faltering of our vigilance. Sometimes Stanley visits me in my sleep, covered in the dust of the fallen tower. We mostly talk about football games and he never brings it up, about me balling his wife, for which I am grateful, and he occasionally says things that encourage me. 'Keep paying your taxes, big guy – we're smoking those sand-niggers.'

Yes, we sit on our porch and listen to the crickets. There is no need to say too much to Martha, because she knows already. She finishes her beer and says, 'Don't know about you, honey, but I'm all beat,' and I nod and follow her into the house. While she's on the can, I lock the doors and switch off the lights. I look in on the children for a moment, sleeping peacefully, and there can be nothing more beautiful than that. Then I use the bathroom and wash my face and brush my teeth and get into bed beside her.

'Honey,' she says, 'don't forget the PTA meeting tomorrow.'

'Sure thing.'

'You know?'

'What?'

'I'm thinking we should try that new diet. The fruit and high protein one Roy-and-Sally were talking about. I mean, don't take it wrong . . .'

'What?'

'We're both getting a little bit tubby . . .'

The way Martha's been swelling up, in a couple of months she can join the circus.

'Maybe we should just buy a bigger bed, honey.'

We both laugh. Martha's a good sport. She can take my little jokes. We roll toward each other and there is the wet sound in the dark as our lips slap together. Then we roll apart and sigh. We are so close to each other, it is hard in such moments to believe in the evil, the terror, of the world. It does not seem true. And yet the struggle depends on people like us, on our quiet work.

'Goodnight, honey,' she says.

'Goodnight, hon.'

'You Believe in God?'

Thomas could feel that the back of his neck was burned. He closed the door of the hotel room and took off his baseball cap. He stood still for a moment with the cap in his hands, examining it. It had been new and white that morning when he had left the hotel and now it was dirty. Whether it was pollution from cars or fine desert dust, he did not know. He put the cap on the bedside table, alongside the book he had picked up at the airport. He sat on the bed and removed his shoes. His feet were sore.

He spread out the map of Cairo fully until it covered a large part of the double bed. The streets were a dense web of fracture lines before his hot eyes. The area he had walked was only a tiny section of the city. It hardly seemed possible that such a place could exist. Twenty million people, living hand to mouth.

He had walked along the Nile, northwards, then veered east from the river into dirty backstreets where barefoot children called out to him, extending their hands for money, so many of them, and he had looked away in shame. He had grown tired, hungry and thirsty, but was intimidated by food stalls and hole-in-the-wall restaurants where he could comprehend neither script nor numerals. In the end there was nothing to do but to return to the centre, where it was easy to be a tourist.

The map of the city stared dumbly back at him. He had walked among the poor and it had not been interesting. He could not make it mean anything, like a story he could tell to somebody else. He slowly folded the map back into a neat rectangle and set it beside his cap and the book.

He undressed to shower and looked in the mirror. The sun had turned him into a clown. His reddened face and arms clashed madly with his grey-white torso. It had never been a body to admire. Cycling and swimming had kept his muscles strong but he remained blocky and overweight, unable to shed the stubborn flesh. He showered, then lay down on the bed, covered with a sheet, and picked up the book. He had bought it on impulse, attracted by words such as 'wisdom', 'mysticism' and 'ancient' on the back cover. He opened it at random and began to read of a philosopher called al-Ghazali, who had analysed the passions, one by one. If improperly indulged, the passions lead to perdition. The devil enters the human heart through the senses, the imagination and the carnal appetites. The devil enters through words – the use of the tongue in conflict, lying, mockery and flattery. The devil enters through the passions of anger, hatred and jealousy.

Thomas read several pages but could not concentrate on the words. He put the book aside. It was medieval, all that talk of the devil. He closed his hot eyes.

He was lost in an infinite city. Small boys surrounded him and put their hands in his pockets and he had to push them away. Other times they tried to help him, to give him directions, but he could not understand their language. His shoelaces kept coming untied as he walked.

He woke with a jolt, certain he was late for work. In the first moment he did not know where he was. Then he saw the baseball cap, the map and the book. He propped himself with pillows and picked up the remote and brought the screen to life. A number of the stations showed Arabic music videos and he stopped at one with a very beautiful singer. It was tame enough, her stylized gestures of longing, and yet it was clear that she needed a man, and could not wait. He uncapped a bottle of duty-free whiskey and poured a good holiday-measure. After a few drinks he turned off the television. He was hungry. He had not eaten since breakfast.

The street was altered with the coming of night. There were old people, young people, couples hand in hand and parents with small children. The crowd overflowed the footpaths and the cars in the street had to nudge tentatively through. The windows of the fast-food restaurants and ice-cream parlours and tea shops were colourful with bright electric light and their doors were wide open to the busy street. Thomas moved through it easily, the whiskey glowing in his belly.

It was listed in his guide book, the restaurant-café. But the door was locked and a sign in English said it was closed for refurbishment. He peered through the window. Several middle-aged men – writers, intellectuals, perhaps – sat at a table, talking, as in a silent film. When he turned, a man was standing near him. Thomas had not noticed him approach. The man was bald and paunchy and had a moustache, and he was smiling.

'*Sprechen Sie Deutsch?*'

'*Nein.*'

'*Nein!*' repeated the man, laughing. The laughter made his eyes small and bright. 'You are looking for something to drink?'

Thomas hoped it was not on his breath. 'No.'

'I have very nice perfume shop. Come see.'

They shook hands. Introduced themselves. Thomas and Muhammad. Thomas explained that he did not wear scent. For your wife or girlfriend, said Muhammad. I do not have a wife or a girlfriend, said Thomas. Maybe you will have one very soon, said Muhammad, laughing. Just come see. No obligation.

Thomas allowed himself to be led through a narrow alley. It opened unexpectedly into a broad courtyard where men sat at tables beneath big trees, sipping tea and coffee, playing back-gammon, smoking water pipes. The transformation was extraordinary. An island of peace, after the noise of the street, which he had thought inescapable. There must be many such places in this city, he reflected, but they are hidden from me.

Muhammad nodded to the teenage boy who had been mind-ing the shop, and led Thomas inside. The walls were lined with mirrored display cases containing bottles of scent. Thomas saw his face reflected everywhere as bottles were placed before him and he was invited to smell them. One he liked more than the others and he put it on his skin. He bought a small quantity, feeling extravagant to be buying perfume at all.

Muhammad invited Thomas to have tea with him in the courtyard, and again left the shop in the care of the boy. Muhammad ordered flower tea. Thomas ordered black tea and a water pipe. Muhammad said he himself was not allowed to smoke, and put his hand on his fat chest above his heart. *Haram.* The water pipe was brought and a boy came with a tray of live coals and picked them out with tongs and placed them on the foil on the bowl of the pipe. Thomas exhaled the thick clouds of cool pale smoke upwards into the dark air. From other tables came the murmur of talk, the bubbling of other pipes. Muhammad was inquiring about Thomas's job, and Thomas was saying that it was not such a satisfactory job, not such a satisfactory life in general.

'You believe in God?' asked Muhammad, gently dropping sugar lumps into his tea of flowers.

The smoke stimulated Thomas's heartbeat. His hunger had

subsided and he had regained the edge the alcohol had dulled. He became aware of many things at once. He was aware of the conversations taking place around him, the men at the other tables, the kind of people they were. Voices came through an open window from a house above the courtyard. What had a little earlier been strange was now being disclosed. He saw ordinary lives. And yet the scene retained a note of distortion, as if people he had known for a long time had simultaneously appeared in unusual dress. He sniffed the scent on his arm. He forgot his own pale flesh.

'Yes.'

'You know the five things you must do if you are Muslim?' asked Muhammad, looking into his cup, from which steam was rising.

Thomas shook his head.

'I will explain,' said Muhammad, stirring.

The first pillar of Islam was the declaration of faith. Muhammad said it first in Arabic and then translated. No God but One, and Muhammad is his prophet. Then there was prayer, five times a day. Fasting during Ramadan. The pilgrimage to Mecca. And, not least, there was *zakat*, the giving of alms.

Muhammad explained that he set aside a proportion of his profits for the needy. He would walk into a poor neighbourhood, knock on doors and hand over envelopes containing money. You did this, but did not talk about it afterwards or say how much. It was between you and God. You did it for others, but you did it as much for yourself.

'Do all Muslims do this?'

'Those who believe. But anybody can take this step. Even you.'

Thomas wanted to give. He wanted to give love to a woman, to care for her completely. But this had not happened.

'Thomas,' said Muhammad – pausing to raise the glass to his lips and sip – 'there is always something we need to buy, some place to go. Our money is never enough. Our time is not enough. And so we try to grip it in our fist, hard, like this, and doing this is our life. But when you give, you are free. You become rich. You understand what I am saying?'

Thomas nodded. He heard the rattle of dice across a backgammon board, the wooden click of counters being moved.

As though he had been handed a key and a door had swung open before his eyes, it was revealed. It was no longer a riddle, how that immense city could function in the face of such poverty. The people who lived there were united by a religious bond. The knowledge of living under a common mortal sky. Giving – that was what broke the spell of the world.

'Muhammad, I think this is a good thing to do.'

'How much money is not important,' said Muhammad, shrugging. 'It is between you and God. Important is to begin. I can also bring you to mosque, show you. You have *jalabaya*? Not important. Afterwards we can go my home, eat real Arabic meal.'

Thomas nodded. He saw his new friend leading him into neighbourhoods of litter, open sewers, barefoot children. Saw the dispensing of useless wealth.

Thomas left twenty minutes later, when his water pipe was exhausted. He paid for both of them, and because he was with Muhammad the waiter did not try to rip him off.

He decided not to stop and eat at any of the fast-food places. He was a little hungry, but that was not important. He liked the feeling of being hungry without having the need to push food nervously into his mouth. Perhaps he would skip breakfast. Some fruit juice only. They would not recognize him when he went home. He would be another man.

Lying on his hotel bed, his heart beat fast and he was very awake from the water pipe. He picked up the book again, and on this occasion the words were perfectly clear. He read again al-Ghazali's description of all the ways the devil entered the human heart, and this time it spoke to him as a simple but systematic analysis of the ways in which a human being could poison his own existence. Through the carnal appetites, through lies, through ambition and the desire for wealth.

There was an intimate relationship, he read, between acts and the dispositions of the soul. Or, to state it differently, between external observances and the spirit in which they are undertaken. Good character is strengthened by right action. Almsgiving should be performed out of a desire to obey God, and from a sense that the goods of the world are of no account.

Giving, an act that was between you and God, could free you from your insatiable worldly nature.

And he read of the Sufi, ascetic wanderers on the holy path. The traveller needed the guidance of one who was further along the path. The disciple followed his master implicitly. He should be passive as a corpse beneath the hands of the washer of the dead.

The next day, Thomas visited Muhammad in the shop, among the rows of scent. The boy brought them coffee on a silver tray and Thomas told Muhammad of his intention to give *zakat*. Muhammad smiled. 'Nobody is pressuring you.'

'No,' said Thomas. 'This is something I want to do. For myself.'

They arranged to meet the following day to decide what was to be done, then Thomas broke his fast. He had not eaten solid food for over twenty-four hours. In an ordinary neighbourhood restaurant, he pointed at what he wanted and gave a small banknote and received change, and the man at the counter smiled at him, as did the other customers, because it was not a place where tourists went. He ate crushed beans with bread, standing at the counter. The beans were served in a blue plastic bowl, and he cleaned it with the bread, and he felt well after eating this meal. Then he went outside into the noisy street, feeling part of the city, feeling he could lose himself in it and be safe. The sun that shone on his face, the same sun that shone on them all, was the sun that allowed the plants to grow, that had made the food he had just eaten. The sun itself now ran in his blood and was part of him.

Muhammad was standing in front of his perfume shop the following morning. They shook hands and he was ushered inside again among the mirrored walls and bottles of scent.

'Wait one minute, I get coffee,' said Muhammad.

'Don't trouble yourself, Muhammad.'

'No trouble! For me, no trouble!'

But when he returned several minutes later, he did seem troubled, and when he had set down the tray before Thomas he took a handkerchief from his pocket and dabbed at the sweat beading and running from his forehead.

'I am fat, ha ha! Bad for heart!'

Thomas was not sweating. He did not even feel hot. Muhammad was now talking quickly. 'What did you see? Nothing! Sleeping! Aha, very good, I wish I can sleep more. But I must work! I have family! And your Arabic, how are your numbers? One, two, three. *Wahid, itneen, talaat . . .*'

Muhammad counted to ten, making Thomas repeat the words after him.

'Aha. Good. You are very good, pronounce-ation not bad. Well.'

41

Muhammad rose and walked over to a black plastic sack and rummaged through it, extracting small pairs of trousers, jackets and sweaters as he spoke.

'Tomorrow is very good to see orphans. You come back here tonight, seven o'clock, we arrange transport. We go together, tomorrow. You see for yourself how happy will be the orphans, and grateful. You can take picture of you with them.'

Muhammad handed Thomas a little jacket. 'Good quality,' said Muhammad. 'Just because they have no parents, don't mean I give bad quality. These cost twenty-five *giné* a piece, but I know the man and he give me them twenty *giné* a piece.'

Thomas examined the jacket. It was new. A tag hung from it. He had foreseen walking into a poor neighbourhood with his mentor, knocking on doors, handing out envelopes to the heads of needy households. Now he was buying clothes.

'I'll take twelve pieces.'

'Fifty pieces here. Why not all fifty?'

Thomas calculated. 'I'll take fifteen.'

'You have the money now?'

Thomas handed over three crisp notes.

'Thank you,' said Muhammad, putting the money away. 'Thank you for helping the people.'

In the street, walking back to his hotel, Thomas began to ask himself why it should have made any difference to Muhammad whether he bought twelve pieces or fifty.

Another man was waiting in the shop that evening. Muhammad introduced him as Sayeed. Sayeed's car keys were in his fist and his fist rested on his knee. The pointed end of one key, the one for the ignition perhaps, projected out of his fist between his index and middle fingers. Sayeed was tall and thin and slightly stooped, as though he had been waiting too

long for something that did not come. Thomas declined
tea.

Muhammad could not accompany Thomas to the orphanage
the next morning, he explained. He had to work. But Sayeed
would take him there, he would see how happy the children
were. It was in Giza, so he could go on to visit the pyramids,
or even the pyramids at Saqqara. In fact, Sayeed could take him
anywhere.

'I don't want a tour.'

'No problem, never mind, I understand. You don't like noisy
tourist place. You can go to Fayyum. Oasis. Very many farmers.
Palm trees. Very quiet place, very nice.'

'Muhammad, I don't want a tour.'

'Price the car, only one hundred and fifty *giné*, all the day.
Hmm?' said Muhammad, raising his eyebrows. 'It's good for
you?'

Thomas looked up from the ground and saw his own reflection. He looked at himself between rows of bottles of
perfume. His bloated pink face, his strange reddish hair. He
visualized himself standing up and leaving quickly. It was clear
to him now that the next morning there would be a problem
about visiting the orphanage and the clothes would already
be 'delivered'.

'No. It's not good for me.'

Muhammad and Sayeed exchanged glances. Muhammad said
something in Arabic. Sayeed shrugged in sad resignation.

'Maybe special price,' said Muhammad. 'Because you help
the people.'

Thomas said nothing.

Not a problem, said Muhammad. Sayeed would deliver the
clothes to the children; he lived in Giza.

'Do what you want,' said Thomas, standing up.

'Thank you! Thank you for helping the people!'
Thomas nodded and left.

Thomas stopped into a kebab shop and fed himself properly, angrily.

Wherever you travelled in the world, no matter how strange it seemed, an inevitable sameness forced its way through. People smiled at those who handed them money, despised those who had none. There were no miracles any more. No shortcuts to redemption.

I am a fool anyway, he reflected, for wanting to buy it like that. For wanting it cheaply. He recalled the moment when Muhammad had mopped his sweating brow and said: 'You have the money now?'

He wiped his mouth and tossed the soiled napkin onto his tray.

He walked back to the hotel and went to his room. As he entered, he saw on the bedside table a baseball cap, a map and a book. The cleaning woman had straightened up the room and the objects were arranged in an orderly fashion. He closed the door and sat down on the bed. He stayed that way for a long time, staring at the dark screen of the television, in which his own face was reflected.

He took off his shoes and lay down on the bed and closed his eyes.

The Alchemist

Pablo Conejo crested the scrubby Andalucian hill and beheld the valley below, green in the low evening light. The stream would provide water for his sheep. A ruined church stood by the stream. Its roof had long ago collapsed and a tree had grown up between its walls. It would be a good place into which to herd his flock.

As if reading his thoughts, the sheep began to spill over the crest and to flow down the hillside, their individual shadows lengthening across the land.

I am leading the sheep, thought the boy, and they have got so used to me they know my ways. They know what I want even before I know it myself. But perhaps it is I who follow the sheep, who know their own needs.

When the sheep had drunk from the brook, and Pablo had drunk too, upstream of them, of course, and they had settled for the night under the stars in the ruined church, Pablo lit his candle and read from a book.

When he was too tired to read, he blew out the candle and listened to the peaceful stirring of his flock. He watched the stars for a time, and then fell asleep.

They had been standing outside their humble home, the day Pablo broke it to his father about his desire for a wandering sort of life, sleeping beneath the stars and so on. The old man thought about this. He took his cap off and wiped his brow with a hand rough from labouring in the fields. He looked across their stony hectares, towards the horizon, and, after some reflection, said:

'Listen, son, we all feel like that when we're young. It's part of growing up, to think that happiness lies somewhere else, in something new. But, you know, the women here are as good-looking as anywhere. You should choose one you like and stick with her, and you can have a happy life and children of your own.'

'Father, I wish to travel and see other villages.'

'You may think it's a cliché, Pablo, but people really are the same wherever you go. They're motivated by pretty much the same urges. Sex and money mostly, and seesawing between a desire for stability and a desire for novelty. You're at the novelty end of the seesaw right now, and I just don't want you to end up disappointed. The only people around here who travel are shepherds. You meet them in isolated places if you go walking and the batteries are going on their transistors. The last one I met asked me to light his cigarette, but my lighter wasn't working either. He probably waited another two days for a light.'

'If the only ones who wander are shepherds, then I too will tend a flock. I must follow my own path in life.'

'I'll tell you one thing about sheep that makes them smarter than us. They know every day is the same. You can walk them this way and that way, but it makes no real difference to them. All they care about is food and water. Humans have to walk down a lot of roads before they sense any kind of a pattern emerging. One day you'll end up back here, and I'll be saying, Told you so.'

'I'm not going back to college.'

Seeing there was no point talking to the boy, old Mr Conejo went out and bought some sheep. Two days later he stood on the roadside and wished his son luck on his travels. Along with the sheep, his father presented him with a small leather purse.

'Here's three gold coins I found in a ditch. Perhaps they'll help you out of a jam someday.'

'Thanks, Dad.'

'Listen, Pablo, I know you don't think much of my opinions, but there's something important you should know about shepherding. Shepherds do not "wander" per se, but mostly practise transhumance between summer and winter pastures, and most grazing places are traditional property of nearby villages. The long-distance driving of sheep too, from pasture to market for example, follows well-defined routes. I'm just telling you this because I don't want you getting in any trouble.'

Still, Pablo did get in a fair bit of trouble. Other shepherds would come running long distances across hills, shouting and shaking their sticks, and he took a few beatings from landowners.

He woke before dawn in the ruined church, having had a very strange dream. Perhaps it's a sign, he thought. But he did not know yet what the sign signified. Only that it was pretty definitely a significant sign. I should really find me a Gypsy and get it properly interpreted, thought Pablo. That was quite a dream, and it's worth giving it a go.

He got up and began to rouse the sheep. Some of them did not seem pleased about having to resume their wandering, but they were getting to their feet. That's strange, thought Pablo, they do not wish to rise, and yet they do, with very little prodding. Our destinies are as one. It is as if they know what I want before I want it myself. We are all just part of nature, like the rocks and the stream and the stars.

The morning sun was red as Pablo set to the open road.

God was everywhere, in the sunshine and in the flowers and in every bit of dirt on the roadside. These were just the physical manifestations of the masterpiece that was creation. Pablo possessed some sheep, a wineskin, a book and a jacket. He did not even have a change of underwear. But he was living his dream.

The road is full of dreams, thought Pablo, and that is what makes life interesting, the feeling that a dream might come true. Then he remembered hearing that an old Gypsy woman in the nearby town interpreted dreams.

Just as well I remembered that, thought Pablo. Otherwise we would have missed each other. I would have gone on to another town where the Gypsy woman does not live, or perhaps there are no Gypsies at all, and I would have missed an opportunity to get my dream interpreted. I wonder if it is not perhaps significant that I remembered in time?

The sheep continued down the road, towards the town.

It is as if they know where they are going, thought Pablo. It is as if they are leading me rather than I the shepherd guiding them. As if we are all part of a mysterious Force.

'Hello,' said Pablo.

'Hello,' said the old Gypsy woman. 'What do you want?'

'I wish to have my dream interpreted,' said Pablo. 'I want to know what it means.'

'You'd better come in, then.'

She led Pablo through a dirty corridor to a small room at the back of the house, open to a courtyard at the rear of the building. Most of the furnishings were very old and dusty but there was also some hippie gear, such as coloured beads hanging in the doorless doorway and brightly coloured textiles decorating the walls. She also had the Sacred Heart of Jesus, a bottle of water from Lourdes and an assortment of Blessed Virgins from the Iberian peninsula.

'Interested in a camera?' asked the Gypsy. 'Straight from the factory.'

'No thanks.'

'It's not stolen.'

'No.'

'This stuff is fresh in from Morocco. Go on, give it a sniff. Look how sticky it is.'

'I wish only for you to interpret my dreams.'

The Gypsy woman sat down at a small round table and invited Pablo to seat himself opposite her. Pablo recounted his dream. She listened attentively, nodding from time to time.

'In my dream I'm with the sheep and this young child appears. I don't like strangers turning up and worrying the animals, but in this case the child is small and they allow him to frolic among them and seem to enjoy the company. Well, this goes on for a long time, the child and the sheep, and then the child walks up to me smiling and takes my hands and transports me to the pyramids. The pyramids of Egypt!'

'I know where the pyramids are.'

'Then, as we're standing looking at the pyramids, the child says to me, "If you come here, you will find the treasure." Just as he is about to show me the treasure, I wake up.'

'Well, dreams are the language of God. It's a symbolic language. I don't think the sheep symbolize anything, though. I think that bit is because you're interested in sheep and spend a lot of time with them, being a shepherd. Probably they were baaing in your sleep.'

'But how did you know that I'm a shepherd?'

'The smell isn't as bad as goats, but it's pretty pervasive.'

'Oh.'

'But the other part of the dream, about the pyramids, that's symbolic. God is telling you to go to Egypt to find the treasure that will make you rich.'

Pablo thanked the woman, paid and left, unimpressed by her interpretation. It struck him as a little too obvious and simplistic.

Where the town dissolved into the hills, with a good view over the sea to the south, Pablo sat and read his book. But there were too many people with strange Russian names on the first page. If I ever write a book, thought Pablo, I won't introduce more than one character every three pages. That way the reader can get used to the new person and will not confuse them with any others. I'll make the characters very distinct and significant to the story. I won't have characters who turn up for no reason, the way they do in real life.

An old man had appeared beside Pablo, picking at his teeth with a piece of stick. The old man cleared his throat but Pablo put his head deeper in the book. He wanted to read and did not want to have to make conversation with any old men.

In my book, thought Pablo, if a new character appears you'll know it has something pretty important to do with the destiny of the central character. Even if the protagonist does not real-ize immediately that the new character is significant, the reader would have to be really slow not to get it. Yes, thought Pablo, if I write a book I'll make it easy on people who have learning disabilities. And it will have big print so that even people with thick glasses can read it.

The new arrival sat down beside Pablo. Pablo pretended not to notice, even when the old man cleared his throat again and this time spat a raucous gob of phlegm. How annoying, thought Pablo, pretending to read.

'Mind if I have a sip of your wine, young fellow?'

Oh no! thought Pablo. A dirty old wino!

Pablo passed him the wine sack and the old man squirted the liquid down his throat, pressing the sack greedily until he had to take a pause for breath. He arrested the flow expertly, without spilling a drop. Pablo frowned into the pages of his book.

'What you reading there, sonny?'

Pablo sighed and rolled his eyes a bit and showed the book to the wino.

'Young fellow, this book just repeats the lie of the world. Restates it in dramatic terms. You'll get discouraged if you read that kind of stuff. Don't get me wrong, it's an elegant piece of literature. But uplifting it's not. It's full of characters who believe in the lie.'

'What lie are you talking about?' asked Pablo.

'That we are not responsible for our own destinies. It suggests that we're ruled by fate, that we can't choose which way to go.'

'Not me,' said Pablo. 'I wanted a free life on the road so I became a wandering herder of sheep.'

'Good for you,' said the old man.

'Where are you from?' asked Pablo.

'A universe far, far away.'

Probably, thought Pablo, he's one of those Romanian Gypsies. Well, at least he didn't pretend he's Italian.

'It was nice talking to you, but I have to get along now and look after my sheep.'

Pablo watched with displeasure as the old man helped himself to the wine sack. This time a dribble went into his white beard, staining it pink.

'If you give me one tenth of your sheep, I'll tell you how to find the treasure.'

Pablo sat down again. It was his turn for a blast of the vino. The old man was dressed very strangely, Pablo observed, and his beard was of prophetic proportions. It would be best to hear him out.

'The Force is strong in you, Pablo. You must follow your Destiny.'

'What do you mean, the Force? What do you mean, my Destiny? How do you know who I am?'

'Pablo, when you are young you have dreams, and our path in life is to follow them and meet our destiny. If we couldn't follow our dreams it would mean that God put us on this earth as some kind of bad joke. But some people do not always read the signs. They are swayed by the dark side of the Force. See that man over there?'

The old man was pointing to a baker, having a smoke in front of his shop. Pablo nodded.

'He dreamed of travel once, just like you.'

'If he wanted to travel, why didn't he become a lowly herder of flocks, as did I?'

'Oh, he wanted to be a shepherd, but people laughed at him, so he became a baker instead.'

'He had no faith in his dream.'

'I have to be really blatant with some people. I send them easy-to-read dreams and leave very symbolic things in the road for them to pick up. But even then I might be wasting my time. You just can't do much with certain individuals. Like that clown there.'

'Maybe I can have a word with him.'

'Good luck. But about what we were discussing, do we have a deal?'

'A tenth of my sheep?'

'Yes.'

'Can I get the treasure first, then give you the sheep?'

'Doesn't work like that. Same place, same time tomorrow, bring the animals. I'll tell you where the treasure is.'

The old man took a last squirt of wine then stood up and walked away. He turned a corner and was gone.

Pablo walked over to the baker and bought a loaf. It was still warm and smelled good. Pablo broke the crust. It was lovely bread. He chewed a mouthful in front of the baker. Pablo met the baker's eyes. The baker was watching Pablo.

'Is baking your destiny?' asked Pablo.

'Something wrong with the bread?'

'I'm wondering, baker, if you have truly followed your dream.'

'There's other places you can buy bread. I have plenty of customers, they like it.'

'I was going to college, but then I became a shepherd instead.'

The baker shrugged and blew through his lips and went back into his shop without saying goodbye.

The old man is right, thought Pablo, as he rounded up his flock. That baker is an idiot. The sheep moved along obediently, heading for pasture outside the town.

The sheep seem to know what I'm thinking even before I think it, thought Pablo.

'Baaaaa,' said the sheep.

The next morning Pablo sat on the hill, looking across the sea. He had sold most of his sheep but kept six for the old man. It was not easy parting with the sheep. They had been together for so long and it was as if they could feel his feelings before he felt them himself.

Dolly had looked at him beseechingly as she was being led

away, and that had torn him up a bit. She was not as good-looking as when she was a lamb, but that did not matter to Pablo. What was her destiny? Hopefully she would not end up on a barbecue, being devoured by a gang of drunken louts. Yes, they had been very close. She had a special way of feeling his feelings before he even felt them himself. He could never express his sentiments for Dolly to another person. Not that he had done anything shameful or unclean. It was not that sort of relationship. No, he could not talk about Dolly because of the cheap jokes people made about shepherds and their sheep. He had heard enough of those remarks in the villages. The jokes were not even funny. The men who said such things were insecure about their own masculinity and unable to relate to animals on an emotional level and for that reason picked on the easiest target there was – the humble shepherd with his flock.

The old man appeared very suddenly beside Pablo and picked up the wine sack and helped himself. Pablo was amazed. He had not seen the old man approach.

'Hello, youngster. I see you've brought the sheep. Thanks. Your next stop is the pyramids, as you probably guessed. You'll find it easier now that you've no animals. I don't really want any sheep, by the way. We don't use them where I come from. But I needed you to demonstrate your desire to follow your destiny.'

'To symbolize that I was really serious?'

'Yes, it's symbolic. Do you know the difference between a symbol and an omen? I'll run through it very quickly. Omens are symbols but not all symbols are omens. Symbols signify something other than themselves. So God might talk to us through symbols, like in dreams. But also if you were writing a book, say, you'd use symbols for extra atmosphere. Like the thing here with the sheep. It wouldn't be important for the mechanics of the story, the structure of which is rather loose anyway, since you could have just rented out the sheep, and promised me you'd follow your destiny. But this way it's clearer and more interesting. So that's a symbol, but omens are what I really wanted to talk to you about. An omen is something symbolic of the future, and if you read it right it directs you. It's a sign down the road to your destiny.'

'Omens could turn out very useful in my journey to Egypt. I've no idea how to get there.'

'They will be useful, but you have to be careful, because they help you to choose, but do not necessarily hand you easy choices. Beware of the dark side of the Force, and the world will conspire to help you fulfil your destiny.'

'It will?'

'Absolutely. It's like beginner's luck. The first time you sit down to cards you're bound to win. The world wants to help you along.'

'Does it really?'

'Yes.'

The old man took a dirty little nugget out of his pocket and handed it to Pablo, who looked up at him inquiringly.

'This,' said the old man, 'is the bone from the little toe of Napoleon's left foot. Napoleon followed his destiny and won a lot of battles. For a long time he was extremely lucky. But he ended up stuck on a very small island, and that's what people remember, with a great deal of satisfaction.'

'What does this mean, old man?'

'Most people are losers and it irks them to see someone else do well. So they always like it when someone rich and famous ends up badly. There is a whole universe of negative vibrations out there. It's a manifestation of the dark side of the Force, which hates positive thinking and a can-do attitude to life. But you will have to negotiate a path through these people. When you wish to make a crucial decision, place Napoleon's toe in the crack of your behind and hold it there for at least thirty seconds. Close your eyes and ask a simple question. If the bone vibrates pleasantly, the answer is yes. If it gives you a small electric shock, you had better watch out.'

'But why between my cheeks, Master? Isn't that un-hygienic?'

'You're no longer a shepherd, Pablo. Time to start washing more regularly.'

'I still find the idea odd. I mean, the crack of my . . .'

'Free your mind from preconceptions and arbitrary categories. Pablo, let me tell you a story . . .'

And this was the tale that the old man told:

Once upon a time a Searcher after Truth was directed to the Palace of King Solomon. The Seeker travelled many moons through the desert and at the end of his journey reached the Palace of the Wise King.

'Oh tell me, Great Sage, what is the secret of happiness?' asked the Seeker, when he was brought before Solomon.

'Seeker after Truth,' said the king, 'if you wish to know the answer to this question, first you must see where I live. Tour my palace and its gardens. But I must ask you one thing. Take off your robes and place this spoon between the cheeks of your buttocks. Hold it there with a clenching action. As you walk about, do not under any circumstances let the spoon fall. You will walk funny but it's not impossible.'

After several hours, the Seeker after Truth returned, with the spoon. He had completed his task.

'And tell me,' said the king. 'Did you see my Persian tapestries and my Chinese vases and the rare orchids in my garden?'

But no, the Seeker after Truth had seen none of these things – he had been too busy concentrating on not dropping the spoon.

'Young traveller,' said the king, 'how can you learn the secret of happiness if you embark on a journey and yet return having seen nothing? Here, put the spoon back there again and have another go.'

Several hours later the young Seeker returned before King Solomon, and the eyes of the Seeker after Truth were bright with wonder at the palace of marvels he had witnessed.

'That is all very well, young man,' said the king. 'But where is my spoon?'

When the old man had finished his tale, they were both silent for a time. They looked across the waves, where Pablo would soon be sailing.

'I'm starting to understand,' said Pablo. 'I must see the world, and yet not drop the spoon. It is like being a shepherd. You must wander freely, yet not misplace your sheep.'

'The Force is strong in you, Pablo,' said the old man. He stood up and opened his robes. His chest was covered with metal and buttons and flashing lights. He pressed a button and spoke a lot of numbers.

Then he disappeared. The six sheep were gone too.

That was strange, thought Pablo.

He looked down towards the coast. A small boat was being loaded and men were milling about on the beach. Probably they're going across to Africa, where Egypt is, thought Pablo. He rose and descended to the shore.

Pablo wandered the twisted alleyways of Tangier medina as night fell, and he became conscious of many eyes upon him. A number of men approached him, offering guided tours, carpets, hashish and clean girls. Footsore and tired of saying, 'No thank you,' he stepped into a small tea house. The men eyed him suspiciously as they puffed on their hookah pipes. Pablo ordered a glass of tea and was sipping it when a man called Ahmed, with a scar down his right cheek, approached him and made friendly conversation. Then he said:

'Want hashish? Opium?'

'No, thanks,' said Pablo, in a loud voice, addressing the tea house in general. 'But I wouldn't mind playing cards for cash with some of you fellows.'

A scuffle involving a number of the patrons ensued, and the owner of the tea house shoved Pablo out the door, swearing. Pablo could hear things breaking inside, then the door flew open again and many bodies tumbled out into the alley. The struggle continued on the cobbles. Men pulled other men down to the ground and climbed over them in an effort to get closer to Pablo, then would themselves be pulled down and climbed over, which created an interesting rolling effect in the very narrow alley, which Pablo observed, walking backwards. The ultimate winner of the altercation was Ahmed, the man with the scar, who brushed himself off and told Pablo breathlessly that he knew a nice place to play some cards.

They went down winding alleyways with smelly open drains that Pablo had to be careful not to step in, now that it was dark. Finally, they ascended a rickety flight of stairs to a small room lit with a single candle. A bearded man was asleep on the floor. Ahmed nudged the sleeper in the ribs with his boot and spoke in Arabic. The man woke and rubbed his eyes. He looked Pablo up and down and produced a battered pack of cards from inside his *djellaba*.

★

So much for beginner's luck! thought Pablo, next day, berating himself severely. Those scoundrels weren't playing by the rules!

He had spent a bad night in an alley, pining for Dolly. He wiped the tears from his face and found a quiet place and slipped Napoleon's toe between his cheeks. He waited for about thirty seconds, and then formulated his question.

'Napoleon,' he intoned to the alleyway of high shuttered windows, 'I'm taking a break from cards. Do you think I should join the army, either in ballistics or as an ordinary foot soldier, or do you think I should go back to Andalucia and resume sheep-herding in the hills, or do you think I should learn a trade such as plumbing or baking?'

Pablo received a rude shock.

He picked himself up off the ground and wiped the sweat from his face. He was trembling. The nugget dropped out of the end of his right trouser leg and onto the ground. He re-inserted it and prepared his question more humbly.

'Should I get a menial job so I can afford to buy food?'

Napoleon's toe vibrated pleasantly.

That's decided, then, thought Pablo.

He was getting hungry.

With his last coins, Pablo bought a second-hand copy of Dick Schultz's *Sell Yourself: Ten Steps to Success in Marketing: Meeting the Sales Challenges of a New Millennium*.

Destiny has led me to this sage, thought Pablo, observing that, although they used different words, the old man and Schultz had the same philosophy. Instead of 'Destiny', Schultz talked about 'Success', that was all. You failed to make a sale not so much as a result of external obstacles, but because the dark side of the Force was strong in you. This was what Schultz called 'negative thinking'. Schultz had many examples of people who had been down to their last dollar, and had seen an opportunity to exploit and had done so and as a result had become million-aires, fulfilling their destinies.

Pablo entered the shop of the seller of glassware and offered to clean up around the place. The proprietor, a thin man who rolled his own cigarettes, shrugged and handed him a broom. After he had swept the shop properly he mopped the floor. The man brought him some bread and a bowl of chick pea soup and Pablo ate hungrily.

'Eye-level is buy-level,' said Pablo. 'Ever heard that one?'

The owner frowned and pulled at his little cigarette.

'That means,' continued Pablo, 'putting your most saleable products on the shelves where people can see them as soon as they enter. Not necessarily the most beautiful or expensive pieces, but high-turnover items that people shouldn't have to go looking for. It's standard practice in the supermarket trade throughout the world.'

'It makes no difference,' said the shopkeeper. 'Nobody comes in here anyway. This shop is in the wrong part of town.'

'Look,' said Pablo, 'your windows are so dirty the customers can't even see in.'

'It doesn't matter. I have no customers.'

'And you need a little air freshener, to take away the musty smell.'

'Waste of money.'

'And maybe some music. Pan pipes, something like that.'

'I've been in this business for years, I know what I'm talking about. You can wash the windows if you want, but I can't pay you. All I've got is this soup.'

Pablo set to work with a bucket of soapy water and a rag. He whistled as he worked, and to anybody who passed in the street, he smiled and said things like 'Nice day' and 'Howya doin'?'

Just as Pablo was finishing his work and the display windows were gleaming, a bus full of German tourists pulled up down the street and Pablo hailed them with '*Guten Tag!*' and a friendly wave. Then the shop was full of Germans, buying souvenir glassware.

'That was incredible,' said the shopkeeper, at the end of the day. 'I made more today than in the last six months! Maybe there is something to what you say!'

'The next step,' said Pablo, 'is to upgrade your display cases and your stock in order to reach a wealthier segment. We need to repaint the walls in bright colours and get in the sound system with the mood music I mentioned, and diversify into other ethnic arts and crafts and have a section for glossy coffee-table books. And then we need to break through the back wall and open a coffeeshop-slash-bistro that also sells a range of over-priced smoothies.'

'What's a smoothie?'

Pablo explained that by liquidizing combinations of exotic fruit you could entertain the consumer's insatiable desire for novelty, and at the same time jack up the price to keep out people who wore tracksuits.

The owner hired Pablo as an adviser and they split the profits fifty-fifty. Within six months Pablo was a wealthy man.

On the edge of the Sahara Desert, under canvas awnings, Pablo read through the contract while flies buzzed about and tried to drink from the corners of his eyes and the camels groaned and made life difficult for the drivers who were trying to load them with supplies for the journey. The title page of the contract was headed:

HARDWAY TOURS — EXTREME ADVENTURES
Why take it easy when you can do it The Hard Way?

The contract absolved Hardway, represented by Ali, of any responsibility for any accidents in the desert, including fatal ones.

There was a tall Englishman with a crate of books. He was dressed in khaki and wore a helmet against the sun. He read his contract rapidly and signed it without hesitating, then stared out across the burning sands to the wavering horizon.

I'll bet he's following his destiny, thought Pablo. I'm sure we'll have good conversations.

A sob came from the next table. It was Greg, an overweight American teenager. He said he had never felt life to be beautiful until that day; he realized he was soft, and he wanted a challenge that would make him a man. He signed too.

The Japanese formed a compact group of nine, including two women. They all wore glasses. They pored over the contract and would search out words in their English–Japanese dictionary, and grew increasingly distressed and fractious as the deadline for signing approached. But they too signed in the end.

The last to sign it were Tina and Louise. Tina had piercings all over her face. Why is that ugly girl dressed up like a man? wondered Pablo. Louise was pale and more delicately built and broke into tears after reading the Death from Dehydration clause. 'Fucking sign it,' snarled Tina, who threatened to dump her on the spot.

When the money was handed over, Ali stood on a rock and waved his sword about. He was dressed as a Bedouin but wore sunglasses.

'The desert is a cruel mistress! She will drive you insane! She makes you fall in love with her so she can torture you! Hahaha!'

There was a flurry of dictionary-work among the Japanese.

'And now I am taking you to look into her eyes! She will test you! If you obey my orders, there is a chance you will live! I am the master of Life and Death! Hahaha!'

Ali put his sword back into his scabbard, then stepped forward and punched Greg hard in the gut. Greg collapsed to the ground.

'That was uncalled for,' muttered the Englishman, but not very loud. Ali glanced from face to face, hand on his sword.

'Anybody got a problem with what I just done?' he asked.

Apart from a little subdued chatter from the Japanese, nobody said anything.

They set off towards evening and Pablo, just as he had anticipated, had an interesting conversation with the Englishman, who told him about the philosopher's stone and the elixir of life, and about alchemy in general.

'There is no such thing as coincidence,' said the Englishman.

'I agree entirely,' said Pablo. 'There is only a chain of events, as you read the signs and follow your destiny.'

'Yes,' said the Englishman, 'and when you follow your destiny you are in harmony with the Soul of the World.'

'That's exactly what I think,' said Pablo.

They were becoming great friends. They listened to the eternal wind and the hoofbeats of the animals and felt small in the face of the elemental force of the majestic vastness. The desert seems old and wise, thought Pablo. Perhaps it can teach me something. Probably if I pay attention I can learn the Universal Language of the Soul of the World.

The Englishman told Pablo about the alchemists, men who sought as their final goal the Master Work, which would let them understand the Soul of the World. They spent lifetimes in their laboratories, transforming matter through flame. The liquid part of their goal was the elixir of life, which promised perpetual health and youth, while the solid part was the philosopher's stone, which converted base metals into gold. Pablo told the Englishman of the writings of Schultz, and the tales of those wise men who used their last dollar to make a million. Yes, agreed the Englishman, such stories show that those who can read the omens are in tune with the Soul of the World. The camel drivers read the omens, and the caravan and the desert speak the same language. The soul of the caravan speaks to the soul of the desert.

'The desert is truly majestic in its vastness,' said Pablo.

'Yes,' said the Englishman. 'But she's a cruel mistress.'

Days passed. There were incidents. Greg suffered from bad diarrhoea and had to be executed. He was losing weight and would not have made it anyway. Ali took him behind a dune and they all heard the shot ring out. Then Ali returned alone, with his gun.

'That was uncalled for,' muttered the Englishman.

'Anybody got a problem with what I just done?' asked Ali.

Nobody said anything.

Several nights later there was an incident involving Louise, and she also had to be shot. Tina had taken to sharing a tent with one of the Japanese women, and Louise's sobs would rack the camp and disturb the camels. So Ali dragged her behind a dune and, once again, they heard the report ring out through the darkness. After that they all slept better.

'Have an awful feeling the brute ravished the poor girl first,' the Englishman confided to Pablo, between gritted teeth, the next morning.

Pablo said nothing. He was listening to the eternal wind. He felt close to the Soul of the World.

After several months, as they neared their destination, mysterious hooded Bedouin appeared on distant ridges and picked off the Japanese with their rifles at a rate of one per day.

'No talking Japanese, no taking pictures, keep yourselves well covered,' Ali advised the last three surviving Orientals, a woman and two men, who were very nervous as they set out that morning.

'Why do they hate us?' cried one of the men.

'They don't hate you,' said Ali, mounting his camel. 'They think you taste better.'

They carried on. The guides read the signs of the desert. The soul of the caravan spoke to the soul of the desert. They became one. Towards evening they lost another Jap to a sniper.

That evening, by the light of the campfire, Pablo studied the Englishman's texts on alchemy. He could make no sense of the symbols and figures. It was not like Schultz, who had bullet points and numbered steps to success. This was a secret code.

'I don't quite get it myself,' said the Englishman. 'When we arrive at the oasis of al-Fayyum, I must find an alchemist.'

The next morning, within a day's march from the oasis, their final destination, the two remaining Japanese were unable to look each other in the eye. Both were suffering fits of retching and had to be coaxed onto their mounts.

After perhaps an hour a shot rang out and the body fell to the ground with a dull thud.

They rode forward. Nobody spoke.

'Rotten luck,' said the Englishman, eventually breaking the silence. 'But the Nips can be a cruel lot too. I shan't tell you what they did to me in Burma.'

A line of green appeared on the horizon. This was the oasis. A cry of joy went up among the guides.

On arrival at the oasis, Ali was assaulted by Tina and badly injured. He had passed a remark about eating sushi to the surviving Japanese woman, to whom Tina had become very attached.

'I say, let's make ourselves scarce,' said the Englishman to Pablo as the police and ambulance arrived.

They wandered around the oasis asking if anybody knew of the Alchemist. It was as big as a city and by evening their feet were sore. People would say things like 'I'm afraid I don't know what you're talking about' and 'Would you like to buy a carpet?' – but most hurried away rapidly without speaking.

'Let's just ask this little thing,' said the Englishman to Pablo, referring to a girl drawing water from a well. The girl had her back to them. Pablo was tired and dispirited. The girl turned around and their eyes met. When he looked in her dark eyes, he knew she was his destiny. He was her destiny and she was his. Their souls spoke the same language, the language of the Soul of the World, which is the soul of love. They both knew they were made by the one hand. Their destinies were intertwined. Their names were written together in the same book. She smiled. She had good teeth too. It was the omen Pablo had been waiting for. He felt something he had never felt before. It left the thing with Dolly in the shade. The Soul of the World surged within him.

'Let's meet tomorrow,' said Pablo. 'Same time, same place.'

'I don't know,' said the girl. 'It's not the done thing here. We could both end up getting stoned.'

'She seems rather forward,' said the Englishman to Pablo, in English. 'Look at the way she's grinning at you. I'd be careful.'

'There is no danger,' said Pablo to the Englishman. 'For we are as one.' And then to the girl: 'I'll be waiting.'

She turned and walked away, bearing her water jar on her shoulder like an Old Testament beauty. She wore a *hijab* and long robes that covered her body, but she had an eloquent sort of walk.

'My goodness,' said the Englishman. 'Some things just can't be hidden, even if you throw a sack over them. Wait a minute. Ask Girlie if she knows where the Alchemist lives.'

Pablo called out and the girl turned around.

'Do you know by any chance where the Alchemist lives?'

She did, as it happened, and she gave them his address, which was in one of the sandy neighbourhoods south of town.

The next day Pablo was hanging about the well, waiting for the girl. To his surprise, the Englishman was hanging about too. He had been to see the Alchemist.

'Well, he told me I should go for it, the lead to gold transformation, stop reading so many books.'

'So why don't you?' asked Pablo.

'Maybe I shall, maybe I shall. Only . . .'

'What?'

'I don't know. It seems too easy, that's all. Abracadabra, gold! If that's all there were to it, everybody would be doing it.'

'I'm sorry, Englishman, to seem rude. But I have a date.'

'Yes, well,' said the Englishman, seeing the girl approaching. 'Mind the sand. It gets everywhere.'

The Englishman took his long face elsewhere. What was he talking about? wondered Pablo. He seemed a bit like that foolish baker, afraid to follow his destiny.

'Hello,' said Pablo, as the girl put her water jar on the ground. 'I just wanted to say one thing. I love you and I think we should get married. You are my destiny.'

'Hello. My name's Fatima. It's a common girl's name round here. What's your name?'

'Pablo,' said Pablo. 'I want to marry you because you are worth even more to me than my treasure.'

'What treasure?'

Pablo told her. Fatima said she didn't mind waiting. He could get the treasure and come back. She'd respect him more that way.

'The desert winds sculpt the dunes, and the dunes are always changing,' said Fatima. 'But the desert is always the same. And so will be our love. I am a woman of the desert. I know you must fulfil your destiny.'

'How about we get married and spend some time together? I've been moving around a lot and never really got to enjoy that side of life. Then I can go get the treasure.'

'No, for your destiny calls you and you must follow. You must wander as free as the wind. That is what we expect of our men, us women of the desert.'

Pablo saw another hard journey ahead, with the omens of the desert speaking and him being part of the Soul of the World.

'And even if your bones get bleached in the desert,' said Fatima, 'you will become part of the desert and the wind, and you will return to creation, which is in every grain of sand, because All is One. Goodbye, Pablo. Good luck.'

'Goodbye, Fatima.'

*

Pablo loaded his camel with supplies in preparation for the trip across the desert to the pyramids. But first he made a short detour towards the place where Fatima had said the Alchemist lived.

After an hour he came to a small encampment. The sun had set and the silver disc of the moon was rising large and luminous over the desert. A milk-white horse stood tethered near the Alchemist's tent. The Alchemist was dressed in black robes. His beard was black and his dark eyes ferocious and intelligent. He was stirring a small pot of beans on the stove.

'Hello,' said the Alchemist. 'Have you eaten yet?'

'Greetings,' said Pablo. 'Are you the Alchemist?'

The Alchemist continued stirring and did not reply. Perhaps I have offended him, thought Pablo.

'Go wash your hands,' said the Alchemist. 'Then we'll eat.'

Soon they were eating together by the Alchemist's campfire, before his tent. The beans were the best Pablo had ever tasted.

'These beans are the best I've ever tasted,' said Pablo.

'Yes,' said the Alchemist. 'Just because something's simple doesn't mean you can't cook it well.'

'What's your secret?'

'There's some basic things to bear in mind when preparing beans. They should be soaked in water for at least twelve hours prior to cooking. When you bring them to the boil you should discard the water at least once. This makes them easier to digest, if you know what I mean. Then you let them simmer again until they're tender. You shouldn't add salt until the beans are cooked, because it makes the skins tough. As for the flavour, don't be shy with the onions and garlic, and these can be added fried at any stage of cooking. Bay leaf is also crucial, and thyme and red pepper. Fresh peppers and tomatoes make the sauce particularly rich. And some fatty mutton, cooked so slowly it begins to disintegrate. And the dish is always better reheated, the second day. It allows the flavours to mingle and intensify. These are the basics of bean cookery, and once you get that much right you're set up for life and you can branch out and experiment with other flavours and ingredients.'

They ate for a little while in silence. These beans really are good, thought Pablo, but perhaps I should get to the point.

'Alchemist, what do you advise me to do? On the one hand I'd like to stay around the oasis and get to know Fatima better, and then get married, settle down, maybe have some kids. I mean, I have a little money, it shouldn't be so difficult. On the other hand, perhaps I should follow my destiny and find the treasure.'

Pablo described his meeting with Fatima at the well and their conversation.

'I know that Fatima,' said the Alchemist. 'Men hang about her house like dogs, sniffing the wind. You're probably better off getting the treasure first. Tomorrow we'll go towards the pyramids of Egypt. It is foretold in the Soul of the World.'

As they travelled by night across the desert, beneath the moon, they would converse.

'Can you really turn lead into gold?' asked Pablo.

'That's why they call me the Alchemist,' said the Alchemist. 'Among other reasons.'

'How do you do it?'

'The code is written on an emerald tablet. But really, immerse yourself in creation, because all creation is in every grain of sand. Also, listen to your heart.'

'My heart?'

'Yes, your heart can teach you the language of the Soul of

the World, then you can read the omens and follow your destiny. The real treasure is following your destiny.'

'Yes, I agree. Still, being able to make gold is very impressive.'

Pablo listened to his heart for a while. It told him all kinds of contradictory things.

'Alchemist, my heart is telling me to follow my destiny. But also to go back to Fatima, right away, because I miss her terribly. There's things I'd like to do to her, I don't even have words.'

'That's fine,' said the Alchemist. 'Keep listening. When you get to my age you have all the words but the business itself is not nearly so interesting.'

'Alchemist, I fear suffering, defeat, sadness, age and failure.'

'That is the dark side of the Force, Pablo. Do not yield to fear. Fear of suffering is worse than suffering itself.'

'Alchemist, I am full of fear, because men are approaching us in large numbers, on horseback!'

'The Force is strong in you, Pablo. Control your fear!'

'But, Alchemist, they have guns!'

As they were led into the encampment of the savage tribesmen, Pablo could not help noticing that there was a lot of Japanese camera equipment scattered around the camp, and pairs of glasses. Their mounts were seized and Pablo's money was taken from him. Pablo observed that the Alchemist was unruffled by their mistreatment. They were manhandled into a large tent and pushed to their knees before the chief.

'Who are you and what are you doing here?' demanded the chief.

'I'm an alchemist,' said the Alchemist. 'And this is Pablo. He's following his destiny, and if you get in the way of his destiny, there'll be trouble.'

The chief laughed.

'You can laugh,' continued the Alchemist. 'But, I assure you, if you continue mistreating us he will destroy your camp.'

'And how will he manage that?' asked the chief, looking at Pablo.

'He will turn himself into the wind.'

'He couldn't blow out the candles on his birthday cake.'

'He will turn himself into a storm that will flatten your camp. By using the Power of Love.'

'"The Power of Love"?'

The Alchemist explained the concept to the barbarian. Love was what made the world go around and conquered all. The Soul of the World was made of Love, pure love. Everything, by following its destiny, transforms itself into something better, and makes the world a better place, for you and for me. Everything is striving upwards, like a plant in the sun, towards God's love.

The barbarian stroked his beard a bit. 'Listen, I don't believe what you're saying about your magic tricks, but I'm prepared to argue this on its theological merits. What you're proposing is the destruction of my camp, causing the death of many people. Fair enough, we're barbarians and we stole your money. But these people have been brought up to be barbarians, they don't know any better. The menfolk are trying to provide for their families and want to give their kids a brighter future. Some people say we should head for the city, but there's a lot of drugs and prostitution and gang-related crime there, and it's not a healthy environment in which to raise children. So, granted, destroying our camp might solve your problem, but why should the Soul of the World care one way or another?'

Pablo rose to his feet and pointed his finger at the barbarian chief. 'You people eat Japanese tourists!'

The chief rolled his eyes. A guard struck Pablo with the butt of his gun, forcing him back down on his knees.

'We don't eat them,' said the chief. 'We just play with their camera equipment. But the batteries run out so fast, and then we have to get more.'

'You cook them and eat them!' insisted Pablo. 'You dirty Arab!'

'Pablo,' whispered the Alchemist, 'no ethnic slurs! I'm an Arab myself, and proud of my heritage.'

'You've got three days to use the Power of Love to turn yourself into the wind,' said the barbarian. 'Then I'll take personal pleasure in sticking knives into you. I was actually going to just take your money and let you go, but I've decided to torture you to death instead. Take them away!'

Late that night Pablo said to the Alchemist:

'Alchemist, I got a bit carried away there. I'm afraid I have no idea how I'm going to get us out of this. You're an alchemist – can't you do something?'

'Conquer your fear, Pablo. Fear is the dark side of the Force.'

On the third day something very strange happened. Pablo was having an agitated dream involving Fatima, who spoke to him in the Universal Language of the Soul of the World. The wind picked up and eventually flattened the entire encampment. The Alchemist and Pablo were among the few survivors, and wandered about afterwards, inspecting the damage. A hysterical woman was trying to dig her husband out of the side of a dune but it seemed hopeless, as only his feet could be seen protruding from the sand. Nearby, a small orphaned child screamed at the sky.

They recovered their mounts, which had been miraculously

spared, and rode away from the devastation, not looking back.

'Now you understand the Power of Love,' said the Alchemist.

'Yes,' said Pablo. 'This stretch of desert will be safer now for Japanese tourists, after what has happened here today.'

They rode towards the pyramids.

After they had been riding through barren country for a long time, without speaking, the Alchemist asked, in a gentle voice:

'Something is troubling you, Pablo. Tell me what is on your mind.'

The moon shone high above. Pablo watched the ground as they moved forward. Then he said: 'Alchemist, who is my real father?'

They rode on a little further. The question hung plaintively in the air, with the silver disc of the moon.

'That is a very difficult question, Pablo. Are you sure this is something you want us to go into right now?'

'I have to know.'

'Very well. But why do you ask? Do people say things about your mother?'

'It's not that. It's just that my father does not seem special in any way. He's just a farmer. He's a rather common sort of a person. He just takes care of a farm.'

'Pablo, this is a hard question. But generally when you grow up in a house with people who claim to be your parents, even if they're farmers, you have to take their word for it.'

'I see. I just thought . . . Never mind.'

They rode on.

*

They had a quick stop at a Coptic monastery, where the Alchemist used the stove in the kitchen to turn some lead into gold. He gave a bit to a monk for the roof-repair fund and a piece to Pablo in case it took him longer than expected to turn up some treasure.

'Goodbye, Pablo. Follow your dream. May the Force be with you!'

'And with you, Alchemist. Thanks for teaching me about the Power of Love!'

They parted. On the horizon could be seen the shapes of the pyramids.

Pablo dismounted under the pyramids. A man approached him and offered to be his friend, his guide and to get him discounts on souvenirs.

'Go away,' said Pablo. 'You're annoying me.'

'Very good perfume shop nearby.'

'Oh, please! By the way, why are you walking that way? Don't your shoes fit properly?'

'My shoes are fine. The police pulled me in last year for attending a demonstration against the ruling oligarchy, which keeps us all in poverty while they do filthy deals with the Americans and Israelis.'

'If you want to make anti-Semitic comments you're talking to the wrong person.'

'And they put a broom handle up my rectum and manipulated that for about fifteen minutes while I writhed on the floor screaming.'

'I'm very, VERY sorry, whatever your name is, but I am NOT interested in politics!'

'You don't need to be. They recorded it on their camera phones and put it on the internet.'

'Will you please, please stop harassing me?'

'Then I was put in jail for six months for resisting arrest.'

Pablo put his hands over his ears and said, 'NYA-NYA-NYA-NYA-NYA-NYA-NYA,' very loud for over thirty seconds. When he had finished, the Egyptian man was walking away with that funny walk of his.

Pablo wandered around the pyramids a bit, listening to his heart, while the anti-Semitic agitator irritated him by watching from a distance. Finally he found a place and his heart told him to dig there. So he dug with some persistence until a policeman came over to him and said:

'Excuse me, sir, this is an archaeological site, possibly the most important one in our country. We're very proud of it. I'm going to have to ask you not to keep digging there.'

Pablo slapped the dust from his trousers and listened to his heart.

'You see that man over there? He's a fundamentalist. He was talking to me about politics just now.'

The policeman got an eyeball on the suspect, then lifted his walkie-talkie and spoke into it while walking slowly in the direction of the hustler. From the other direction, a police van was raising dust on the dirt road as it drove towards the agitator, who began to twitch, then to retreat, as if it were possible with that strange walk of his, the result of his shoes, or the broom handle, Pablo didn't really know. Pablo was back in the dirt, digging furiously. Sweat was pouring off him. And what if I do find treasure here? he wondered. They will only say it belongs to the pharaohs and put it in a museum. Pablo tried listening to his heart, but his heart said, yes, that's probably how it is, Pablo, it'll end up in a museum!

Pablo took a break and looked at where the cop and the van had converged on the hustler. There was a cursory interrogation and the man was invited into the back of the vehicle. Several policemen got in behind him. The doors were closed and the parked van began to bounce vigorously.

Pablo resumed digging. He thought about all he had invested in this moment, about the flock he had left behind, about how Dolly would gaze at him in the low glow of the dying campfire in the Andalucian hills. He thought about his successful career as an entrepreneur in Tangier. He recalled the dangerous crossing of the Sahara, his meeting with Fatima, woman of the desert, and his vanquishing of the barbarian encampment. He thought of the Alchemist, who had instructed him in the Power of Love.

Pablo listened to his heart, but his digging was coming up with nothing. The policeman who had arrested the subversive was approaching him again, in no particular hurry. Pablo, breathing hard, threw aside his small shovel and sat on the lip of the crater he had created.

'Listen,' said the cop. 'You're going to get yourself in trouble. If I let you dig holes here, they'll all be doing it and the place will look like a building site. Move along before I have to take measures.'

The tears of defeat welled in Pablo and overflowed his cheeks and he could not help but share his pain with the stranger standing before him.

'I dreamed it was my destiny to find treasure here beneath the pyramids!'

'Yeah, well,' said the policeman, twirling his baton. 'I keep having a dream about a ruined church in Andalucia, with a tree growing up in the middle of it, and I dig under the tree and find treasure. But that doesn't mean I just run off when I feel like it, leave the wife and kids. Now if I come back in ten minutes and find you still digging, there's going to be a problem.'

But Pablo was already out of the hole, and walking towards the exit. His tears had turned to laughter. Because now he knew where his treasure was.

Pablo opened the wooden chest and showed his humble rustic father the treasure that had belonged to a conquistador who had plundered a large area of South America.

He told his father the entire story, from his dream in the church to the journey to the pyramids and back to the ruined church.

'I don't know why you couldn't have just dreamed in the church that the treasure was there,' said Mr Conejo. 'It would have saved you a trip.'

'Then I'd never have seen the pyramids,' said Pablo.

'That's true. I meant to ask, what are they like?'

'Very big up close. It was wonderful to see the remnants of an ancient civilization.'

'Yes,' said Mr Conejo, examining the loot in the chest. 'These are pre-Columbian artefacts. I imagine the museums will be interested.'

'Actually, Dad, don't go telling anyone, because if I melt it down to sell I can invest the cash on the stock exchange. Then there's a girl I must go find.'

Pablo told his father about Fatima.

'I agree, it's about time you had a woman,' said Mr Conejo. 'I didn't find it easy at your age. But I don't know why you can't find yourself a wife in this village. The women here are as good-looking as anywhere. All your talk about destiny, I don't know what it means. This place is good. I was born here and this is where I'll die. That's my destiny. I was restless once, like you, but it passed. I wanted to learn everything. And then when you were born, I understood I wasn't so important and I was happy here. We have all we need. The soil is good and the water is plentiful. I know it is not like this everywhere, that there is injustice in the world, that the rich laugh in the faces of the poor, so I was grateful to have this land. I knew the day would come when I would be old enough to love the grave and all desire to stay here would leave me. But this no longer seemed so terrible to me when I saw you, my son. I no longer wished to learn everything, and I only hoped I could teach you something practical that you might be resilient and accepting in the face of the suffering we all must go through. But then you started on about the sheep, and I could see there was no point speaking to you. Now, all this about Destiny and the Power of Love, and this crate of gold you plan to melt down. I don't understand any of it.

'There's no point talking to you. I have work to do. I have my vines to tend, and weeding and fixing fences. God gives us enough to live. He gives us fruits in every season. If God is everywhere, as you say, why don't you sit still and listen to him? Why do you run around like a cat with its ass on fire?'

The sun was growing red and swollen as father and son sat outside their house, looking over their gentle ancestral fields. They were drinking a little of Mr Conejo's old wine, and Pablo was not disturbed by his father's words. On the contrary, he just smiled and listened to the familiar intonation and enjoyed the sound of his father's voice. Indeed, his father had a beautiful voice, and there was no need whatever to listen to what he was actually saying.

A Note from the Publisher

Dear Reader

We hope you enjoyed this tale and that it inspires you to follow your destiny, but there are a couple of loose ends to tie up, or at least mention, because they trouble me a little bit.

There's the bit where Pablo's father says, 'Here's three coins I found in a ditch. Perhaps they'll help you out of a tight corner someday,' or words to that effect. And then we never hear another word about these coins!

Of course, Pablo's father mentions the coins in an offhand sort of a way, but we are not fooled, because a father giving a son gold coins at the beginning of a story is bound to be significant. So we find ourselves waiting for Pablo to save his skin at a crucial moment by suddenly remembering the gold coins. It makes me uncomfortable that this never in fact happens, and I'm sure other attentive readers feel the same way. Perhaps the coins were gambled away in the Tangier incident. But shouldn't we have been told?

Then there is the matter of Napoleon's toe. A big fuss is made about this bone, and indeed Pablo gets to use it once. It then disappears from the narrative. If its services aren't required in the latter half of the story, fair enough, but what happened to the item? Did Pablo lose it? Give it away? Does he retain the bone and plan to use it in the future?

And what about the Englishman? He enters the story significantly, but he leaves without saying goodbye.

Still, these are minor details which do not detract from the overall inspiring nature of the tale, and I'm sure future editions of the story will clear them up, along with any spelling mistakes.

The Song of Songs

She was getting off a bus with about twenty others when he saw her. If you don't fuck this one, thought Joey, you can toss yourself off the balcony. Though Joey did not like big asses specifically, there was something special in the vast twin rotundities atop short solid legs like triangles, down to the points of her heels tap-tapping the asphalt as she negotiated her way through the profane human mess. She wore loose semi-transparent cotton trousers – well, maybe cotton, he didn't really know – and her thong panties made a tiny triangle of fabric over her tailbone. He was looking at a big naked ass, basically.

Motion was the holy spirit that gave the language of the ass, the ass-song, its poetry, and hers was the soul of sex in motion, rolling and flowing to the mad music of the heavens. Joey mouthed the words:

> Love is as powerful as death;
> Passion is as strong as death itself.
> It bursts into flame
> And burns like a raging fire.
> Water cannot put it out;
> No flood can drown it.

It was a hot day. He felt that if he rose forward on his toes and held his breath, it would happen, that he would float above the people and the traffic.

81

Everybody was getting out of work, determined to get back to the buildings where they ate and slept. People struggled with each other to board buses and made it very hard for the people getting off. The people on the footpath hurried to connect with other buses, with trams, and walked into those going the opposite direction. Joey pushed his way through the human obstacles and followed her.

At the intersection she did not join the throng waiting to cross the road. She turned left. The people were fewer now and he followed at a discreet distance. Her generous haunches set off a slim waist, delicate back and narrow shoulders.

Some women had the shape but did not have the motion. This one, walking ahead of him, had that very pure lateral gyration, the sideways switch of the hips on the horizontal plane, inflected only slightly by the nodding vertical motion of each buttock. Women, Joey figured, didn't just bleed to the moon and wake to the sun: the movement of their backsides, like all heavenly bodies, could be described on a series of planes. The annual journey of the earth around the sun could be described on a horizontal plane, relative to which the daily rotation of the globe occurred on a vertical axis. These two axes intersected at the earth's centre. On the axis of the horizontal and lateral movements of the female backside, Joey also posited a central point. He did not know whether it was in her cunt or up her ass, but this was dead bones anyway, like mathematics, irrelevant to the fact that the world spun, women shook their buttocks, and it was all magical and sad.

About a hundred metres after a shack made of aluminium, or some kind of metal, that sold booze, chocolate and cigarettes all night, she turned left towards the entrance of a block, rummaging in her handbag for keys.

Joey grunted and leapt the steps, caught the door with his

fingertips just in time. As the ass disappeared round a corner, he slid into the cool shadows of the hallway and pressed his back against the cold wall. He heard her opening the lift door and entering and pulling the clunking door after her.

She ascended in the metal box, and Joey strode forward. He watched the lighted display as she rode past the fourth, fifth, sixth floors. It stopped at the seventh.

He called the lift and rode to the seventh.

There were four apartments on the floor. He pressed his ears to the door closest to the lift. There was no sound. At the second door a man and a woman were talking. He reckoned a new gearbox. She thought the bathroom should be retiled. Joey moved on. At the third door the television was on. The newscaster said it would be a very hot week. Some people were going to the mountains, but most people were going to the coast. There would be a special report, random citizens giving their accounts of hot weather. Joey moved on to the last door. He heard a toilet flush. That was her. He knew it. He knocked.

– Whozat?

– Joey!

– Who?

– Joey! The windows man!

She opened the door. Her face was nothing special. Round and kind of stupid. No matter. Her hallway was still painted with the cheap greyish mud they sprayed on the walls when the block was first built, thirty-something years before. Linoleum on the floor. Probably she rented, and worked in a government office where there was not much to do.

– Special offer for PVC double-glazing, said Joey. Do it in the summer, you'll be glad in the winter.

– No, thank you.

– Colossal savings on utilities. Free estimates.

– Not interested.

– Here, let me give you my card, case you change your mind.

Joey went through his pockets but there was no card, because he had never had any printed.

– I can come back.

She closed the door.

Joey took the stairs back down, two at a time.

That night he woke from the dream, the moon shining in his window.

> I will stay on the hill of myrrh,
> The hill of incense
> Until the morning breezes blow
> And the darkness disappears.

He stood up and knew it would happen even before it did. He rose up on his toes and just kept going, gently, like a balloon, and put a hand up and touched the ceiling. He pushed gently against the ceiling and came back to the floor. It was a simple matter of concentration. With practice he would learn to control it, surely, and fly as high as he liked. He could probably launch himself off the balcony and float down to the street, five floors down. But he did not think he should try that trick just yet.

He knocked on the door. He could hear the after-work noise of the television. He closed his eyes, ignoring the sound as best he could, and breathed, reciting:

I have come down among the almond trees
To see the young plants in the valley,
To see the new leaves on the vines
And the blossoms on the pomegranate trees.
I am trembling; you have made me as eager for love
As a chariot driver is for battle.

He felt the lightness and pushed off gently from the floor.
The door opened.

– Holy fuck! said the woman.

He opened his eyes. He was levitating very slightly. He felt
it wavering and brought himself back down.

She looked around the hallway.

– I come in peace, said Joey.

– Yeah right. How do you explain THAT?

Joey sighed.

– Do not be afraid. It's a gift. I don't understand it yet
myself.

– Wait a minute, aren't you the windows man?

– It's true, I can do windows, but that's not why I'm here.
Can I come in a minute?

She looked around, suspicious.

– Listen, said Joey, you're going to have to trust me. Do you
believe in angels?

– Alright, then, you'd better come inside.

He entered the hall and she closed the door. He introduced
himself. They shook hands. Her name was Maria.

– Pleased to meet you, Maria.

In the hallway the good smell of the meat and onions she
had been frying in old grease. On the TV they were moving
through the ads.

– So, get to the point, said Maria.

– I've chosen you, said Joey, from amongst all women.

She raised her eyebrows and opened her mouth.

– Is this some kinda –

– You saw me fly, didn't you? You think it's easy to do that?

– I saw some kinda trick, don't know what it was. Wasn't flying exactly. Floating a little bit maybe . . .

Hard to impress some of these ladies, thought Joey.

– Want me to do it again, huh?

– Wouldya?

– If I'm not interrupting your evening's viewing.

The television was on very loud, advertising instant soup. They went into the small room where she lived. There was a narrow mattress on the floor.

– Do it again, so, said Maria.

– Help me out a bit. Can you turn off that racket? Got anything to drink? Some nice music?

Maria switched off the set and indicated a small cassette player. She went to the kitchen and Joey looked through the cassettes. They all showed stocky men wearing tight tops, grinning horribly. Adrian the Wonder-Boy, one was called. Keyboard and drum-machine pop. He turned on the radio and tuned into a classical music programme and got lucky with a Chopin nocturne, in B-flat minor. The sun was going down and from the window it looked like half the city was on fire. Fine by him if it really was. The fire engines could howl down through the smoky twilight streets and they could all go to hell. Maria returned with a litre of red wine and two water glasses, and Joey felt it was going to all work out. He emptied a glass and poured another.

– Okay, then, you going to do it or what?

The piano notes surged upwards, sure of their direction.

– Yes, Maria, I certainly am. I'm going to fly specially for you, but you'll have to turn round for a moment.

– Hey! What's the big idea?

– Just for a moment, till I'm airborne, then you can look.

She turned to face the wall and Joey took another good swig. He stared at her miraculous ass. He felt it welling in him. He spoke softly:

> *You, my love, excite men*
> *As a mare excites the stallions of pharaoh's chariots*
> *Your hair is beautiful upon your cheeks*
> *And falls along your neck like jewels.*

He inhaled and pushed off and felt it, more surely this time, and was able to direct his body so that he tilted forwards a little as he gained height, floating in the middle of the room with his arms outspread.

Maria turned her head. Her eyes were popping.

– Jesus fucking Christ! Howja do that!

– Don't turn around!

Too late. Joey veered right, into the doorjamb, and crashed to the floor. Maria was beside him, her hands on his face.

– Sweetie! You OK?

– I'm still getting the hang of it.

He smiled wanly. Her hands caressed his sore head.

– Maybe you shouldn't drink when you fly, hon.

– Booze helps. Gimme some more.

He chugged another glass down, the two of them kneeling on the floor. Then he stuck his mouth on hers and reached around with his left hand and grabbed some haunch while working with his tongue. It was a good combination, with his eyes closed. When they took a break they were both breathing hard, and transfigured.

– Tell me how you do it, she murmured.

– Well, it's been a while coming, but I'm only learning how to harness my power. Actually it has something to do with you. With the essence of your womanliness.

– Hey, don't go poking fun.

– Really. When I saw you today in the street I knew you were special. But your face distracts me. Maybe I'm still a bit shy, but I need to see you from behind.

He got her onto the mattress and had his hand under the elastic of her trouser-things. He had almost worked a couple of digits into her snatch but she bucked him out of it.

– Hey, Joey, don't you think this is moving a bit fast? We haven't even talked about stuff.

– The speed feels about right. We've got something magic here, can't you feel it?

– Yeah, I can feel *something*. Joey, fly for me one more time, baby.

– Let's get it on, then I'll do loop-the-loops for you. I might leap from the balcony even.

– Listen, let me go freshen up. First you fly. Then we make love.

– Sounds good.

Maria went to the bathroom. Joey sat up on the mattress and drank some more red. He heard the water go on and thought about it flowing all over her.

When she came back she was wearing something see-through that came to just below her pussy, and fresh thong-panties.

She lowered herself onto the mattress and lay on her side. Her hips were a fine rounded mountain range with the bedside light making a Himalayan shadow onto the back wall. Her tits were nothing special.

– Listen, Joey. I want you to know this isn't something I usually do. I usually like to get to know a guy first. To go out to a restaurant and talk about things, like where we grew up and what we expect from life, and to find out if we're compatible. You know what I mean?

Yeah, I know exactly, thought Joey.

– Maria, you are the only woman I have ever flown for.

– Do it again, Joey. Do it for me.

– OK. Lie on your front. That's it. Take your panties off.

He could see it all anyway with the bit of material on but she obliged him. He took off his shoes and socks and trousers and shirt and stood there, lordly, in his shorts. Life would never be the same again for either of them, he was sure. Once he got this flying thing under control, there would be no looking back. Just ignore the face, he told himself. Concentrate on the centre of gravity. Luckily the station was doing a run of Chopin nocturnes and he had one in D-flat major that was just perfect.

The winter is over; the rains have stopped;
In the countryside the flowers are in bloom
This is the time for singing;
The song of doves is heard in the field.

He pushed off gently with his toes, giving a little more with the left for torque. He kept it going until he was right above her and felt his head graze the ceiling, then held it there above her. Gradually he came down until he was trembling above her, not touching, with his face before her ass. He rubbed his face against it and kissed it, reached down and caressed her hips, while his feet were hanging in the sky. This is it, thought Joey. This is how it is supposed to be. He felt her ass up for a good long time, not wanting it to end.

– It's OK, Joey, she said. I'm on the pill.

He murmured:

I have entered my garden,
My beloved, my bride.
I am gathering my spices and myrrh;
I am eating my honey and honeycomb;
I am drinking my wine and milk.

Flying was good, but when he was in her, giving it from behind and getting handfuls, feeling up the sun and the moon – all the stars in the sky sparking up his mind – that was the real thing too.

– OOH! UUH! Joey! Aaa!

– Huh! Huh! Huh!

– Right there!

– UH! Uh!

– Now, Joey! Now!

All the heavenly bodies rushed together and exploded briefly. There was complete darkness and one shooting star fell through the black sky like a drip from the ceiling. It went very quiet for a moment, then the radio said they would be back again at the same time next week. The ads came on. Does your deodorant ever let you down? Joey disengaged and fell off to the side, which was the floor, because the mattress was not big. The blood pounded in his head.

– You're a special guy, no doubt about it, said Maria, reaching for her smokes. She offered him one and they lit up.

He sat up properly on the linoleum and looked around. There was a row of paperbacks on a shelf of a unit. He couldn't read the titles properly but one was definitely by Paulo Coelho. On another shelf she had made up an arrangement of empty perfume bottles. It was some kind of shrine. He took a few drags of the cigarette. Maria was talking:

– Nobody ever flew for me before. I've met a lot of creepy

guys. Most guys think they got a big dick or a car they're hot shit. Fuck them sons of bitches. You're the real thing, Joey. Flying, that's real magic. And you know poetry too. You don't look like much, but with this flying we've got it made. You just need a haircut and some decent clothes. Maybe if you got some exercise too, worked out or something.

Joey began to put on his clothes.

– Got to go, he said.

– Oh well. Here, gimme a big kiss.

He gave her a big kiss, just to be nice.

– Fly one more time for me, 'fore you go.

– I'd love to, Maria, but I'm pretty whacked.

– Just float a little. Nothing flashy. Here, I'll lie on my front the way you like.

She flopped onto her belly and stuck her ass in the air and wiggled it a little. He sighed.

– Why don't I leap off the balcony for you?

– You can use the front door like everyone else. Come on now! Three! two! One! Lift off!

He looked at Maria's big fat ass. It said nothing to him. It was a dead jellyfish on the beach. He concentrated on his breathing but he knew it would not work. He did a lame little jump on the linoleum, but that was all it was.

– Hey, what was that?

He shrugged.

– Seems like I'm just like everyone else again, huh? Well, you can blame me, I can blame you, but that won't get us out of it. How about I just say thanks for a good time and we leave it at that?

He heard the glass hit the wall behind him. He was out the front door before she could throw the second one.

Back in the street the light was gone from the sky. He decided to pick up a couple of bottles of beer to drink at home. He was sad about the flying because he didn't think it would be back soon. But he didn't want to get stuck with Maria, flying or no flying. If he could get airborne for any woman, or get women by getting airborne, that would be a trick. But he knew it would not happen. There had just been something special about Maria, briefly, and that was all.

Somewhere, on a street parallel, a fire engine was screaming its way towards a burning building. The 24-hour sheet-metal shack was coming up on his right. Joey put his hand in his pocket and felt his money. At least that was still there, thank God.

Uprooted

The evening promenade – couples young and old, baby-buggies, tracksuited headphoned joggers, dogs on leashes. Spring air gusting across the sandflats and lowtide rocks. The fluent limestone strata of the hills across the bay sculpted in slanting light.

Eoin is caught up in the flow, radio tuner drifting across crackling frequencies, catching scraps of conversation. Then the native old-time God-bless-you beggar standing before him, tangled beard and swollen nose, overcoat open to the seaweedy breeze. Change for a cup of tea? Eoin digs his pocket.

You're after getting out, says the man. Of the hospital.

Today, says Eoin.

It's hard on you. But thank God for the weather.

Eoin looks across the bright-topped waves and nods. Thank God, he says.

They put me out in the rain, says the man. I coulda cried.

The man pockets the change, raises index to temple to tip a hat that is not there.

Eoin proceeds along the promenade, the evening ritual of the coastal constitutional, towards the town.

Before the breakdown he did a lot of walking. And drinking. Could not stop his thoughts. Writing poems for her, whole notebooks full. He presented the poems to her, and when inside received a letter, compassionate, thanking him. He read her letter without hope. The circus had left town by then, the excitement had expired. You offered them your veins and they mixed what they wanted with your blood. You started at the bottom again, in playschool. Lithium and basketry.

Those who have been here, he told himself, will know Christian pity for those forsaken, for the homeless, for hearts that are splitting with grief. There were those worse off, he discovered. People tormented by voices, people who fought themselves, who were afraid at a door opening, at a door closing.

The busy part of town, bridge over the ever tumbling Corrib, hectic overspill of vast mysteries of inland lakes. Quay Street, pedestrianized, surging with human forms.

A girl's voice from behind asks him how he *is*.

He stops. She strides onwards, shouting at a telephone.

A scatter of individuals in the oncoming crowd fall into step together, speak into phones simultaneously, identical left-hand gesture. They threaten to form a unit, break into dance, like in an old musical film. Eoin stops and looks at his shoes, concentrates on his breathing. Looks up, focuses on a tame clump of tourists assessing seafood options posted in the window of MacDonagh's.

When he looks around again, the crowd is behaving normally.

Moving on. Tí Ó Neachtain – exceptional public house, where a man can order coffee without shame – and left down Mainguard Street, across O'Brien Bridge this time. Knots of girls, their strange ecstatic dialect in the darkening air. They are destined for the night. Towers of empties stacked on tabletops.

No more alcohol. A fundamental resolution. And to pray, another. These commandments, and Prozac.

Turns right down Nun's Island, towards the cathedral and the dull turquoise gleam of its copper dome. Halfway down the street, a crowd of young people before a Protestant church, desanctified.

DANGEROUS LIAISONS!!!

– says the poster.

Buys a ticket, takes a seat. The lights go down. Communion of strangers attending a mystery. The stage a pregnant space.

A long time ago, in another country.

He leans forward when he sees her, comprehends that this is the tale of good and evil. Valmont, the corruption of the world, sets a snare for a virgin called Cécile.

A butterfly, blinded by sunlight, dancing towards a web.

A spider tiptoes across his strings.

Eoin wants to cry out: Look behind you!

Poison kiss.

Conan, from the final row, cannot see Cécile as well as he could wish. He pulls the wisps of his blond beard between thumb and index until the last hairs slip from between his fingers. Then again, from chin to longest wisp. He has seen her before. Monday night poetry readings at the café, perhaps. Or a face from one of the crowds gathered about his juggling act. Maybe she has dropped a coin in his hat on Quay Street, and smiled.

Cécile comes on stage. Ah, joy of theatre, permission to stare! Jonathan recalls a stag night, a Dublin stripclub. Then his wife, perky through his hangover, presenting issues: low self-esteem of sex-workers, forced by economic conditions, and so on. A Latvian woman cleans our house, he says. Later apologizes for justifying himself.

Cécile performs the bedroom scene in a simple white night-dress, fleeting hints of silhouetted curves as the lights catch her from behind. She is a barefoot dancer, eloquent restraint of loose garments twisting on her body.

Valmont closes on his prey. Jonathan twists his wedding ring in the dark. Jonathan is for Valmont. He identifies.

Watching Cécile move, Aidan thinks of ballet. The point of which is not technical difficulty or athleticism, but the creation of a space untouched by this graceless world. Angels, perfect of form, their motions set to music. Humankind in its ideal; young and strong. And you stare.

This is what we dream, thinks Aidan. A beauty not of this earth.

The difference between art and life?

Art is easier to take.

Leaving the theatre. Jonathan and Sean:

J: Cécile has talent.

S: Her acting's good too.

(Her name is Kirsten. German. Sean knows her, kind of, knows a flatmate. Does Irish Studies, even speaks the *Gaeilge*. Jonathan twists his wedding ring.)

J: Not the typical German. Unconventional. Spontaneous.

S: That's a kind of German. Germans become fully German being anti-German. Tour around, saying they hate Germany, always end up back there.

J: Goods and services.

S: No place like Babylon.

J: So. A pint.

Eoin, next day, standing in a café doorway, watching, petrified. A man paces the parapet of the roof of the building across the street. Then someone, from a top window, sends up a cable tied to a stick. The man takes the cable, unties it from the stick. Eoin folds his chin onto his chest, and sighs.

Come inside, says the doorway.

Menu *as Gaeilge*. Twenty kinds of tea and coffee, salads with nuts and avocado. *Ceapaire ar arán donn le prosciutto crudo agus cáis emmenthal*. A ham and cheese sandwich. Two students behind him discuss globalization in Irish but he gets stuck on *idirlíon. Líon*: Net. Of course. Orders the ham and cheese, *más é do thoil é*. Catches himself commenting *as Gaeilge*. Wishes for a settling, not to be caught up in the talk of strangers. Not to assume suicide the issue when a man is only laying a cable for the *idirlíon*. Pu-leez! says a girl at another table, and I'm like, she so isn't! Syntax scrambled in the ether. Perfectly harmless, everybody imitates, we're all receivers, *buíochas do Dhia*. Tank God fer de wedder. The expensive sandwich arrives. Not as big as he could wish.

She asks for the milk. He passes it, recognizes her face. Or voice. Recalling the girl is like trying to remember a story, or a dream. A premonition. In the old church in the dark. Cécile sits next to him, reading. Her very fine blonde hair is tied up with a mechanism he does not comprehend, involving varnished wooden sticks.

Rehearses lines, finds his character, prompts himself. Leans in. Excuse me . . .

She is vegetarian, looks at him with clear blue eyes and tells him food should be pure. Impure food burdens the blood with toxins. This happens when we consume animals that have suffered, she explains. She is against torturing living creatures. He tells her the importance of prayer. She does not believe in religion, she says, because of terrible things done in history, wars and so on. But she is interested in spirituality. They agree that there is 'something out there'.

They drink their coffees, walk down the street together. She says goodbye, it was nice meeting him, and she walks with her bicycle respectfully through a pedestrian street, her little satchel on her back, becoming a figure in a crowd.

Immaculate milky skin of one whose blood contains no toxins. *Gan smál*. Full of Grace.

He goes to the cathedral to pray. The Blessed Virgin holds the child to her robes.

And then his final walk through the darkening town, shoppers, employees in the moments after their release, tasting the free air of the breezy streets. He feels a quickening. Something crushed regenerating. The opening of a bloom.

Trust the Captain, Aidan thinks, sudden westerly picking up as the boat leaves the harbour. It will be bad in open sea.

Waves smash starboard. The windows are white foam. The boat rises, hangs, crashes into troughs, lurches to extreme angles, unexpectedly, repeatedly. The fairground feeling at open sea upsets the regulars also. They hold onto the seats in front of them. Women bless themselves. Aidan reads an old book.

Art is life, he thinks, refining the thought. Art is life, by the spoonful, in digestible form.

The boat bucks savagely. Somebody begins to vomit.

The island is a long narrow ridge, an animal stretched full length, lying low in the water, and he would usually go on deck to see it taking shape as a complex piece of solid earth, and to identify his own house, on the mainland-facing coastal strip.

In the lee of the island, the waves ease.

They disembark under electric light, grateful. The world continues swaying, even on the solid concrete of the quay. The joyful lights of the village make a break for open sky, then come back to earth.

His cottage, twenty minutes on foot. The storm blows hard,

though his side of the island is spared the worst Atlantic weather. The cat twines itself mewling between his legs as he opens the door to the cottage in the darkness and the rain starts, lashed by gusts. He turns on the light of the room and is gladdened. His stove and his chair and his books. And his work. The pieces of wood, some already sculpted, some yet to find their form. The room he lives and sleeps in, because it is too hard to heat the bedroom also. Feeds the cat to get it from underfoot then takes a torch to fetch fuel from the shed. All that is left is an old wooden cartwheel. His boot splinters the rotten spokes.

He watches the flames. He eats a sandwich, drinks some whiskey.

The nagging things, tiny splinters under the skin, become unimportant as he drinks and watches flames, listens to the wind howling in the empty sky. He likes the sound of the storms. One blending into the next in winter, the pauses between them growing in the spring. He likes the rain against his windowpane, the slow indifferent passage of time and the vacant evenings. It is the company of the uncongenial that wearies the spirit. The noise and the machinery of the city, the anxiety at time running away.

Jonathan, working, rain flecking the plate-glass windows of the university library, the grey morning beyond. The storm has blown itself out. He is dressed in black. He likes other colours. But not on him.

Days you bow your head, plough like a mule. The obstinate will inherit the earth. Become junior lecturers. Then tenure. And then your wife might come live in the same city as you. You purchase a house, please God, and find a vein of Irish literature to exploit.

As he heads from the checkout desk with his books, she

almost walks into him. He says hello, thinking he knows her. She responds, too blankly he feels, until he remembers her from the stage, introduces himself. They laugh. She looks at his pile of books, is most interested in Synge's *The Aran Islands*. She's going out to the islands. He insists she borrow the book. It took Synge many years to get the book published, he says. Nobody had wanted it.

Aidan wakes. Mizzle spitting on the windowpane, milky mist trailing between small fields of stone walls. The stove is cold. He never relights it in the morning. Bad dreams have followed him into the day. He puts on his cold clothes and washes his face in cold water. He fries eggs on the gas cooker in the frigid little kitchen, eats them with brown soda bread, washes it down with good coffee.

The feeling of desolation will burn off like vapour under the gathering power of the sun. He puts on his boots.

Chill mist pours across the spine of the island. The mainland is hidden. A white calf in the lee of a stone wall, its front legs folded beneath itself. Its mother, inured, grazes at a distance. Epochs of men clearing rocky fields, building chains of walls. And the same beast staring down the same cold spring day, beneath shifting skies. He passes Saint Kevin's Church, a thousand years old, from the days of the monks. Sometimes a defrocked priest and his wife hold services for believers in Celtic spirituality, whatever that is – Aidan visualizes guitars strummed to the heavens in the roofless ruin.

He ascends the steep narrow path, follows tracks through fields. He reaches the cliffs. Gulls quiver on the wind, swoop, rise again, wheeling in the updraught. Fresh seaweed by his feet, carried up by the storm, though the ocean is a hundred metres below, waves crashing and foaming on titanic slabs of cliff-fallen rock. He has often on a bad day watched the wind picking up the crashing swell at the cliffs of Inis Meáin, propelling it half-way across that island as salt rain.

The mist is slowly lifting, revealing his island. The vantage gives him everything – cliffs and sea and land, and in the distance Inis Meáin, and now the mainland, hazy. The dream is dispelled, mostly. Now it is only a matter of descending, returning to work.

The day brightens from the west. Conan, making a cappuccino, sees her already through the café window. She enters, approaches the counter, asks what teas they have. He recites the list, from China to Ceylon, from Raspberry to Blackberry. And congratulates her on the play. Her smile increases his appreciation, retrospectively, of her performance. She knows him also, has seen him performing. They are each other's fans, meeting for the first time.

Aidan throws open the doors and windows, picks up his tools, approaches the block. A relationship he has got into that has good days and rough patches. A matter of working the material, chipping away until a form emerges. A solitary apprenticeship, without end. An escape as much as an act of bravery, such obsession. Awaiting a moment when you put doubt aside and trust your hand. And that is a humble thing, finally, to lose yourself in the work, and then to step back and find it is well done. State of grace.

It does not happen that way often.

Sometimes, frustrated with wood, the limitations of a grain, how it splinters and cracks, he is bitter at using what is cast up on the shore, and imagines kinds of wood that will give him what he wants, easily. But, in his heart, he knows all material is unforgiving of errors. He thinks of those sculptors who work marble, those who cast bronze. Terracotta would be malleable but must be fired. No perfect material, only conditions imposed by nature.

He sets to work, reciting:

> *Ár n-aithreacha bhíodh,*
> *Is a n-aithreacha siúd,*
> *In achrann leis an saol*
> *Ag coraíocht leis an gcarraig loim.*

Conan sits with her by O'Brien Bridge. The storm has passed and the only reminder is the Corrib in flood, the headlong waves tripping over each other in their hurry to the sea. He tells her of his travels from Australia, always passing through. Stepping off a train or bus or boat or plane, walking into a new city with your bags and knowing there would be a new set of people. And coming finally to the old stone city in the west, with its cold salt air and its seabirds and monument to Columbus, who might himself have passed through once. Having gone steadily westwards for over a year, he has reached the edge of the world. There is no more land.

So he stops and looks around, where the drinking houses are convivial, and where students and tourists gather and toss coins into his hat.

He wears a yellow scarf and hers is red, and he is happy. He describes for her the baked-dry outback where he grew up, a shed behind the house where he made pottery and fired it in a kiln he had built himself, trial and error. A one-man civilization crafting its artefacts, because hands must be busy. The absent father, the ill mother, a house of books. A shipwrecked savant discovering the world alone, from clues left behind.

Though he admits he was bored, hiding from the sun, she closes her eyes and says she imagines it, and the rows of pottery, growing, and him painting, designing objects that nobody used. His journey is noble.

And then the degree in physics, an academic career thrown away, learning circus arts, the juggling, the unicycle.

He is a vegetarian too, he tells her. He will cook for her soon, he promises. Her mobile rings. When she finishes speaking it is time for her to go to her lecture.

After she has left, he watches the river. He would not mind staying in that city, growing into it, letting it grow into him. He walks home, goes up to his room, masturbates efficiently. Then makes seed bread according to a Scandinavian recipe.

Each day Eoin looks for her among the faces in the college cafeteria. Metal tables and plastic cups. People carrying folders, exchanging notes. If he meets her he will say he was using the library. Useless signs posted by the catering company demand that the students stop stealing the cutlery. Soon, they say, there will be no cutlery. The cafeteria's big plate-glass windows look onto a flagstoned terrace and wooden picnic tables. It is now warm enough to venture outside. Undecided spring, black and white clouds scrolling the sky, moments of wind and darkness alternating with bursts of sun, and the green grass and the new trees.

Her headscarf is knotted behind, a Gypsy fortune-teller. The scarf is shiny blue and her blonde hair flows out underneath, down her back. It is amazing, the length of her hair. She wears a long loose dress, deep blue as the sky when the first star appears.

She smiles and rises and says his name like he is a long-lost friend. She is going into town, has to meet someone, but they can walk together, if he has time.

Outside, he holds her bag of books as she unlocks her bicycle from the rack. She wheels the bicycle; he carries the books. Gentle student traffic on university pathways, cyclists and pedestrians bearing their essential bags and bundles.

They cross the road outside the campus, take the canal path. Willows drooping branches in the water, soft breeze rippling the surface. She lays her bicycle upon the grass and they sit on a bench. A duck pulls a chain of ducklings. Clouds tremble in the water.

He tells her about the hospital. The words he has spoken to no one. But he knows he can tell her what it is to be nobody, to reach the bottom and have to rebuild yourself again, knowing that from then on standing or falling is not in your hands, but is something you have to trust as you walk through the world. He tells her of the other ones, the ones who really suffered. When he stops speaking she says his name, leans into him, puts her arms around him, rests her head on his shoulder. This is embarrassing and he looks at indifferent ducks pecking pondweed. She is overdoing it a little. And it is enjoyable, her hair tickling his neck, and the smell of her, like nothing on earth.

She pulls back, tells him he is very brave. He shakes his head, knows this is simply untrue. I didn't mean to speak of it, he says. You're very brave, she repeats. Brave to keep going, courageous to tell me like that. People, she says, are scared to reveal themselves.

She wipes a tear. He hopes she will not cry. He does not know what to do with a crying girl.

People, she says, think I'm tough, that I'm happy all the time. But I'm not. Not at all. There's things I can't tell people. That's why I say you're brave.

Her mobile rings. The theme from *Titanic* scares the ducks. She closes her eyes, lets it ring a little more.

Hate this phone, she says, submitting, putting it to her ear, eyes still misty. He feels her travel far away from him as her voice changes, far from the canal with the trees dripping their branches in the water. Nooo! she says. Dooon't be silly! Yes, I will! Get out of that! Dooon't be silly!

It goes on like that, the conversation with the invisible person, and he with ducks for consolation. A passing cyclist looks at them. Perhaps the cyclist thinks he is with his girlfriend.

She finishes the conversation, puts her phone in her bag. Looks at him.

Sorry.

Doesn't matter.

They look at clouds in water. He wonders how they can return.

Do you want to tell me? he says.

Tell you what?

What we were saying. Before.

She closes her eyes, shakes her head. No, she says, and he feels ashamed, as if he has brazenly demanded a kiss, and been refused.

She jumps up. Late! She rights the bicycle and mounts. Wait! Give me your number. Mobile in hand, ready to key it in. But he has no number. She rummages for a pen, writes her number on her notepad, rips the page and gives it to him. Byeeeee!

Robes rippling, billowing as she rides away. The sun breaks out and lights her blonde hair, escaping from under her head-scarf. Chaste and extravagant.

That night, returning from the pub, a *síbín* down an alleyway, having drunk three moderate pints, which she has matched, Jonathan lies on his back, hands clasped across his chest, right foot crossed over left.

Her smiles, the eye contact, the way she would touch his leg or arm for emphasis – and that was before she had drunk anything. And the farewell hug, her breasts compressed against his chest. Yes, beneath that baggy clothing were large breasts, and a backside that would ripple with the slap of flesh against it.

He takes from his pocket his wedding ring and puts it on his finger again. He has never done such a thing before. No intention of creating secrets. Solely curious whether it would be possible, in this instance, were she interested. It was something forgotten, something that was in a play, or a ballet, or the words of a writer such as Synge – in the days before such words had become his work – back then when they cut him and surprised him and awoke in him things that he felt fully because they had been formulated beautifully in words.

Walking down a small road, slowly, in the sunshine, shawl about her shoulders. The hem of her dress, dark blue like a late evening sky, trailing the road. Stone walls and small fields. The sun, warming the left side of her face, prepares to meet a rocky hillcrest. To her right, an ocean view towards the mainland.

She wants to walk down that road forever, for the sun to hold still in the sky. If the shadows could draw out so far and stop. The patterns of the walls, and the sun coming through the gaps in the stones, and the shadows of the walls on the grass.

She comes to a cow and says: He-llo, cow! The cow looks back, and munches.

She walks on and meets a white horse. She leans against the wall, her arms reaching into the field, the hard stones pleasantly cold against her breasts, and cluck-cluck-clucks her tongue. The horse lifts its head a little, notes her, drops its head and crops more good grass.

White smoke trails seawards from an aluminium stove-pipe on the roof of a small house. A short man places planks from a broken pallet against the wall of the cottage, smashes them with his boot. His beard needs a trim. He wears baggy brown corduroy trousers. An axe lies on the grass.

He-llo! she says.

He looks up with little eyes, frowns.

Cécile de Volanges! he says.

Oh, you're an artist! she exclaims, seeing the figures worked from wood.

Well, he says, disliking the inflection.

And she stands before some pieces made of wood, and is charmed by the effect. He has become special to her, he realizes, far too quickly, for the wrong reason.

She is enchanted by his simple house. He lights the fire and they sit in front of it and he gives her bread and honey and later whiskey, and she drinks some, but not as much as he does. He gets drunk, calls her Goldilocks.

It is late. She falls asleep while he is talking. When he lays a blanket over her, he feels he has seen it many times in a film but surrenders anyway to the tenderness of the gesture. He drinks a little more, watches her dreaming innocently. How easily she has fallen asleep, on the sofa that is his bed.

He pulls the mattress from the frigid bedroom and lays it beside the stove.

Awakening in the daylight, Aidan stares at her again, as he stared at her on the stage, because her long blonde hair is spread out over her face and on the cushion, but this time he watches her furtively, that she might wake, and he be caught in transgression.

He gets up, washes in cold water, turns on the boiler for her. He steps out. The clean line of the mainland. A clear still day for her, thank God. He puts a sod of turf in the stove, where embers still glow when the ash is raked.

She wakes, rubs her eyes, looks at him and smiles.

An hour later they walk out of his house together, into the morning, as if this were natural.

They take the unpaved cliff road to Gort na gCapall. The track undulates. The stone walls thread in every direction, geometric designs on the contours of the land.

At the cliffs the island reaches its highest point. A larger mass sectioned by the prehistoric violence of the elements, the windward half collapsed into the waves. Ahead, the ragged wall of rock, stretching the length of the island.

The horizon is the ocean. The end of the world.

She believes nature is good. Eating animals is wrong. Every person is interesting, if you take the time. The information revolution will bring people together. The American empire is a dirty machine driven on oil. Nationalism is absurd, retrograde. Religion, another divisive superstition – her generation has discarded it as unhealthy, along with smoking. Yet drugs should be legal, because it is a matter of personal freedom. Immigration controls are racist. There should be no borders. Everything can be resolved by dialogue. Jealousy has no place in a relationship – you should sleep with whoever you want. (Though she makes love only with those she loves.)

She says she often cries and does not mind who is present. She wants to visit everywhere, because every place has something to teach. She likes Ireland, and particularly its landscapes. This landscape, she says, indicating the fields and walls around them, perfectly balances the natural and human worlds. An organic work of art, written on the land.

Yes, he says. A lot of little fields. And all those rocks placed there by human hands. And you visit for a day and see the beauty. But the people who built the walls did not have your conception of beauty, because they did not receive nature as a pretty gift. These walls were made to clear fields. The only thing to do was to stack one rock upon the other. In some places there was no soil, a field was just rock, and they would make soil from sand and composted seaweed. It was not an easy life. He recites:

> *Aiteas orthu bhíodh*
> *Tráth ab eol dóibh*
> *Féile chaoin na húire,*
> *Is díochas orthu bhíodh*
> *Ag baint ceart*
> *De neart na ndúl.*

She does not know all the words, so he puts it in English for her, and she is delighted.

We like such places, he continues, because they remind us of another time. Nature is never pushed aside here, where you spend the winter cowering from storms. The reality is wind and rock and water, and you, a little pouch of blood and bones, a dreaming creature that does not even last a century. Look at those cliffs there. Look down the strata and you see a geologic record, ticking out the time in stone.

She looks as if she will swoon at his words. In that case, he thinks, it is not what I meant. Not what I meant at all.

Don't you call me spiritual now, he warns, or I'll toss you off the cliff.

She likes to agree and he does not want what he has said put to New Age chill-out music. He does not want perfumed candles or soya foodstuffs or recordings of whales. None of that soul-tourist trinketry of the spiritually unmoored. The pick 'n' mix herbal nirvana of refugees from any kind of rigour. He senses she is doped on that stuff. Her romantic idea of Ireland, and this island that was the soul of Irishness, slotted into this lazy notion. She has plotted the 'artist' in the cottage into the frame, he knows.

But he looks at her and wonders is it something he can profit from, to kiss her lips, or her cheek or forehead, or even her hand. She is leaving on the evening boat, and he is hungry for a little time. The kind of time in which many small fascinating human events occur, such as one person taking the hand of another, and them kissing, and deciding when they will see each other again.

They are walking slowly. Her head is tilted towards him as he speaks, her arms folded under her breasts, clutching her shawl, her robe billowing around her legs.

She asks if he ever married. Kiddo, he says, in his Bogart voice, in this crazy mixed-up world the problems of two little people don't add up to a hill of beans.

They walk on. Dún Aengus, a prehistoric cliff fort, takes shape ahead, on the highest point of the island. He explains that this island, now so peripheral, had in seafaring times been a strategic point from which the west coast could be controlled. Look, he says, you can see every ship travelling up and down the coast, the islands, the bay.

He wants to kiss her, but is afraid to. He continues to talk.

They stand at the cliff and together behold the whole wide world.

*

He walks her to the boat. It is a very clear evening – starlings punctuate the village telephone wires in musical notation, their feathers oily-blue in the low light. A few thin streaks of cirrus describe the vast curve of the sky, and the distant waves on the bay are pure white flecks on green. People outside Tí Joe Mac finish drinks and hurry for the boat. The mood on the docks is celebratory. The weather promises long warm days ahead and still seas and good fishing on the bay. Locals seeing Aidan with the girl say hello and smile as if to say they know what is going on. Speculations will be exchanged around the island. It will be established there was only one place she could have slept.

She is going and he is staying. You're lucky, he says, the crossing will be very gentle. The captain calls for the latecomers to board, and she is last down the gangplank, which they retract behind her. The mooring ropes are cast onto the deck as the noise of the engines rises. She stays on deck and as the boat pulls away she turns and waves and he watches her hair blowing in the wind. He observes her figure for as long as he can as the boat recedes, moving past the lighthouse on Straw Island, towards open sea. In twenty minutes she will be halfway to the mainland.

He is the last one left on the quayside. Well, that is the end of that, he thinks, and turns away.

He walks through Cill Rónáin. At the shop Máirtín pulls up, offers a lift. Thank you, he will walk. *Is tráthnóna brea ea.*

The road shining oily in the last light. The grass glowing edibly green.

The sun falls behind the hill. There is nothing to do. He does not want to pick up his tools and work yet. He does not want to read. Unused to being so much with a person, talking, he is unable to return to himself. He is turned outwards to the world. Something moving in him that has long been still.

It becomes dark. He lights the fire.

He wishes he were in the same room as her, wherever it may be. I will indulge it a little, because it is pleasant, he tells himself, and then it will pass. Dreams, good and bad, dragged into the open, burn off like mist beneath the sun.

He puts the cat off his lap, stokes the stove, closes the air valve for slow combustion, then puts on his coat. He steps into the cool night air, leaving the light on for his return.

He takes the road down to the strand. He walks up and down the beach several times. Waves gush tirelessly, fizzing on the sands. Clouds drift before the pale face of the moon. Another night or two and it will be full again. A string of lights twinkles along the Conamara coast. Individual houses of Gorumna, An Cheathrú Rua, Baile na hAbhann. Indreabhán too perhaps, like a faint constellation. And then the dull orange glow of Galway staining the horizon in the east. That is where she is now. He wonders has the island stayed with her. Then he walks back.

He sits before the fire and eats bread and butter and blackberry jam and drinks some whiskey. The first taste of the whiskey is cutting after the sweetness. He drinks slowly and watches the flames.

And when his thoughts come unhurried and he is sleepy, he puts the blankets and the pillow on the sofa and stokes the stove and undresses and lies down. He lies down and her scent is on the pillow and there is nothing he can do about it, as he puts his head down to dream.

Let me put my arms around you, the night is getting cold, out there among the hard-hearted stars and the rocks and the dark restless waves.

★

Days pass. Eoin is afraid to call her number. The only route from the college into town is now along the canal. He sits on their bench. There, he can smell her again. Her embrace, her breast pressing his shoulder. Solid and soft at the same time, dizzying. In the last light of bright evenings he walks along Nun's Island, past the converted church where she performed, and wonders about her sad secret.

I'll call her when I finish this cup of coffee, he tells himself one evening, alone in the café where they met.

The situation of the first public telephone he finds is wrong. It is not propitious. He walks on.

At Spanish Arch the street disgorges pedestrians and the river spills into the Claddagh and the big sky bears high streaks of cloud in the final light. Prowling students, smelling the beginning of the alcoholic night, bear down on their destinations. Here the phones are tolerable.

She answers. Loud music, voices behind her.

He hangs up, walks across the bridge, down to where the Corrib opens fully to the bay, where the swans swim. High tide wavelets slap the stone quays. Lights in the row of houses on the far side. He imagines the inhabitants as similar to each other and very different from himself. People who go to pubs at night, people who do not pray. He wishes he were a little like them on the surface, wishes for a room in a renovated old pastel house, overlooking the water, one of those squares of light to be the bedroom where he sleeps.

The green postal van stops outside the cottage and Aidan puts down his chisel, meets Joe Pat at the wall and takes the letter. Elegant script on the envelope. Fountain pen, blue ink. Old-fashioned touch. He likes that. He knows it is from her. He sits down on the armchair by the cold stove and rips it open. The cat jumps on his lap. It is a one-page letter.

She had a wonderful time. Wonderful twice underlined. Most of the sentences end with at least one mark of exclamation. Large, extravagant handwriting, the loops on the *g*'s and *f*'s decorative events. He turns the letter upside down, holds it at arm's length. It radiates the same enthusiasm. He smiles, reads on.

He is invited to a party. Exhorted not to be a smelly old bear. To abandon his den and come to town.

He puts the letter down, sighs. It's no good. He is in the trap. He has to go. He strokes the cat. It purrs.

Semi-detached, parcelled-out suburbia, each unit bought and sold and bought again as the contestants jostle for a better piece. Each blocky house fronted by its patch of grass and the strip of concrete for the car that takes you to the job. Aidan has picked up someone more lost than himself. He approached the tall, thin young man for directions, to find that they were both heading for the same address. The young man – Eoin – has a mucker accent, is interested that Aidan lives on an island. What does he do there? Aidan lets it slip.

You're an artist!

Well . . .

I wish I could do that. It must be great, to express yourself, like. I wrote some poems once. I had one published, in the college magazine. And then I stopped.

Why stop, when it's going well?

'Twasn't. Going all that well.

Aidan pulls a bottle of vodka from his overcoat, swigs and proffers.

Ah no. No, I don't.

The music coming from the house. Kirsten opens the door.

Hell-oooo! She hugs Aidan, sooo surprised he could come. Eoin is hugged too but feels less warmth from the hug now. She is promiscuous with embraces.

Stepping into the hall, a creature with a wispy blond-red beard introduces himself.

Onan? asks Aidan.

Conan! repeats Conan, louder, over the music coming through the open living-room door.

Aidan wonders does he live there too, or if he is Kirsten's lover. Just good friends? It would make sense – the floppy blue hat and loose, striped trousers like pyjamas.

In the suburban living room, candles are burning and people lounge in chairs and perch on armrests and on the floor. Aidan is grateful it is not a dancing party.

Young bodies, competing for space and attention. Aidan does not know how to play the game. He does not want to hear anything any of them have to say. Particularly anything a man in pyjamas might say. You get older, then feel awkward as a teenager again. He gives his bottle special attention. Eoin sticks, pest-like, to him. How do you know Kirsten? he asks. Isn't Kirsten great? Aidan nods. Yes, he says, she's a superstar. He drinks from the bottle. He pushes the bottle into Eoin's hands, goes to find her. But she is locked in negotiation in the hallway with the fluffy-bearded jackoff, so he carries on to the kitchen so as not to seem to be seeking her. He stands for a decent interval in the kitchen with people he does not know. It has passed the point where people shake hands and introduce them-selves. Now they drift about, looking to connect with something stronger than what they have left behind. They enter each other's conversations, talk about nothing much, and drift away again. He removes his coat and hangs it on a chair. Then moves on to the toilet, as something to do more than due to urgent need. Then back through the hallway, glimpsing Kirsten and Fluffy – now sitting together on the stairs – and back to Eoin in the living room. Eoin holds the bottle like it is a bomb. Aidan takes the bottle, removes the cap, drinks and offers.

Work away, pal.

Ah, thanks, no, no.

Go on, have a good swig.

Eoin looks at the bottle.

Get on out of that. He pokes Eoin in the ribs with the bottle. Have a fucken drink.

Ah no, I don't. Well.

Eoin takes a sudden familiar swig, upending the bottle and sending bubbles up through it. And then another. He hands it back with a small shy nod of appreciation.

Fuck's sake, Eoin!

Eoin is floating free. Aidan is integrating. Recognizes a face from the play and compliments the actress with vodka-enthusiasm, is introduced to a person who had a small part. He pretends he recognizes her because these things are now effortless. He is introduced to the set designer, a small bespectacled girl of the type often overlooked at parties. They get into a conversation about the Middle East.

Eoin returns from the petrol station down the road with two bottles of wine.

Kirsten still monopolized by Fluffy. Aidan in the kitchen again, formulating a complaint about inviting someone to your home, them travelling across the waves, and being ignored by the cunt, after extending gracious hospitality yourself, fuck it. Fluffy had to piss eventually. Or maybe he'd just bust in, displace him forcibly. A couple are eating the faces off each other, the man leaning back up against the fridge, the girl taller than him. The group of people around the kitchen table find this funny, Aidan does not understand why. He recognizes the man at the fridge as Valmont, the ruthless seducer, but under the kitchen's fluorescent light his skin is bad. It is red and flaking in patches. Aidan recalls that he delivered his lines in too great a hurry.

Aidan passes the toilet, steps out into the back garden. It is paved concrete between breeze-block walls. Unzips, slashes in the dark against the concrete wall. Better to piss in the open, beneath the sky, much better in the natural breeze. Gives a shake and arranges to return to society. The kitchen window, a television screen in a dark room, no, a very large painting. The group at the table, composed with their faces towards him like the apostles at the Last Supper. Five of them, anyhow. Valmont and his conquest against the fridge, another film.

Eoin enters the frame, exclaiming in silent mode. Heads turn. The smoochers too attend the interruption. The drunken apostles listen, unsure. The apostle closest to the door rises and leaves, then another. Eoin beats the table with a fist in emphasis. Then he is alone with the smoochers, who choose not to look at him. Eoin leaves the frame. The girl says something to Valmont. He begins to reply. She pushes her face into his.

The living room, Eoin leaning too close, shouting, eyes animated with the pure and undiluted spirit.

Aidan! Frien'! Wan' tellya something!

Aidan wipes his face of flecks of spit.

You don't have to, if it's private.

I! Love! To drink! I am SO fucking happy! Fuckin' hear what I'm saying!?

I'd never stop if it made me that happy. I wouldn't have it in me.

Wanna tellya something', fucker! What I wanna – You're an artist! We know! We know!

People in a nearby cluster, including the set designer, are giving Eoin space. Aidan steps away and goes to the stairs. Fluffy leaning into Kirsten, oozing sap.

Kirsten, your friend! says Aidan. A couple of drinks, pow!

Eoin?

Yes.

Noooo! He must not drink! He's supposed to pray! It is soooo terrible! O my God!

She talks very rapidly, about a mental hospital, a very sensitive nature. Eoin arrives, spidery, shambling –

Kirsten! Gotta tellya something!

Aidan makes way for Eoin. Even Fluffy yields. Aidan leans against the wall at the bottom of the stairs, the better to observe, finds himself with Fluffy, sorry, Conan. Aidan likes the party now. It is showing signs of fluidity. He can engage with various characters at various levels. It is a story he is getting into, something with more flavour than his accustomed monologue.

Conan is Australian, a street entertainer no less, which explains the get-up. Kirsten, Aidan reflects, has assembled an oddball circus. He is an acquisition, he understands. The cottage. The island. Lumps of wood. Now this one who looks like a hard wind would blow him away. Looks like a dandelion seed, with his fluffy halo.

What brings you to Europe? asks Aidan.

Travelling, ey.

Then back to college?

Nah, done Uni. Have a first in physics.

Slipped on your own shite there, Fluff, thinks Aidan. We don't do that in this country – peasant tradition, not speaking well of ourselves. We're not Americans yet. Next year, maybe.

Oh really? I'm a physicist myself.

What? Kirsten said you were a painter.

Sculptor. But used to teach in the college here. Thermodynamics. But in my spare time working on a book on how the humanities erroneously borrow concepts from science. You know, trying to find, since the eighteenth century, deterministic laws that govern human behaviour. As if human society behaved like matter . . . I didn't want their big salary, the bastards. It was corrupting me. I . . .

Aidan looks up the stairs, from where he catches stray words. Eoin is telling the girl she is an angel. She is beautiful, he loves her. Yes, love has been declared. Kirsten's replies are inaudible, but she is making no attempt to escape. Kirsten gives her entire being, it seems, to whoever is before her. Does she not understand that spilling drunkards need to be stoppered, for their own protection? Does she not know where kindness lies?

The girl who has been kissing Valmont in the kitchen looks about the hall distraught and up the stairs to Kirsten, asks where Eamonn has gone.

The boy with the bad skin who was groping you? asks Aidan. He left a few minutes ago.

Are you SURE?

Out the door, wearing his coat.

Valmont's victim howls.

Kirsten is on her feet. Female emergency.

Kirsten, why did Eamonn LEAVE, without saying ANYTHING?

I suppose he doesn't respect you, contributes Aidan.

Kirsten gives him a withering look. Sisters, sisters, *über alles*.

Aidan goes to the living room, finds his bottle, sits on the sofa beside a bored-looking man dressed entirely in black. He offers the man the bottle. The man sighs and gets up. The party is faltering, thinning out. Only energizing, mood-enhancing drugs can give it a lease of life, but they're mostly not that crowd.

Aidan wants a woman, any woman at all. To have a woman beside him and sleep in her bed. Even the set designer who seemed not very attractive earlier probably has a decent bed. He looks around and does not see her. From where he sits, he sees the Man in Black trying to say goodbye to Kirsten, now distracted by Valmont's latest victim, and Eoin, hanging over her.

Aidan is charged with walking Sharon – the girl misused by Valmont – to find a taxi.

Isn't Kirsten GREAT? she says.

It is a cold starry night. She is very drunk, and whatever else, and leans against him. She wears high heels and has linked arms with him to steady herself. He finds this very pleasant. Her make-up is smudged from crying and kissing, but she is an attractive woman.

Yeah, she's great.

Sharon cries a little more. Aidan pats her shoulder, hails a taxi, puts her inside, regretfully. He would like to comfort her further.

The taxi pulls away. As he turns, Eoin is winding towards him blindly, gesticulating, declaiming.

Eoin!

Ha! Ya fucker!

Eoin, let's get you in a taxi.

Eoin's nostrils flare, fists bunch. Aidan steps out of range. He does not want to have to punch him out. But Eoin wheels and heads townwards. Aidan walks back to the house. He has nowhere else to go, to sleep.

Jonathan undresses, with distaste. His clothes reek of smoke and he is not a smoker. He showers quickly, drinks water, brushes his teeth – admires his own discipline at doing these things, though he is very tired and still a little drunk. He does not want any more student parties. His towel wrapped around his waist, he opens the drawer of the bedside table, extracts a ring and replaces it on his finger.

What was it that the islandman told the poet? That the man who is not married eats a little in his sister's house, a little in his brother's house – he is a donkey straying upon the rocks.

He gets in bed naked, turns off the bedside light, thinks about his wife. He longs for her, across the distance. Wishes to be no longer separated from her by this practical, flexible way of life.

Kirsten and Conan and two girls who live at the house empty ashtrays, collect glasses and bottles. Aidan positions himself at the sink and begins to wash. Conan produces bananas from a canvas shoulder bag. And a block of dark chocolate. Kirsten hands him a frying pan. The electric ring heats. The chocolate slithers across the pan.

They sit at the kitchen table and eat warm bananas in chocolate sauce. The three girls say how great it is. Delicious, says Aidan. He would prefer a burger and some greasy chips, and the sharp sting of vinegar.

Aidan removes his boots, lies on the sofa in the dark. Stale smell of spilled ashtrays and drink. Fluffy and Kirsten alone in the kitchen. Were there a way to get back to the island he would be on the road, travelling at night, to get there sooner. He does not like any of the people he has met. It is not that he dislikes any of them. Simply that he does not care to meet any of them again. Nothing very original beneath the sun, the moon, the stars.

He had seen her on the stage, as in a ballet, and now he lies on a sofa that is too short, breathing the odours of the cigarettes and drinks of students who are now sleeping in their beds, dreaming their dreams. There was a part of your life when the beauty of it was all that was going to happen, when every failure and shortcoming could be redeemed, when the story was a blank page waiting to be written.

His thinking is becoming drifting and peaceful when the noises bring him back to the sofa that is too short. Muffled exclamations. A male noise. A female noise. Above him? The bedroom?

So that is what you have to do. To juggle, ride a unicycle, wear pyjamas by day, to have bananas and chocolate at the ready.

Calculates it will be some four hours until dawn. Fluffy will not rush it. Sensitive stratospheric love. The candles are burning. A foot massage with spiritual oils, then he will tickle her body with his beard.

He is about to get up and leave the house when the front door opens, sees Kirsten and Fluffy enter through the open living-room door. So, that was all. Outside, talking. Fluffy, glumly, putting on his coat. Kirsten languid, sorrowful, beside him. She says goodnight, he says nothing. She closes the door gently after him.

So, chocolate bananas are not the answer. He is glad nobody is having her, while he lies there. This is a girl who conquers widely, surrenders nothing that will deplete her freedom to harvest scalps.

Kirsten, framed in the doorway, the hall light behind her. He doubts she can see him as he lies in darkness, but watches her through one eye open barely a crack and breathes like a sleeping man. He does not want a conversation about Conan, about Eoin, about whoever else. Least of all does he want a conversation about himself. She stands for a brief moment looking into the room, then quietly pulls the door closed.

Eoin approaches a group outside the nightclub, young men and women. Nothing he says will incite them to speak to him. The girls pull their men away. He has moved beyond communication with the people of the world, become a ghost. He follows the artery of most remaining life through the centre of the drunken town, from Quay Street to Eyre Square. At the corner of the square, fast-food establishments offer the final possibilities – salty, deep-fried, covered in sauce – and blurred people swim behind the glass in garish overlit aquariums. A girl is vomiting and sobbing at the corner of the alley that goes to the shopping mall. You're disgusting, Saoirse, says her female companion, you're a fucking pig. The street is littered with paper cups, paper bags, polystyrene and cardboard cartons. Down the road a glass breaks and Eoin looks to the sound, can see nothing, only the tribe of boys, loaded with drink, slouching towards the square. He walks towards them, into them, becomes one of them, does not even feel it, only going down, down in the dark, and the boots kicking him in the darkness.

Conan is not sorry he has told Kirsten that he loves her. Now he is free to leave. He thinks of hot countries, dry clear days, places where you sit beneath fans, trees, because it is too hot to move and you shield your eyes from a light that is too white.

Where the sweat never dries from your skin entirely, and the sea calls you to immerse yourself in it.

Not this damp island with ever changing skies, rolling in from the west, suspended in confusion between something old as the stones and something trashy coming over the airwaves, giddy as a radio DJ with a fake American accent.

The light is returning. Aidan sits up and puts on his boots. He goes and pisses in the ugly little suburban bathroom. He finds a clean dish towel in a drawer in the kitchen, throws cold water on his face and dries himself off. He feels very clear for a man who has slept only a few hours. He drinks a glass of water at the sink and in the grey dawn light regards the backyard for the first time. An ugly quadrangle of concrete in which nothing grows. The shrivelled remains of weeds in the cracks in the concrete. Probably the landlord sprayed them with pesticide. A landlord's garden. He recalls the words:

> *Sinne a gclann,*
> *Is clann a gclainne,*
> *Dúinn is éigean*
> *Cónaí a dhéanamh*
> *In árais ó dhaoine*
> *A leagfadh cíos*
> *Ar an mbraon anuas.*

Steps out into the cool morning, light from the east painting on the clouds. The crossing to the island will be calm. He walks out of the housing estate and onto the deserted promenade, and briskly west along it, to depart the city. He will walk while the citizens lie in their beds, and when alarm clocks are going off in bedrooms throughout the city he will already be approaching open country, hitching an early lift towards Ros a' Mhíl. To his left, the colours of the bay awakening and the sculpted limestone hills of the Burren gaining definition by the moment, like a photograph developing. He will walk out past Bearna, possibly even until the distant black shapes of the islands appear on the horizon of the open sea. The three of them, plotted out on a line: Inis Oírr and Inis Meáin low and rounded, like the backs of whales, Árainn a long sea monster, stretched at rest.

He is alive to the world, as if after a long inexplicable period of sorrow, and he envisions throwing open the doors and windows of his house, cleaning, deciding what must be burned and what is to be sold, clearing out the clutter that he may work again, and better. The winter storms are over and it is time to do the things that have always been done. To catch rockfish from the cliffs. To collect driftwood for the fire. To crack open the earth and ready it for planting. The day is long enough for all these things. It is not too late.

In Another Country

I crossed the border into another country, this time on the Black Sea's eastern shore, and came to another town, and walked around, trying to get a sense of the place. I had a small bag on my back, containing a few things. The coast curved north beyond the harbour and a lush backdrop of hills rose beyond the sleepy streets. Peeling plasterwork drew maps of imaginary continents across walls. The balcony railings of the fine old houses were flaking with rust, and weeds flourished tropically in cracks in the brickwork. It was an outpost of an empire that no longer existed. In the shops and businesses the prudent people hung pictures of an old man who had a private army and ran the place. There was no one to rise against him, and no good reason to try.

I entered the Hotel Beso. A heavy man in a tight dark suit was reclining on a sofa in the lobby, under a large framed photograph of the ruler. I asked about a room, addressing him in Russian, and he got to his feet slowly. He climbed the stairs ahead of me, breathing hard.

That evening, having fixed the water heater in my room, he lingered in my doorway, told me to call reception if I wanted anything. I was lying on the bed, reading.

Anything you need, just lift the phone, he said, rubbing his hands together, as if washing them.

I thanked him.

He put a hand on the door handle to leave, but then he stalled, head hanging. I could not figure out what was wrong with him. He looked up at me again.

'Do you want a woman?'

So I ended up in bed with one, for twenty dollars. And I'd only been in the country a few hours.

Afterwards, she was in no hurry to leave. She talked, perhaps because I did not. Relief that the job was done and had gone more easily than expected. I was out of cigarettes and asked her for one but she had none either. She wanted me to understand that she was not really a whore. She was a ballet dancer but the theatre had closed down because there was no money for dancing. Now she gave some dancing lessons to little girls, but she had a daughter, so to make ends meet she fucked the occasional Turk passing through the Hotel Beso. I suppose I must have given her an easier ride than some of the Turks because she told me I was very gentle. She ran her fingers over my hands, examining them.

'You have delicate hands. Like a girl. Are you an artist?'

'Not really. Sketches mostly.'

She suggested I sketch her and I said I might. It was beautiful in the hills around the town now that spring had come, she said, and we could go there. She wrote down her telephone number in my notebook, then began to dress.

I went inland, to the capital. I got a simple room overlooking the river in a family guest house. It was not much of a guest house. I was the only guest and usually I had to listen to three generations of the family screaming at each other. The worst was the grandmother, a stocky old woman dressed in black. She would live to be a hundred. A dynamo of anger in the middle of her chest powered her whole existence. The only reason it did not explode and level the neighbourhood was because she released the pressure through her vocal chords, like a pneumatic drill that with force and persistence can shatter concrete. It had killed one man already. Her husband had decided underground was the only safe place, and had gone there early. Now the son-in-law was getting it on the top of his bald head.

He was a slight man, soft-spoken, bespectacled. After a couple of days as their guest we had a cup of tea together and talked in Russian about various things and I explained how much longer I could stay, assuming he could let me pay a little less. I paid in advance and it was very agreeable and I went back to my room and lay down. Then the woman started on him. They were speaking Georgian, so 'dollar' was the only word I understood.

'*NYAKNYAKNYAKNYAKNYAKNYAK* – DOLLAR!'
'Mumble mumble.'
'DOLLAR – *NYAKNYAKNYAK* – DOLLAR!'
'Mumble!'
'*NYAK* – DOLLAR – *NYAK*!'

I met Eka in a bar and fell in love with her. I was drinking alone and she was at a birthday celebration at another table. I found it hard not to stare. She wore a simple white blouse and sat very straight, but when she moved it was like a sapling bending in the wind and coming straight again. The drunk brother of the birthday girl invited me to the table. Later, without the others seeing, Eka slipped me her number on a very small piece of paper. Late that night, drunk, walking back to my room, over the dark cobbles of the old town, I memorized the number in case I lost the scrap of paper.

*

I needed a job. I was hired by the editor of the *Georgian Times*,
a tall young man called Zviad Pochkua. He wore a trim dark
suit and a matching buttoned waistcoat and never looked me
in the eye. My job was to rewrite the paper in passable English.
The pay was a joke but they said they would find me a place
to live. My money was running out so I left the screaming family
and slept on the sofa in the office. Because of the power cuts I
was reluctant to get up at night to relieve myself for fear of
stepping in one of the rat traps so I tried to bed down sober.
One time I pissed in a bottle but I forgot to empty it in the
morning and the cleaning lady gave me a hard time. She never
cleaned the men's toilets. She said it was too disgusting. I made
use of the sink there to keep reasonably clean. I was very diligent
about correcting the mistakes but it turned out the newspaper
was all lies anyway. They invented intricate international scoops.
But nobody read it so it did not matter. They lied to me too,
about finding me a place to live, and paying me. After a week
I received a typed note from Zviad saying I was embarrassing
him by sleeping on the premises, so I cleared out. It was a society
very conscious of status, so for my bad manners I got a kick
when I was down. It was all I deserved.

I met Nathan Petrosian, the American, in a whore-bar and restaurant run by Turks. It was quite a nice place, softly lit, white
tablecloths, glitterball hanging from the ceiling. I was drinking
beer, celebrating my freedom. My rucksack was propped against
the wall.

The bar was almost empty and Nathan was at the next table.
He leaned over and asked if I was interested in corruption. He
was wearing a shirt and tie and a cheap rainproof jacket.
He invited himself to my table and told me he was a journalist.
He admitted he could not write but he was committed to the

truth, something most journalists didn't give a damn about, according to him. I said I was a journalist too and agreed with him about the other journalists. He bought me a beer.

He was forty-two. His big gut made him look older and his sideparted grey hair was overdue a cut. The name was Armenian, but he said he was Irish too, and he even had some Cherokee in his bashed-up face. His nose had been broken at least once. He had stories about what had happened to his face, including the bad scar on his forehead, involving him fighting for truth in different parts of the world.

He gave me a draft of one of his articles and watched me while I read it. His sentences were overlong. And other problems, too numerous to mention.

'What do you think?' he asked, as I put down the final page. It was about geopolitics, corruption and everything wrong in the world. I took a swig of beer.

'Pretty interesting.'

'The average journalist is a bastard in a hotel who doesn't stick his neck out, and gives the organization what it wants to hear.'

I agreed with him.

Nathan, personally, was a victim of corruption. When he reported the stealing to the New York headquarters of the humanitarian organization he had worked for, he was fired and vile stories were invented about him and disseminated. Ever since then he had had trouble getting steady work in the country. He had even done a stint at the *Georgian Times*. They had ripped him off too. He told me Zviad was a refugee from the Abkhazian war. He reckoned the Georgians from Abkhazia funded the paper, to dish dirt at the Russians. Refugees could be the worst bastards, he said, because they'd had it so tough.

I excused myself and used the facilities. Turkish-style but sweeter-smelling than those at the *Times*.

When I got back I asked Nathan about Georgian women. I had been ringing Eka's number for over a week and getting no answer.

'Depends what you want from them.'

'I'm feeling romantic.'

'You need to go take another shit. I'll tell you about Georgian women. I was in love with one, really in love, and after a while all she'd talk about was going to America. So I got the money together. I took her to America.'

He paused and swigged his beer and set the bottle back down.

'She dumped my ass at the airport.'

Nathan was now married to two women at the same time, technically speaking. Shortly after his disappointment at the airport he had married a Georgian girlfriend in the US, mainly because she needed residency papers. Then he returned to Georgia without her and got into a more serious marriage. Now he lived in a block on the outskirts with his wife and mother-in-law. He said he didn't believe in not being married. It wasn't practical.

It was dark when we went outside. We took a taxi to his home. It was on the eighth floor. I had my rucksack on my back and when we entered we took up the whole of their little hall. It was a small apartment. He told the women that I was staying a few days.

If Elizaveta or her mother had any misgivings about me they were good enough not to let it show. Food and drink appeared on the table and we all sat down together. I was very grateful for the kindness.

They were Armenians. The Armenians of Georgia had adopted the Russian language in the last century, I learned, but had not forgotten they were Armenians. Elizaveta spoke to

Nathan in English. She was a doctor, a radiologist. The Armenians were intelligent people, unlike the Georgians, said Nathan. I asked if he had been there. Doesn't exist, he said. The modern state of Armenia, I clarified. He shrugged. Just a rock.

On one wall was an old framed photograph of a man in a suit. It was Elizaveta's deceased father. With his neat moustache and lean good looks, he was a 1940s movie star, smiling for the camera. Elizaveta's mother told me he had worked for the customs, on the border with Iran, and that he was incorruptible. On the wall opposite the photograph was a stain of red wine, a glass he had smashed during a party. It had been left there in his honour.

Sitting there, on the edge of that ruined city, as Nathan forked meat into his mouth, it felt to me like these two women were the last representatives of a race of aristocrats. If they had offered me a new religion I would have joined it.

One evening, Nathan wanted to introduce me to a woman he knew called Mancho. We arranged to meet her in the Turkish bar, but when we arrived she was sitting with some well-cut suits and blanked us.

'Sorry about that. I'll find you another.'

'Doesn't matter.'

I had no money and nowhere to take a woman anyway but he was stuck on the idea. He went away and several minutes later came back with one of the less expensive ones. I got rid of her politely.

We drank. Then we were in a taxi, Nathan up front, me in the back, coloured lights streaming past the window, and he was telling me how he had shot down a Russian helicopter in Afghanistan in his special operations days.

'Killed sixty men. A thing like that changes your life.'

We stopped outside the bar. He paid the driver and we got out.

We went inside and got beers. We talked of a couple of different things. I went to take a leak. I was staring at the wall, urinating, visualizing the shooting down of a helicopter.

I went back, sat down. We clinked bottles and I asked why he had told me the story.

Scenery was rearranged, junk discarded, clocks reset. All in the moment required to take a pull from a bottle.

'Hey, I knew you wouldn't believe that shit.'

'Really?'

He tried to change the subject but I kept coming back to it, so he would think twice next time. I did this because he was my only friend.

We finished the beers and were in a taxi again. We got out in front of a club. The bouncers nodded to Nathan. A regular. It was a very big basement. Loud. Flashing lights. Men and women dancing. The women were prostitutes but outnumbered by the men, so it was just like an ordinary nightclub, you were supposed to compete. Only the expectation of a fuck-transaction held it together while the drinks got drunk and money filled the registers. Nathan soon had a couple of girls at our table. I didn't speak to them. I looked around. It was like watching corpses dancing. Nathan pulled one of the girls to her feet, bumping into people as he led her to the dance floor. He had sweat rings under his armpits and the back of his shirt was hanging out.

The girls split. I got Nathan out of there. Elizaveta was in a dressing gown when we came in the door. She had waited up.

Nathan staggered past her towards the bedroom, struck the

doorframe with his shoulder, collapsed on the conjugal bed. Through the doorway I could see his feet hanging over the edge of the mattress, and the sad frayed ends of brown laces on respectable black shoes.

I sat on the sofa-bed Elizaveta had made up for me in the living room. She sat on a straight-backed chair. Nathan was snoring already. She asked if I had met Mancho.

'That whore!'

'Didn't you know?'

'Mmm, I suppose . . .'

'Why is he so drunk?'

'He drank a lot.'

'You're not drunk.'

'I am. But I'm trying to act sober.'

'Why?'

'I don't know.'

Elizaveta's lips appeared to tremble even as she smiled. I could picture her bursting into tears for no reason. She had that face.

'He's a strange man,' she said, 'but he's my husband. My first husband, he was a doctor. We met in medical school. He was the only man I was ever with. He died of a heart attack. He was thirty-two. I thought my life was over. For ten years I was alone, here with my mother. Then I met Nathan. And now this is another life.'

She went to bed.

I took a last look at the photograph on the wall, at that incorruptible man smiling down from a better time. I found it reassuring. I turned out the light and got into bed.

I lay in the dark, listening to Nathan snoring in the next room.

*

I stayed for several nights with Nathan and Elizaveta, then Nathan brought me to see my new accommodation. It belonged to his other wife, the one in America.

We turned off the main road where the Armenian church stood – it was the Armenian area of town – and into a dirt and gravel alley. We entered a yard. A few trees and bushes grew there. It had been a beautiful house once. A wooden stairway ran up the outside of the building to a wooden gallery on an upper floor. It was subdivided between many families and each had a room or two. Laundry was strung out around the upper floor and on slumping lines above the dirt and weeds of the yard.

We stopped at a ground-floor door and Nathan turned a big clunky key in the lock. He pushed the door open. I followed him inside. It was very dim. He pulled the curtains open. One window looked directly onto the alley and one onto the yard.

The room contained a table, a chair, a sink and a bookcase. Old copies of the *Georgian Times* were piled on the table. The bookshelf had books in Russian, Georgian and another strange script, Armenian, I supposed, and even a couple of paperbacks in English. There was another room at the back that was even smaller. It contained a bed.

'What do you think?'

I looked at the sad room and shrugged. It was a free place to live.

'I lived here six months, when I got back from America. Until I got married to Elizaveta.'

On the bookshelf was a picture of a pretty girl. Nathan picked it up to see better and held it with both hands. I supposed it was the one who had ditched him at the airport.

'The one you were in love with?'

'Still am, I guess.'

He must have had the picture there, looked at it, those six months in that room, until his marriage to Elizaveta.

'We've all had our troubles,' he said, setting the picture back in its place. 'I suppose you have too. But what can you do? You got to keep going, keep moving on.'

He showed me an item resembling an egg-beater. I could plug it in and boil water in a basin. I would need it. There was no shower.

It was dim and musty in there. I stared through the greyish net curtains and for a moment I had trouble recalling my own life. It was all in another country, a long time before. My memories were old wallpaper. I looked out at the shithouse in the yard. It looked ready to topple.

'What about the toilet?' I asked.

'Somebody has a key.'

It had a patched, backwoods look, some of the planks having fallen off and been replaced with other planks. There would be a stink and flies and shit-stained bits of newspaper in Georgian script. Why the key? Nathan explained that too many vagabonds had been coming round, overflowing it with their crap. There was only so much a hole in the ground could take.

We were two fuck-ups. Nathan was inspirational to me, being a bigger fuck-up than I was. If he could keep going, then I could too.

A couple of nights earlier I had been lying on the sofa-bed, listening to him and Elizaveta arguing. It was about the other woman he was married to. It sounded like an old argument.

'But Elizaveta,' I heard him say, 'when I was in jail it was her who helped me out.'

I woke up one fine day, after I had been in the room about a week. The sun was shining and the birds were singing in the courtyard. I rose and pissed in the sink then splashed water on my face.

It was warming up and I was not going to beg the neighbours for the key to their fragrant shit-shack. So I put an old *Georgian Times* down on the floor and crouched over one of Nathan's articles. My bed was at eye-level and various household items stared at me. I heard voices in the alleyway. Shadows passed across my curtains. I felt vulnerable, like a dog in the street.

I wiped with another of Nathan's articles. I began to laugh, remembering the earnest way he had awaited my verdict on his work. Plumbing beats writing, I would have told him, and right now we haven't much of either. I folded the newspaper cleverly and put the package in a plastic bag.

I performed my ablutions ingeniously at the sink, got dressed, pulled the curtains, then went out to meet the morning. I walked jauntily down the street, swinging my little bundle, and dumped my dump in a dumpster.

I stopped at the square that faced the metro station and the Armenian church. Rows of haphazard kiosks were strewn across a concrete wasteland. I dialled Eka's number. The phones were battered lumps of junk, only one in three would work, and then you had to dial three or four times to get a tone. I played around with a few phones, but as usual there was no answer. I lost some coins along the way.

Several days before, somebody had answered. I asked for Eka and the voice of an old woman told me to wait. I waited a very long time. I closed my eyes and heard the sounds of a rambling dream-building of long corridors and wooden stairways and interconnecting chambers. And then I was speaking to Eka. She explained that the phone had been broken. I told her we had to meet immediately. I must have sounded crazy. It was eleven o'clock at night and they were sweeping up in front of my metro station. She told me to call next day.

Next day it began again. Never any answer.

I bought *khachapuri* and *lubiani* for breakfast and took the food back to my room. Of the fast-food I can't complain. *Khachapuri* are flat bread baked with a layer of salty cheese. *Lubiani* are the same thing but with a filling of spicy mashed red beans. You eat them warm.

I made use of an old contact and started scripting brief radio reports for listeners far away.

Once upon a time there was an empire, and very suddenly it disintegrated into many little pieces. One of those pieces was Georgia, which in turn crumbled into smaller pieces. There were different ethnic groups and religions, and their armies and militias fought. The economy collapsed and there was no law, and the biggest mafia became the government of what remained of the country. Under these conditions, ordinary people still tried to believe in basic decency and order, in friendship and family, and to celebrate as best they could the birth of their children and the weddings of their young people.

This is how I came to be writing about arms smuggling and met the Chechen, Ahmed Baiev.

I saw the Chechen twice. The first time was in Nathan's apartment. I called Nathan to arrange to take a shower and he told me to come by taxi, there was a man I had to meet. He would not say more. He liked to pretend his calls were listened to. I took the metro.

Ahmed Baiev was sitting at the table, smoking, television on behind him, sound turned low. Several long wiry grey hairs sprouted from otherwise dark eyebrows. Vertical crevasses ran from his cheekbones into a reddish beard that was turning grey. He wore a cheap grey jacket and a musty smoky smell came off him. Mid-forties. He rose to shake my hand and looked me hard in the eye like we were both serious people, which I doubted. There was a cold pot of tea on the table, left over from breakfast. Probably Nathan did not know where the tea was kept. The women did everything for him.

Nathan explained in Russian that I was an important foreign journalist. Then he ran through Baiev's story, in English, to me, switching to Russian from time to time to check details with Baiev. Nathan spoke basic Russian, mangled by a very bad accent. Baiev put out his cigarette and lit another. They were cheap stubby cigarettes.

Baiev obtained arms for his comrades in Chechnya. The best source was a breakaway province called South Ossetia. The Russian peacekeepers were often the purveyors. South Ossetia was Georgia's duty-free, selling everything from chocolate bars to tankers of fuel to rocket launchers. Too many people close to the government were getting a cut for the government to do anything about it.

Baiev had been dealing with an ex-colonel of the Georgian Army called Tristan Kikadze, who had been dismissed for selling his army's heavy ordnance. But not convicted. The judge said he had not sold anything really big and, anyway, the colonel was a patriot. Kikadze fronted for somebody higher up. Baiev had paid Kikadze fifty thousand dollars but had not received the goods. He no longer believed he would get the weapons, or his money back. Baiev and his colleagues would have liked to kill Kikadze, but he was too well protected. So they were going to expose him instead, through the press. Nathan believed a contact of his who presented an investigative news show for the Rustavi II television station would want to break the story.

Baiev left, having again shaken hands with me gravely.

'What do you think?' asked Nathan, amazed at his luck.

I looked out the window at makeshift garages and a few trees and more blocks like the one we were in. I asked Nathan if it didn't seem odd to him to be elected by such an individual as an instrument of retribution. Hell no, Nathan knew Baiev from previously, when he'd written articles on the kidnappings and disappearances of Chechens living in Georgia. Baiev believed Nathan was an important international reporter.

'It's not like he's forgotten to pay his taxes, Nathan. Perhaps the best thing to do is walk away.'

'Chechens don't walk away. They take on Russian tanks with their bare hands.'

Nathan's plan was to let the television people run with the story. We would watch from the sidelines. Then sell it internationally. Shady weapons deals in a country receiving American money. For counter-terrorism. Nathan had some contacts. *Washington Post, New York Times.*

I thought of that as I looked out the window. And I thought of the money.

When I got back that evening a good part of the male Armenian population of the city was gathered on the concrete wasteland in front of the metro station, as if enacting an ancient ritual. They had been congregating there at that hour from the time when it was a market or a cathedral square, before the architectural degeneration of the place – the squat metro station like a concrete bunker, the fast-food shacks, the Ladas farting along the road. The buildings rose and fell, the trees greened and shed their leaves, the days and nights flickered like a strobe light, and the men gathered in knots on the square under the darkening sky.

I gave Eka's number a go and my heart came alive to what

was surely her voice. But she did not understand what I was saying.

'Is that you, Eka?'

'Nyet.'

I asked if Eka was home and the voice replied in Georgian. It was very strange for someone to understand no Russian. Perhaps it was Eka and it meant she couldn't talk and I was to call her later. Perhaps I had misdialled. Or perhaps Eka now regretted giving her number to a man in a bar. Or maybe she did not need me because she had somebody else. That final thought made me feel terrible.

I hung up. All I could do was call again the next day.

I bought *lubiani* and *khachapuri* and brought them back to my room. I also got a bottle of red wine.

It got completely dark. I ate. I opened the wine. I had no glasses or cups so I drank from the bottle. The nightly power cut came early and I lit the candle. I took off my boots and lay on the bed. For a cheap one the wine tasted quite good. I pulled a blanket over my legs.

The next day started typically, the birds singing and the newspaper and so on. I went out to get some breakfast, dropped the coin into the battered metal phone box and dialled. No answer. Then I dialled another number. She was American. I'd read her column in a local English-language magazine and called her up one day, one journalist to another. She looked not bad in the picture and had a rich musical voice.

I got a dial tone on the first go.

'Hello, Tiffany.' I reminded her who I was.

'I was waiting for you to call!'

She practically sang the sentence, rising towards the end, with the final word containing about three notes.

I felt cool and sure talking to her, yet my chest was at the same time nervous and tight as we made arrangements. I hung up, looked about and rearranged my erection skywards. I put my hands in my pockets and walked home.

We met in a bar that evening. She was big. But not tall. Any shorter and rounder, she would have had to roll down the street. Pale flab is grey and lumpy like uncooked dough, but she was dark – African-American father – and nice and rubbery. I wanted to see what kind of a place she lived in. We discussed Nathan Petrosian. He had no credibility with the international community of Tbilisi, she said. He was a loudmouth and a liar. I listened politely. Tiffany sipped her drink and lowered her voice, confidentially. It was like this, she had been working with young prostitutes, there was this particular family, she knew the girls by name, their mother made them do it, it was terrible, and one day she saw Nathan Petrosian going down the street, drunk, with these girls. The younger one was only thirteen years old!

I didn't comment. Nathan seemed to enjoy the company of prostitutes, but generally did not spend money on them. Not even on the big ones, who were past taking orders from mother.

We went to another bar, down in a basement, and drank some beer. It was a bohemian sort of place. They played one of Dylan's more obscure recordings. We seemed to be getting on well and she invited me back to her place to drink vodka.

She lived nearby, on a quiet street parallel to Rustaveli and up the hill, and we were walking there when a soundless explosion occurred. The earth lurched.

Some people stepped out of a shop and looked around for an explanation. Like me, they looked at the sky, for a sign. But the sky said nothing. The planet continued spinning on its excellent axis.

We picked up a couple of bottles of vodka and something to eat.

We entered her building, a handsome old construction with peeling walls and the classic background tomcat-hum in the resonant stairwell, and walked up to the third floor. Neighbours were sweeping up dust and plaster after the tremor. It gave the evening a lot of character.

Tiffany's apartment had been recently renovated. No loose plaster. Big freshly painted high-ceilinged living room. And sitting there on the sofa soon after entering, with a vodka in my hand and no other women to compare her to, she didn't look that fat at all.

From the living room two glass doors opened onto the bedroom, and to a big bed with white sheets and a brightly coloured bedspread. Another big set of glass doors in the bedroom opened onto a balcony overlooking the street. I imagined the sunlight coming through those windows, hitting the bedspread. It was fine. I could cook and make myself useful. I'd even eat her pussy. Maybe.

We sat around and listened to music and talked about nothing much and it was nice, though she was full of shit, really. I'd met fifty like her, though not so fat of course. College-educated Americans, flying into the Third World for a personal taste of the run-down scene. They end up visiting orphanages and relating to especially needy elements, such as Gypsies, if there are any to be had. They like the discomfort and corruption and general craziness. For a couple of years. Then they go back to America, enriched by the experience.

We talked about the country and were great friends. We were

drinking shots. I had a nice dense buzz going, clear and calm with just the right degree of nervous jangle, oscillating at a good low frequency. None of the bloated sloppiness that digesting litres of gassy beer gives you. It was the lucid peak, you hold it as long as you can before the inevitable slide down into the mists of drooling incoherence. And Tiffany wasn't slumping or slurring yet either.

We had another. Straight vodka might as well be intravenous. You knock it back, exhale, then something hits you on the side of the head. I was pretty impressed that she could match me shot for shot. Maybe it was her weight advantage.

We opened the second bottle and listened to Tom Waits singing 'Blind Love'. Ain't no love but stone blind love. We drank another glass. It was getting late. The good sharp edge I'd had two shots back was dissolving. Maybe I should make some kind of move on her before I lost it entirely, was dealt a knockout. Sure, I'd eat her pussy, no problem with that at all. In fact, I was looking forward to it. I saw her stretched out on her back on her big bed, quivering like a jelly, my head lost between her fat thighs. Forget the beautiful women, plug yourself into the wild charge coursing from the sexually neglected. It was all cunt-energy, uplifting and holy, the source of life itself.

'Hey, Tiff, you're not going to kick me out in the street tonight, are you?'

''Course not!'

'You're not going to make me sleep on this sofa, are you?'

'No!'

A tongue-lashing she'd never forget.

We had another shot. I imagined her sitting on my face. What if I suffocated? She'd be singing to the ceiling, grinding my skull into the mattress as my little fists rapped her thighs, unaware she was killing me.

I started laughing.

'What?'

'Ah, nuthin.'

We finished the bottle and got into bed. She turned her back to me. I pressed my hard-on against her big fat ass and nibbled her neck.

'Go to sleep,' she said.

She told me that in a week I'd have a Georgian girlfriend, slimmer and more attractive than her. Her voice was sad. I thought of my little Eka, straight-backed, supple as a sapling.

'But Tiff, love is an abstraction. Reality pokes you from behind.'

I was unable to say the kind words that were needed.

We fell asleep.

We weren't badly hungover next morning. We breakfasted on *khachapuri* from the shop across the street. I used the shower and the toilet. Perhaps my hungry vagabondage was not appealing to folks further up the real-estate ladder. Whatever I had, she did not need it.

She had got money out of me before going for the *khachapuri*. I had paid for the drinks too. Whatever about the nice apartment, she was tighter than a cat's anus. I finished my breakfast and told her I'd be around next morning at ten to take a shit. She didn't laugh. I left.

My brother wired me four hundred dollars through Western Union. I didn't know when I would be able to pay him back. I got an apartment on the hill above the parliament, a ten-minute walk from the centre. All for a hundred and fifty bucks a month. So I still had over two hundred left.

The afternoon sun shone through the leaves of the trees outside my big second-floor windows. Everything in it was new. I had a bathroom and kitchen. It was recently wall-papered.

In the meantime, the thing with Baiev had turned out to be very interesting and provided material for my radio reports. I felt I had underestimated Nathan. His TV station contacts had set up and filmed a meeting between Baiev and Kikadze in which an arms deal was discussed. The meeting had not gone to plan: the camera crew's cover had been blown and the meeting was cut short. It was not going to be possible to film a handover of weapons, which the television people had initially hoped for.

I was sitting at home, scripting my report, drinking some wine, when an earthquake happened. The lights went out and I could hear my walls shuddering and cracking and bits of the ceiling falling to the floor. The building might have been about to collapse but there was nothing I could do but sit there and listen.

It lasted no more than ten seconds, though some people later claimed that it was a minute. Time stretches out when you think you are going to die. I sat in the dark for a few moments listening to children screaming in the apartment below. Then I got up and felt about for matches. My feet scrunched dust and plaster.

I lit a candle and inspected the damage. In one place the wallpaper had ripped from floor to ceiling and the wall was now in two sections that did not fit together.

I went out and walked down the hill towards Freedom Square for more wine. A lot of masonry had been shaken loose and a couple of old wooden balconies had collapsed. The entire neighbourhood was in the street, chattering. The earthquake had reawoken a sense of community. 'Did you feel it?' asked the middle-aged woman in the wine shop, eyes shining, like she'd just got laid for the first time in a decade. She crunched across broken bottles and fetched a survivor from the shelf.

I went back to the apartment and opened the bottle. The phone rang. It was Nathan. I asked how it had been for him. Yeah, a mirror had fallen off his wall, seven years' bad luck, but that wasn't what he was calling about. Baiev was in the hospital with broken bones. He'd been attacked in the street, beaten almost to death.

The next day Nathan brought me to Rustavi II and introduced me to Akaki, the presenter of the programme. The previous presenter of the programme had been shot dead, the year before. Akaki spoke English with an American accent. He'd been to university there. Princeton, no less. We watched the film where Baiev meets Kikadze and sets up the arms deal that never happened.

The film is poor quality, shot from inside a vehicle, looking through the window of the restaurant where Kikadze and Baiev are meeting. The wire is on Baiev, and he gets Kikadze talking about weapons, about how he's well protected from above. The sound is also very bad and I could make out little of what they were saying. Akaki kept rewinding and translating into English for me and Nathan.

Kikadze is still putting Baiev off about the weapons, and Baiev is begging for something straight away. At the point at which they agree that Baiev will go to South Ossetia for some cases of ammunition, police appear in the street and order the camera crew out of the car, demanding to know what they are doing. This is what you see in the video, though there is no sound from the street. Kikadze notices the commotion and breaks off in mid-sentence and accuses Baiev of setting him up. Baiev turns the accusation back on Kikadze, who swears he knows nothing about it. They cut the meeting short. Two days later Baiev is attacked in the street.

But now Baiev was in hospital, and Rustavi wanted him safely out of the country before they broadcast the report.

Nathan and I took the lift down and walked outside. We felt like we had completed a job. We could get something to eat, perhaps. Or sit around drinking and talking.

'Why does Akaki do it?' I said when we were in the street.

'The guy who was killed before, the presenter, there was a big noise about it. Akaki's safe enough. Much easier to kill someone like Baiev instead. I think the Americans are behind Akaki too, give him money. He acts like he can get out of the country fast.'

'What do they get in return?'

'The Americans? Information, I suppose. Lots of people give money to lots of people. Doesn't mean much, necessarily.'

'I should go visit Baiev.'

'Good. He's probably gaga. You might learn something interesting.'

'I was just thinking of bringing him oranges.'

'Yeah, he needs his vitamin C. Maybe take him some flowers too.'

A shittier-looking hospital I've never seen. Too few windows and they were economizing on lighting. There were beds in the hallways. There were a lot of hallways. And stairways.

Baiev's ward had some other broken legs, but mostly they were immobilized old people lying on their backs looking at the ceiling, sucking their gums in an atmosphere of disinfectant and piss.

I recognized Baiev by his reddish beard. He had taken some blows to the face. One eye was purple and swollen shut and his lip was cut. His right leg was up in plaster, and the left hand and lower arm had also been set. His head was bandaged. He raised his one mobile eyebrow in greeting. I didn't ask him how he felt.

I took a chair between Baiev and an old man in the next bed. The man's mouth was open and he was staring upwards and each gasp for breath sounded like he was counting down to the last.

'Give me a cigarette,' said Baiev. 'Bitches took mine.'

'The nurses?'

'Yes.'

I looked around, lit up swiftly and handed it to him. He ignored me while he smoked, sucking at it like a starving baby at mama's tit. Man and cigarette. He tapped the ash beside the bed. He smoked it right down and handed me the butt.

'Throw it out the window.'

I went and flicked it out the window and then went back to him.

'Now,' he said, 'stamp on the ash and disperse it.'

I stomped and blew.

I sat down again. I waited to see if there was anything else he wanted.

'That was good. Thank you.'

The man in the next bed made a croaking noise. I turned and looked at him.

'Is he alright?' I whispered.

'What do you think?'

'Jesus. What a place.'

'Yes. What do you want?'

I shrugged. At that point I was mostly interested in what was happening to Baiev. I asked him if he needed anything.

He complained about not having cigarettes. When he had

been shot in the shoulder in Grozny at the end of '94 at least he could walk around and smoke and they held onto their weapons in case the hospital was attacked. A good bullet wound will cauterize itself, he said, if it's clean through the tissue. But he'd seen a man who'd got it through the belly, and was begging for someone to finish him off. Baiev had been evacuated south to the mountains shortly after the Russians sent the tanks into Grozny. 'Tanks are useless for close combat. All you need is a small charge to take off one of the tracks, then you smash Molotov cocktails over it and cook the crew. In the end they had to level the city, pretty much.'

He was quiet for a moment. Then he said: 'I also hate the bedpan. Humiliating.'

I indicated the man opposite with both arms in casts up to his elbows. 'At least you can wipe yourself.'

'Wiping is disgusting. You should wash. It says that in the Koran.'

'The Koran says to wash your hole?'

'Basic hygiene.'

I met Nathan in the Turkish bar that night.

'Anything interesting?'

I told him what it said in the Koran.

'Good advice. Anything else?'

'I just let him talk. He wants a quiet life. Knows he's beaten.'

'Haha. Beaten.'

'He was glad to see me. They took his cigarettes.'

'Smoking is bad for you.'

So was the Georgian legal system: Baiev, I told Nathan, was willing to testify about Kikadze, but the police did not want to hear. He was being charged with affray, for fighting in the street.

I was starting to have doubts about the thing, from the truth and justice point of view.

'It was that or he'd try and kill Kikadze, or fuck with him some way. I'll feel better when he's out of the country, though.'

'He wants to go to Baku. He thinks his wife is there.'

'Married, huh. Hard to imagine.'

'He hasn't seen her for years. There was the war, who knows what else. Probably she has another man, that's what he said.'

'Shit. A heart to heart. What else did he tell you?'

'Nothing, really. Oh, he told me I should get married.'

'You should. I don't remember ever not being.'

'To at least two women.'

'Elizaveta, I'm going to grow old with that lady. Can you believe it, I didn't touch her till we married. That's Georgian women for you.'

'Some deal.'

'You're uptight, that's all,' said Nathan. 'What about her?'

'You're treating me?'

Nathan invited her over. Nino wasn't so pretty or so young, but shortly I liked her enough. I liked that she didn't try to ingratiate herself. She didn't do an act.

Nathan handed me twenty bucks.

'Thanks, Daddy.'

I took her back to my place. I had nothing to drink, so I made a pot of coffee. She admired my split wall. I admitted I was proud of it. We smoked and talked about different things. She was thirty-four, divorced. She asked where I was from. I told her it was a medium-sized island in the Atlantic, damp.

'Do people speak Russian there?'

'No.'

I explained I had lived in Petersburg once. That impressed her. I asked about the scars on her arms. When she had been a teenager, she said, her mother refused to let her go to the coast, so she slashed herself.

'Did she let you go then?'

'Yes.'

Since then she'd done pretty much what she wanted. For my twenty I had her until morning, so I was in no hurry, and it was pleasant to sit around, talking. On my black and white TV Robert Redford was speaking Russian and waking up in a beachfront house with big windows and making love and running out past palm trees into the surf, and we laughed, it was a nice stupid film, and then went to bed. She told me she hadn't been able to shave her legs. I said it wasn't important. The water was off for the night, as usual, nothing in the taps. Her smell was noticeable but not unpleasant – another home with limited facilities – and she began to kiss me on the mouth, with the tongue. This is something original, I thought, and worth more than a perfumed call-girl with silicon tits. Easier to fuck someone you don't want than to kiss someone you don't want, as any whore will tell you.

'You don't need the condom,' she said. 'I don't have so many customers.'

'Yeah, but I'm quite promiscuous myself,' I said, putting it on.

We had a good tangle, then she was asleep within two minutes, snoring.

There were so few people you met who you could truly admire. But here, finally, was one. She'd earned some cash, with more playfulness and talent than most people did, and now it was time to sleep. No worries about a strange bed or a strange man or the coming morning.

I couldn't sleep. Perhaps it was the snoring body, or the coffee, or the thing with Baiev. I got up and scripted another radio report.

In the morning we had another go. She rode above with her eyes closed. Her skin flushed pink and a fine sweat broke out over her entire body when she came. She really did need a shower then. Fortunately the water was running again, and I turned it up full and left her alone for a few minutes, then got in behind her and washed her back. After which she washed my back while I sang a bit of Dalla's *Caruso*. ('*Guardò negli occhi la ragazza, quegli occhi verdi come il mare . . .*') Then she got out and I showered alone and sang some more. She was lying on the bed naked, smoking, when I got back to the room, and I had to climb on for a last go. It was good and quick. Sometimes you'd rather just work one off, like a dog.

She went away, sweeter-smelling and a little richer than when she had arrived. She left me her number. We did not dislike each other but we weren't going to see each other again. I couldn't afford it, unfortunately.

The phone rang. Nathan had just been speaking to Akaki. Ahmed Baiev was never going to make it to Baku. Some men had taken him from the hospital during the night.

I delivered my radio report over the phone in my best voice. I hope it held my listeners' attention while they woke and put the coffee on. I noted that Georgia had a free media but that a free media was a useless decoration in bandit country.

Ten days after Baiev's abduction, his body was found dumped in a place called the Pankisi Gorge. He'd been shot in the back of the head. Some of the newspapers carried it in small pieces in their inside pages. Rustavi broadcast their exposé.

Nathan wanted to meet up, to talk. I didn't feel like it but he begged, said he'd buy. So we ended up in the Turkish bar. For long stretches we said nothing. Just sucked our beers. I was sick of him.

'Our mistake was going to Akaki,' said Nathan. 'Too much noise. We could have done it quieter, no cameras, just got the information. Stuck it to Kikadze, but got ourselves clear first.'

I nodded.

We drank our beers. There was one girl there; she had a mobile phone on the table and was for special friends of the house. She was sipping a glass of wine. She was beautiful. But I was no friend of the house and I had no money anyway.

'I'd love to nail the bastard,' said Nathan.

'Kikadze?'

'Nail him good.'

'He's more likely to nail you.'

Nathan was getting drunk. He was surprised when I got up to leave and I felt sorry for him because he had nothing to do and would end up in a hotel bar, drunk, boasting to expatriates of how he had nailed an arms smuggler with ties to the police, an ex-colonel no less, in his latest article about corruption.

Tristan Kikadze. I'd never even seen his face. I'd seen the back of his head in a piece of bad film. He walked around, free.

My part in the whole mess had been minor enough, but I did not feel good about it and I kept to myself for several days, looking at the walls. It rained most of the time. But I was glad of my apartment with the cracked wall. I sat listening to the rain pattering on the leaves, watched it running down the windowpane. In a few weeks I would have to move out.

Then the clouds blew over and I went over to Nathan's place and we ate from pots of food prepared by Elizaveta and her mother, and I read what Nathan had written to milk the Baiev thing. He emphasized certain violent incidents and linked it into geopolitics. Georgia was the second-biggest recipient of US aid in the world, per capita, after Israel, and on top of this was due to receive sixty-four million in military aid. A first instalment. Counter-terrorism, they called it. Military advisers were arriving. It was all about an oil pipeline being laid from the Caspian to the Mediterranean. The most direct route to the sea would have been through Iran, but that did not appeal to the Americans. So Georgia had suddenly become very significant.

'A million barrels a day,' said Nathan. 'Operational within three years, by 2005. Not OPEC oil, not Russian oil. American oil!'

We drank a bottle of wine, some good stuff left over from a christening. Then Nathan decided we were going out.

'The women will be back. They don't like me drinking in the house. I'll take you to a really sleazy place.'

As if that was new.

It was a weekday night and there were just a few men and two whores and Chris de Burgh was singing 'Lady in Red'. We took stools at the horseshoe-shaped bar.

There was foreigner-paraphernalia on the wall. Australian and British flags and rugby jerseys and pictures of rugby and soccer players. There were oil company people in Georgia, said Nathan, but not the ones who got it under their nails, and they needed somewhere to order drinks in English.

We got a couple of beers. A group of three foreigners, wearing the kind of sporting jerseys which hung on the wall, were leaving and shouting goodbye to the barmaid. Regulars and nice fellows, on assignment abroad.

This left two very drunk older men next on our side of the bar and the two chainsmoking whores on the other side. The attractive one came round and asked me to buy her a drink. I shook my head. She said something unpleasant and went back to her perch.

Later, feeling benevolent, I sent her a beer. I didn't suggest she join me. The drunken Brit, slurring, was telling me they were lovely ladies, lovely ladies. Since you think so, I said, and told the barmaid the Brit was buying for the old one with the bleached hair. She ordered one of those whiskey-cream liqueur things. The Brit paid up but used some bad language in my direction. I turned my back.

It was strange, I said to Nathan, about Baiev's body being dumped in the Pankisi Gorge, far from Tbilisi.

'Bush says Al Qaeda is operating there. In a speech he made recently. March, I think. He didn't say precisely that Osama Bin Laden was there, but he hinted it was one of the places he could hide if he felt like it.'

'If George says so.'

'Right, a bunch of bullshit. Al Qaeda doesn't mean anything, they don't have membership badges. The more they talk it up, the more local groups spring up, say they're Al Qaeda. A world power needs a worldwide enemy, right? But Pankisi, that's stretching it, because it's a Chechen area, and the Chechens are fighting the Russians. That's where Baiev would have sent his arms through. But the Americans have to make a big deal about the Gorge, because they're giving a lot of money to the Georgians, sending in military advisers.'

'So why dump the body there?'

'Because it's full of terrorists?'

'Exactly. Full of terrorists, and no journalists.'

He showed me a recent *Washington Post* article describing the Gorge as a 'lawless' place 'even the security forces fear to tread'. The article had been filed by the paper's Moscow correspondent.

After five beers we decided to go to Pankisi. We were sure we'd never make it in. But I still hoped to sell a story that would keep me in my nice apartment. I didn't want to go back to shitting on newspapers.

We got into Pankisi. We took a taxi from a nearby town and were waved through two Georgian Army checkpoints. We got out in the village of Duisi, which was Chechen. Combat fatigues were the men's fashion. We knew nobody, had nothing to do there, so we walked up the valley, past farms and fields.

It was striking that there was no gorge in what the president of the United States and the big newspapers called Pankisi Gorge. We continued walking down a narrowing gravel road. It began to drizzle. A bearded man in fatigues, Kalashnikov over his shoulder, stepped out of a gateway and walked ahead of us along a winding country road, in misty spring rain. We let him gain some ground. He turned into a courtyard, spoke briefly to someone, then turned back the way he had come, towards us.

'*Salaam aleikum,*' he said.

'*Wa aleikum salaam,*' I replied. And peace be with you.

The rain eased off.

Then there were no more houses, just the river and open country, and a track upwards into the forest. We would keep going until there was no more Pankisi left to walk. The track before us went into the foothills of the mountains. The mountains the Chechens crossed when they went to fight the Russians.

★

The army officer marched briskly into the room and put his face too close to mine:

'Why didn't you say you've been here before?'

'I haven't been here before.'

He smiled humourlessly and nodded. 'We know you were here before.'

'You're mistaken.'

'We know.'

I shrugged. It seemed we were under arrest. There was no point trying to leave, that was clear. The Georgian Army had picked us up at a checkpoint in the forest and brought us back to the barracks at the mouth of the valley. The bad-tempered officer who believed I'd been there before questioned us for hours. We could not prove we were journalists. He came and went, sometimes with someone new. But the questions were always the same. They refused to believe we had entered Pankisi the way we said we had. It was too awkward for them to concede that journalists could just walk into their top-security Al Qaeda training ground. We did not mention Baiev.

I stood up and walked back and forth across the dusty floorboards. The officer didn't mind. Part of the act was him pretending to be nice, us pretending to be having fun too. It was a good game and we'd been playing it for hours. I went and leaned my elbows against the sill of the window. The day had cleared nicely and now the sun shone warmly over the fields, and I could see it from the window, the sun getting heavier and shadows stretching across the grass. I had no idea how long it would go on.

Then we were standing on the road, waiting for something. It was a pleasant evening and I preferred to be out in the open, looking at the road and the fields, expecting to leave. It was better than being in the room. A jeep arrived and took us to the town. It was the local Interior Ministry police, and a driver. The policeman was wearing civilian clothes and he was very drunk.

When we got into town the policeman wanted us to come up to his office. It was getting dark. Nathan refused. Ten minutes, said the cop. I went up while Nathan waited downstairs. It was getting dark outside and he had to light a candle. He took my address. I told him the name of the street but gave the wrong number for the building.

It was completely dark when we got to Telavi, the nearest town of any size. The power was out there too and we stumbled blindly through the streets. Behind us, across the plain, thunder boomed periodically. The storm was moving in as we took wrong turns in the dark. The hotel was the biggest building in the town and we would see it on a hill illuminated garishly in dry flashes of lightning. A road would force us to veer away, we would become disoriented, and then with another flash and rumble the hotel trembled on the hill like a horror-film castle, but not where we had expected it to be. We were moving in circles, sometimes getting closer, sometimes further away.

Another flash and we were under it. There was nobody about, no lights, no noise but the crashing of thunder. We felt our way around the building, looking for an entrance, and came full circle. We stepped inside through windows that held no glass. We shouted for someone and our voices echoed back at us. Lightning flared, showing the empty shell of the ground floor.

We found the man in a small room off a hallway in an annexe. I saw a crack of light and pushed the door. He turned, mouth opening in surprise. There was a candle on the table. The shadow of his head and shoulders wobbled across the wall.

We took the stairs together to the ninth floor. The lifts did not work. All the lower floors were occupied by refugees from Abkhazia. We lit a candle and the man left. There were two single beds. There was a bathroom but no water in the taps. We put sheets on the beds and stretched out. We fell asleep in our clothes.

In the morning the sun shone and the room looked out over the plain stretching north to the mountains and smoke drifted up from the chimneys of the cooking stoves of the refugees. The refugees had been there for over a decade. Many had fixed winches to their balconies for hauling up wood.

Nathan put on his shoes. I put on my boots. We were pleased with ourselves. We went down the stairs. No lift. No electricity. Ever, it seemed.

Outside the hotel was a tap, for the entire building. A man was filling containers of water. He stood back to let us wash our faces and drink.

The town was very easy to negotiate in the daylight. We found a small restaurant and went in. It had a concrete floor and we were the only customers. We had not eaten since breakfast the previous day and ordered fried eggs, bread, salad, beef stew and a jug of wine. It was local wine, red. An old woman served us. She must have thought we were crazy. It was nine a.m.

'Another jug? You haven't finished this one.'

Nathan emptied it into the cups, his spilling over, trickling onto the floor, and handed her the jug.

We were celebrating. Surely the *Washington Post* would be keen to know the truth. That there was no Pankisi Gorge, no bandit country, except insofar as Georgia was a mafia state. The Al Qaeda thing was a convenient mirage, convenient for the Georgians and the Americans while the military aid poured in.

As long as Al Qaeda were in Pankisi, journalists would not be visiting there. Except that we just had.

We spooned down big chunks of meat and got the gravy with the bread. We ate plenty and got good and drunk.

Two days later, back in Tbilisi, there was a hard knock on my door. I looked through the peephole. It was a very big guy in a black jacket. He had a shaved head. There were two others behind him.

'Who is it?'

'Police.'

They looked more like racketeers. I asked for ID and something was held up to the peephole, all Georgian squiggles. It could have been a library card. I opened the door.

They invited themselves in and the big one with the shaved head, younger than the other two, demanded my passport. The one with the moustache was slighter and looked like an intellectual, relatively speaking. A country schoolteacher. He wore a tie. An older one with grey wavy hair inspected it. He had a thick neck and didn't speak. The shaved head looked into my bedroom. He took a tour of the house. I heard a drawer opening in the back room. I took a few steps and looked down the hallway at him. He raised his hands innocently as if to say, Just looking. I still wasn't sure they were police. The shaved head came back. He had a bouncy, jerky walk.

'Nice place.'

I nodded.

'This is eighteen. Not twenty-eight.'

He asked why I'd given the wrong address. I told him it had been written down by a drunk man.

'Come with us.'

'Where to?'

'Driving around. Talking.'

I put my boots on. We went downstairs. The car was parked in front of my building. We got in. Thick Neck drove and I sat in the back with Shaved Head. He took his cigarettes out and I did the same. When he saw the Georgian shit I smoked, he made a face and insisted I take a Marlboro. His name was Dato.

'Pleased to meet you. Where are we going?'

'Around.'

'What kind of police are you?'

'Interior Ministry.'

We went down the hill to the centre. It was a nice spring day. The first time I had been driven around in Tbilisi for free.

'This morning your friend showed us where you lived. Funny guy. Likes to tell stories. Says he loves Georgia. And you? You like it too?'

'There's great potential for tourism.'

'So, tell me. What are you doing here?'

'I'm a journalist.'

'Show me your journalist's card.'

I told him I didn't have one.

'You're not really a journalist, are you?'

'No.'

'What are you?'

We were driving down Rustaveli, past the National Theatre.

'A poet.'

He smiled. He spoke in Georgian to the two up front and they all laughed. Dato turned off his smile and looked at me hard. My turn to speak. I told him about the radio programme. He wanted to know how much money I made doing that. I inflated it.

'That's not much,' said Dato.

'I know. It's embarrassing.'

He spoke in Georgian again and they shared another joke.

'It's hard to believe you'd go to such trouble, for that kind of money,' said Dato. 'Moving about in an area where terrorists are active. You know you can't visit Pankisi without a permit, without a military escort?'

'I heard.'

He asked all the questions I'd been asked in Pankisi and a few more besides. We came up to a big building I recognized as the place where Nathan taught an English class once a week. One of his odd jobs. Probably he talked to them about corruption for an hour.

'That's where the American used to work,' said Dato. 'Petrosian. He doesn't work there now. Problems with his papers.'

We drove past.

They would speak in Georgian and then we would change direction. We visited a number of landmarks of my time in Tbilisi. We went past the building where the Rustavi offices were. We went down a street I didn't recognize and they told me Baiev had lived there. We went past the hospital.

Near Freedom Square we stopped for *khachapuri*. We stood eating at circular metal tables in front of the stall and drank strong coffee from little plastic cups. Dato insisted on paying. He was being a nice guy. He advised me against talking to terrorists. I agreed there was no advantage to it. They brought me home. I called Nathan.

'Shit, man, I tried to call, you weren't in. Get out of the house, call me.' He gave me the number of his neighbour across the hall.

'You're paranoid.'

'It's in my family from way back, when the Turks were

wiping them out. They thought they were being persecuted.'

He hung up.

I put my boots back on. There were no phones near my house so I went down to the metro station at Rustaveli. As usual I had to dial several times before I got a tone. The neighbour went for Nathan.

'Sure you're not sitting at home?' he said.

I swore at him and held the receiver out so he could hear the traffic noises. Then he gave me the contact information for the person I needed to talk to.

I met Ismailev in a park from which you could see the river. He told me he had previously received assistance on account of being a refugee. Now the Interior Ministry was getting difficult. The Georgians were arresting people and handing them to the Americans. He himself was thinking of going to Azerbaijan.

'We are going to walk out of this park and down the street. I will show you the building and the number, and tomorrow you can go there to speak with the wife of a man who was abducted. At one o'clock. She has three children. They will not tell her where he is being held. Or if he is alive.'

I was being set up to see the broken family. The suffering wife, the three little children. One would be in her arms pulling at her hair while I tried to find out who her husband really was.

'Was he Al Qaeda?'

'He was a doctor from Jordan, working with the refugees in Pankisi. He was a good Muslim, married a woman from there.'

'Was he Al Qaeda?'

'He wasn't even a *boevik*. He brought money from abroad to set up the clinic. Maybe some of it went on weapons, and that is why he was taken. I don't know. You're the journalist. Write what you think is true.'

I was drinking with Nino in the Turkish bar, waiting for Nathan, and Dato came in with Thick Neck and the Teacher. You couldn't miss him, the shaved head, the twitchy swagger. He was bigger than everybody else. He acted like he didn't see me. They took a table by the door. Thick Neck had a bandage around his head.

'What is it?' she asked.

'Someone I know.'

I suggested to Nino we exchange seats so she didn't have to turn around to check for business. This we did. It was an improvement for her but not much better for me. Perhaps it was a coincidence that they were there. Perhaps they had business in the bar.

'That guy with the shaved head. Recognize him?'

'No. But he's looking at me. I may go say hello.'

'He's police. Interior Ministry. He took me for a ride around town this morning.'

She stopped smiling. I was out of cigarettes. I took one of hers and decided to leave when it was smoked.

'Nino, how about you come with me. Come back to my place.'

She shook her head. Then she stood up and walked away.

I was alone with my back to the room, looking at the end wall. I drained my beer. I would take a piss, and then from the toilets it was a short walk outside. I got up. Dato was still not seeing me as I went past him. He had a small cut on his left cheekbone.

I was rinsing my hands when he came in and shoved my face against the mirror. He held the lapel of my coat securely in his left hand and rapped at my temple with the handgun. The only thing I could think was that it would go off.

'Petrosian lost his temper, bit the ear off one of my men.'

I didn't want someone barging in behind Dato, jigging his arm, my brains splattering the mirror. You're going to listen to me now, he was saying, this time you're going to listen to me, you have nothing more to do in this country, you're wasting your time. On and on. I stared up at a corner of the ceiling. When he got tired of tapping, he lifted me upright and released his grip.

He looked at the hardware then reholstered it beneath his jacket. He was breathing a little faster than usual. So was I. There was a mark on the mirror from my face and a mark on my face from the mirror. 'I want to talk to you,' he said.

We took a table at a little distance from his two friends. Dato insisted on buying me a beer to make up for the incident with his firearm so I ordered two. The waitress was not sure she understood. No, I wanted two for myself, at the same time. I smoked from Dato's pack and it was a very good cigarette. I told him my concerns about guns going off accidentally. He assured me the safety catch had been on.

'Is Nathan alright? Is he locked up?'

'He hurt his head. He's free but we have his passport. The American Embassy knows all about it.'

The beers arrived.

'I won't hold you responsible for the American fucker, but what you are doing now, talking to Chechens, is very stupid, after being arrested in Pankisi.'

'Detained for questioning.'

'You're making it worse. I was telling Petrosian that, and he attacked me. Now he's telling the embassy the police want to kill him. They don't want to hear his stories at the embassy.

We could lock him up if we wanted to. But we don't want him in jail. We want him to go away, to stop talking to Chechens.'

'Fine, Dato. We won't talk to any more Chechens. If you can help us, we don't need to. Who killed Baiev? Interior Ministry?'

He glared, maybe considering hauling me back to the water closet. He had a good glare, all angry-eyeball. I'd say he was good in the interrogation room.

I finished the first beer.

'Forget the Chechen. Nobody wants to know about one dead Chechen. People in the street don't care. The Americans don't want to hear. And I don't want to hear. I want you to go away from Georgia.'

I made a good dent in the second beer.

'Listen.' Dato tapped the table. 'Tomorrow at one o'clock we're going for a drive.'

'You don't get tired of that?'

'You have to explain why you are talking to terrorists.'

'I'm busy at that time.'

'I've cancelled your meeting.'

I emptied the second beer and stood up. I felt like walking. I like that feeling of freedom, when my legs are moving and I don't have to talk.

'Anything else?'

'That's it.'

'You'll come pick me up?'

'Of course.'

Thick Neck gave me a dirty look as I walked past. On the way to the door I was intercepted by the waitress and I indicated my friend with the big shaved head. She looked at him and he gave her a little wave. So I let him pay for my earlier beers too and what Nino had consumed. The Interior Ministry could afford it.

When I hit the street I realized I was very drunk. I hiccuped home, stopping just to buy cigarettes. I got in and took a leak. I was zipping up when the phone rang. It was Elizaveta. She was hysterical. Nathan was in hospital with a fractured skull. The embassy said he would have to go back to America. Nathan said they were trying to send him to Guantánamo Bay. I told her he was saying crazy things because of the concussion. I tried to reassure her, said that the police were apologetic and wanted to sort something out. She was wailing something about not wanting another dead husband. I talked to her for about half an hour, told her everything would be fine. Money worries were interjected in her complaints. The hospital was closing in two weeks and she was losing her job. Did I think she should divorce such a crazy man? No, I said, he had a good heart and would mellow when he got old. This was what she wanted me to say and towards the end she calmed down and by the time I put the phone on the receiver I was sober again and my mouth was dry and I had to take another big piss. It was hard to stay drunk with so much going on.

I was too rattled to sleep. I was hungry. I looked in the fridge. There was nothing but a jar of pickled cucumbers. I ate them with some old bread. Then I sat around and smoked a fair number of bad Georgian cigarettes.

The phone woke me. It was Ismailev. The wife of the Jordanian was not going to speak to me. I asked him to describe the police who had visited her. He hung up on me.

Then I called Elizaveta and found out where Nathan was. It was the same hospital Baiev had been in.

He was sitting up in bed with his head bandaged. He was

cheerful despite the blows he had taken to the face and head. It was untrue, he said, that he had bitten off a cop's ear. The ear was made of cartilage, which was practically impossible to bite through. He had broken the skin, certainly, and may have bitten off part of the flesh at the edge of the ear. He admitted he was drunk when the cops came up to him. The same ones who had taken him for the drive that morning. It was a bar just off Freedom Square, quite a nice place. The big jumpy guy with the shaved head told him to stop talking to Chechens or he'd end up dumped in Pankisi too. Somebody shoved somebody, somebody hit somebody, then he was on the ground, getting booted in the head and body.

'Something you gotta do for us,' said Nathan. 'An interview with the US Embassy, today at four, to discuss my case.'

'Dato and the boys are taking me for the drive around at one. Then if they drop me back at the apartment . . . I don't know.'

'Should be OK. They seem to get bored after about two hours. Don't mention the embassy thing to them. They're holding my passport, embassy won't give me a new one. They're trying to make me return to the States by giving me a temporary document to travel there. Then who knows what they'll spring on me at the airport. I could end up in a legal black hole. It's all about the Pankisi thing. You can use the opportunity to ask some other questions, like why they're funding murderers.'

'Dato's pretty friendly with me. He bought me beers last night.'

'You went drinking with the sonofabitch put me here?'

'After he put a gun to my head.'

'He threatened you in public?'

'In private.'

'That mark on your face, from the gun?'

He meant the redness between my temple and my left eye, from the tapping.

'It's mostly you he's angry about. The American fucker, that's what he calls you. *Pizdyets Americanyets.*'

'Sounds better in Russian. But *pizdyets* means pussy.'

'Cunt, more like.'

'Anyway, I want to know what the US Embassy is going to do about journalists being beaten and threatened at gunpoint by the Interior Ministry. Give them a chance to react, before we go public.'

I told him it was getting harder to do anything. I told him about the wife of the Jordanian doctor, and that Ismailev was talking about going to Azerbaijan.

'We should go too. Till things cool down. Easier to make money in Azerbaijan, now that the oil's about to flow west. The editor of a magazine there, he's published a few of my articles. He has a holiday house on the coast, says I can stay there. Elizaveta's out of a job now, nothing to keep us here.'

'Beats driving around with Dato every day.'

I thought of a home on the coast, living with my friends. Then I remembered Azerbaijan was as fucked as Georgia, with its American-funded dictator, and that oil rigs decorated the Caspian Sea.

'Yeah, well. Come over to my place after the embassy, we'll talk about it. They're letting me out in a few hours, soon's they know I'm not brain damaged.'

I couldn't help smiling.

'Hey,' said Nathan. 'Don't say it.'

*

We had the drive. There were the usual questions but now they also wanted to know why I was interested in Arabs, both dead ones and those still living. I told Dato it was more the way they had been executed that interested me, or why they had been kidnapped and given to the Americans. Ask the Americans, said Dato, if you want to know what they want. We took a turn and went slowly past the park where I had met Ismailev, and crawled past the house of the wife of the Jordanian doctor. After two hours I was becoming uneasy about my meeting at the embassy. I didn't want to mention it. It might have made them extend the drive. Then we were heading back towards town. Fifteen minutes prior to my appointment they pulled up in front of the embassy of the United States and let me out.

'Thanks for the lift.'

I didn't bother asking how they knew. I shrugged and went up to security to be searched.

A young man came to the lounge and pumped my hand. This radiant human being was so pleased to meet me that I felt ashamed, like a member of a race stunted by bitterness and negativity. He had great teeth too.

He took me into a room and we sat down and he turned on the tape recorder. He was sure I understood, it was policy. Used to be the journalist brought the tape recorder, I joked. I had none.

Well, I began, it was common knowledge around town that people were being kidnapped, in operations involving the Georgian Interior Ministry and the CIA, and had disappeared. Those that had not already been shot.

His smile was modified as he inserted the official stick up his embassy ass. He was very sorry, but if I wished to schedule an interview about security cooperation with Georgia, for some later date, he would see what he could do.

'There's a woman here in Tbilisi, three kids, who wonders where her husband is. I asked an Interior Ministry source what he was wanted for and he suggested, off the record, that I ask you.'

This did not provoke him to comment either. Nor would he say anything about the detention without charge of Georgian citizens by the Georgian state on the basis of information supplied by, and possibly requests made by, the United States. No comment on the supply of weapons and training to Georgian security forces. He wasn't prepared to comment on security matters or counter-terrorism operations. Embassy policy at this sensitive time. I asked if the sensitive time referred to the oil pipeline and he said no, the sensitivity was due to the fight against global terror. Al Qaeda was present in the Pankisi Gorge.

'There is no gorge in the Pankisi Gorge.'

'Or it's named after a gorge. I don't know exactly.'

'I've been there. It's not a gorge and there is no gorge. It's farmland. They're farmers.'

'That's what it's called in English.'

'It wasn't anything in English until President Bush made a speech.'

'I'm sorry. Is there a point to this?'

'You're right. I suppose it doesn't matter. I'm just interested because the body of a man I knew was dumped there. And now I'm getting a hard time from the Interior Ministry because I went there.'

His face became very sincere. He spoke quietly: 'You asked to discuss Mr Petrosian and I'm more than happy to do anything I can concerning his specific case.' He allowed himself a little smile.

'Moving on, then,' I said.

'Mr Petrosian is charged with hooliganism. He bit a cop's ear off.'

'Not the whole ear, surely.'

'The consulate has made representations on his behalf, and the authorities will drop charges. If he leaves the country.'

'The police are holding his passport.'

'As they are entitled to do. For our part, we are able to present him with a temporary travel document that will enable him to return to the United States.'

'So he's being pressured to leave.'

'If he stays he goes to jail. We don't want Mr Petrosian to go to jail in Georgia, but there is nothing we can do if he refuses to leave. He has broken the law.'

'How about issuing him a new passport so he can go to a third country?'

'We are unable to issue passports to persons owing in excess of five thousand dollars in child support. Nathan Petrosian's arrears run considerably in excess of that. During his last visit to the United States he was to attend a hearing on the matter. He came to this country instead. The only travel document we may now authorize is one which facilitates his returning to face charges. This rule applies to US embassies worldwide and we are unable to make an exception.'

I tried not to show anything, but my silence in the face of this development was eloquent.

'Yesterday a man put a gun to my head. Interior Ministry. He advised me to leave the country.'

He leaned forward and turned the tape recorder off. The interview was over.

'You have heard of Ahmed Baiev, haven't you?' I said.

He settled back in his chair. 'Listen. They won't shoot you

173

in the head, or an American citizen. But they'll make your life unpleasant and there is nothing a foreign embassy can do on your behalf. There is little to be gained by staying. Nobody cares very much about one dead Chechen.'

'Not as much as they care about an oil pipeline.'

'Terrorists don't inspire sympathy.'

'The terrorists are the Interior Ministry.'

'Very good. Go sell your story. Make the world a better place.'

'I'll give you a story: US official advises journalist to leave country.'

We stood up simultaneously. In fact, he had the jump on me, but I saw it coming and made it appear near-enough simultaneous. We were giving each other little fuck-you grins.

'Stay if you want. I don't give a shit, frankly.'

'Thanks for being frank.'

I got out of that embassy and got a taxi straight for Nathan's place.

Dinner was being served. There was lamb in a sour-plum sauce and chicken in a walnut and garlic sauce, and wine on the table, which was unusual. Nathan wanted to know how it had gone at the embassy but I didn't want to go straight into it. I wanted to eat. Elizaveta looked as if she had been crying and wasn't touching the food. Probably they had been fighting.

The swelling was going down on Nathan's face but he still looked bad. After we cleared the dishes away Elizaveta went into the bedroom and Nathan asked me again.

'Nobody wants to kill you. Nobody even wants to shut us up, because we don't know anything.'

'Why do they want me out of the country, then, if it's not connected to Pankisi?'

'They don't want you in jail. Somebody might make you a cause.'

'Maybe that's what we gotta do. Take it to the next level.'

You could see him thinking about sitting in jail, being a cause.

'You won't be on the cover of *Newsweek*. Maybe some journalists' organization will say something. The ear thing really fucks it up, though.'

'I've no passport. I'm a stateless person. I fly to the States, they pick me up and send me to Guantánamo. What's so funny?'

'Just picturing you. Orange isn't your colour.'

He smiled, though it hurt his face. We went quiet for a bit. I considered going to the window to smoke.

'You're not getting special treatment, you're getting the standard treatment, you son of a bitch. You could have told me about your child-support issues before I went in there, saved me a very awkward moment.'

'How do you think they dug up something from a local court case and got me for it here?'

'Conspiracy?'

'It goes back to when I busted the prostitution ring in Kentucky. The child-support thing, same county. They were bringing in Russian girls and passing them around, even the sheriff. I called in immigration and got my nose broken.'

He pointed to his nose.

'I thought that was a pool cue in West Virginia, exposing vote-buying in the union.'

'I've had my nose broken four times. That's from the pool cue.' He pointed to his forehead. I knew the scar but it was lost in the bruising.

'The problem with our story,' I said, 'is nobody cares about a dead Chechen. A couple of people have pointed this out to me and I can see it myself. The American papers didn't get back, did they?'

He shook his head.

'We've got a story, but we're just a couple of fuck-ups and can't spin it. It's like you bite someone's ear, the embassy will claim that you're a bad person.'

'I was being choked at the time, man. I did what I had to do.'

'And I tried at the embassy but they had their answers ready.'

'Did you tell him about the police telling you to get out? Threatening to blow your brains out?'

'For Christ's sake, Nathan. The safety was on.'

I lit up my cigarette, blew some smoke.

'Could you smoke that out the window?'

'Fuck you.'

'Fuck you too.'

We sat there being glum for a bit, me smoking. Then I got up and went to the window.

'Nathan, I'm not visiting you in a Georgian jail.'

'I'm not going to jail, man. We're going to fight them.'

'No, we're not, because I'm leaving the country.'

'Cutting and running, eh?'

'That's it exactly.'

'So the bad guys win.'

'I'd like to stick around and fight for the truth but I've no money, and I'm sick of the rides around town. I need to go away and get a job, then maybe I'll come back.'

'Yeah, right. You're not coming back.'

I blew some smoke out the window.

Next day I got on a bus for Istanbul.

At the bus station I gave the number a final try. Eka answered.

The phone had been broken. I told her I was leaving Georgia.

'Can't we meet?'

'I was trying so hard to call you. For a long time.'

'Will you come back?'

'Maybe.'

'Didn't you like it here?'

'Yes, I liked lots of things here. I have to go now, because the bus is leaving.'

'Well, goodbye. Have a good trip.'

'Goodbye, Eka.'

Then I was one of thirty or forty people looking through a bus window at Tbilisi disappearing.

It was a 36-hour trip. At the border everybody paid five dollars to the police. Then they found problems with the passports of a number of people and that cost between twenty and fifty. They told the driver to park in a windowless corrugated-iron shed and we sat there for several hours until the last person holding out had paid.

That was the end of that country, and I haven't returned. I went back to the country where I had lived before. Nathan stayed in Georgia. He managed not to go to jail.

Summer came. For a time I was unemployed and then I got a job in an office again. It was the usual thing: boredom, flirtation, backbiting. I travelled back and forth through the city on buses and trolleybuses, on trams, the metro, and the people were crowded together and short-tempered in the heat. I watched on the news about bad things happening in other countries but there were too many countries and the news never told you much, and then it was on to the sports results and the weather. I had a place to live and paid my bills on time. I painted the walls and bought things. Sometimes the sink got blocked and

I unblocked it. I went to the market and bought food and brought it home and put it in the fridge. At the weekends there were people to drink with. After a few months I met a girl. We wanted to be happy together and we succeeded for a while.

Walking Away

Her telephone number remained in the pocket of his funeral trousers for over two weeks. He had not forgotten about it, but he had no particular interest in it either. It was late autumn and the days were getting shorter. The city, people, trees – all these were slowing and turning inwards upon themselves.

The branches dropped their leaves and the people, now wearing the hats and coats that had long hung in wardrobes, boarded buses and tramcars less lightly than before. Listening to their speech, watching them in the streets, he felt he was looking at people who spoke and moved but did not know why and did not care. During this interval he found it hard to be with them in confined spaces. In buses and trams he became agitated and hated every face he saw. He felt much better on the long walk from his office through the cold dark streets to his apartment, observing them from a distance. His route took him past the high walls of the Jewish cemetery, and every evening he noted the handwritten sign on the door requesting a groundsman. And each time he saw the notice he thought it would be good to do such work, to do something at that point with his hands, with the earth, in the garden of the dead Jews. And across the road from the cemetery, through the brightly lit plate-glass windows of the supermarket, he saw people moving down aisles, like sleepwalkers, placing coloured cans and packets in trolleys.

He arrived home that particular evening, the one when he had decided it was time again to do something. He swept the floor and washed some dishes. He ate a sandwich and poured himself a drink then stood by his window with the glass in his hand, looking at the lights of the city. There were streetlights and the lights of moving vehicles, and the bright patchwork of lighted windows from apartment blocks. Towards the centre, perhaps two kilometres away, a flashing giant green and red sign was advertising Beck's beer. Cranes against the horizon were paper cut-outs. The skyline of the city was being altered. Tall new office buildings were going up. Money was being put to work. The city appeared to be getting younger as he got older.

Looking out the window, he recalled how she had stuck close by him on the way to the graveyard, talking rapidly. It jarred with him at the time not only because her way of speaking lacked solemnity, but because the words themselves bore no relation to anything around them, or anything that had happened, as her left breast nudged his arm, repeatedly. He finished his drink, still looking at the city. She was no longer quite so young. But nor was he, and some time had passed since he had been with a woman, and the invitation was a simple one. He thought of her hips, which were becoming heavy. But that was fine too. He felt like holding something solid and imperfect, pulling himself back to earth from those sleepwalking days.

And so, that evening, weeks after the funeral, he picked up the phone and called her. She sounded pleased to hear from him and invited him directly to her home. Though it was not so early, he felt like moving slowly, and did not order a taxi. He took a bus to the intersection with the tramlines, then waited in the cold for a tram. After fifteen minutes two trams came at the same time, both the same number, and not the number that he needed. He waited longer and his feet became cold and then, when he doubted any more trams would come, he took a taxi.

He read the numbers on the gates and when he reached hers he entered the dark garden and approached the house and rang the bell. It was an old house, but well renovated. She opened the door to him, smiling, and he stepped inside. As she took his coat, he apologized for being late and she laughed and said it did not matter. She spoke rapidly, the way he remembered, with that same enthusiasm for speech that had seemed misplaced to him that day, walking in the procession. She could not hear herself as he heard her. This distance between them told him that it would not be complicated. She was not a person he would grow attached to.

They passed from the hall into a small well-heated living room, with a sofa facing a television with the sound turned down, and this room led into a superfluous larger room with antique furniture. It looked unlived in, as if she had only recently taken up residence at the home of a much older person.

They stayed in the smaller room and she invited him to sit down on an oddly angled wooden chair with a long straight narrow back, like an exhibit from an art museum, some kind of play on the idea of a chair. It forced a posture that was not quite natural. He got up and moved to the sofa, beside her. He opened the bottle of wine he had brought and they drank in front of the silent television, which showed a made-for-TV movie. The scenes were lit with such clarity that the objects looked unreal. She took care of the talking.

She had money. She was good at making it, but it was also clear that she had grown up with it, and a solid sense of her own worth. When she travelled she stayed in the best hotels. After she had drunk a glass of wine she told him that when she was younger she had written a novel, and she got up and went to a cabinet and retrieved a box. She sat down again and opened the box and showed him. He leafed through the words, the many thousands of words, and nodded, and could think of nothing to say about it. He put the pages back in the box for her and she replaced the lid. Then she showed him an old newspaper in which two of her poems had been published. They might have been good, but he could not tell because the words required analysis of some kind, or engaging in feelings in which he had no interest. But already she was talking about how she had once gone around with a group of Gypsies and walked barefoot in the streets, asking strangers for coins. She had been good at it. She had not needed the money, but had wanted to experience that side of life. She had done amateur theatre also. Once she had sold vegetables in the market and she showed him a photograph of herself at the stall, dressed as a peasant. Again, it was a part that she was trying. But she had been a very good vegetable seller also. Mostly she spoke, and he nodded. She had opened herself to him. He would have liked to participate, to open himself in return, but he was unable. He had a feeling that there was nothing there to show. He did not believe in any of the things he might have pointed to.

She began to talk about the circumstances in which they had met, and he found he could not talk about that either, though it was the only subject there was. Since the event he had been frozen and felt that if the right words could be found he could unlock himself from the state in which he was trapped, in those weeks when winter was closing in. But he could find no words. The closest he had come was a moment, standing in the street, when he caught sight of two young cats, playing in the shrubbery, fighting, inhabiting their bodies entirely, without thought. That is what it is about, he thought. To live like that. That is what life means. And he felt his own ageing body, slowing, stiffening, and burdened with thought and sadness. He would think about the cats from time to time, and this was as close as he came to clarity.

When the bottle was emptied – she had drunk only the one glass – he made his awkward move. It was reciprocated, and they went to the bedroom.

In the dark, without their clothes, it did not matter who she was or what age she was or what she looked like, and he forgot himself too, which was what he wanted. He forgot about yesterday, and tomorrow. They became everybody else, and nobody. They moved like shadows in the strange room and it became urgent and important. Then it was over, and they slept.

In the morning, before it was fully light, he rose quietly and began to dress, but she awoke and insisted on making coffee. He drank it with her in the semi-darkness, quickly, to preclude unnecessary talk. He wished to be away, swiftly, and not return.

As he put the drained cup on the saucer, she asked him to stay for another little while, but he did not see why he should, now that he was feeling something strong, and his mind beginning to awaken.

Nearly there, he thought, as he felt the weight of his coat about his shoulders, while she stood close beside him, as if wishing to hold him back a little longer. He patted his pocket for his wallet, kissed her goodbye and stepped outside the door. It closed behind him with a definite click. It was a satisfying sound. The air outside was cool in the first moments as he walked away and he breathed it in deeply, gratefully. The garden was crisp with early-morning frost. Perhaps a snowfall was only weeks away. It was possible. The noise from beyond her gate told him the city was gearing up for another day. He was one step ahead already. It was good to be moving, walking away.

The day they had met, walking in the procession, she had

talked about a temple in Thailand, some place like that, one of her sightseeing tours, saying, It makes you think, you know, such places, about what it all means, about what lies beyond. And he did not contradict her, and might even have nodded, as if in agreement with that phrase, *what lies beyond*. But he was in fact thinking, What foolishness, to speak of beyond, when we hardly know what we have here, on this earth, right before our eyes. This is what he thought, as they went to the graveyard to bury his friend, who had been a rare man, good and generous, and had been open to the future, or so the world had imagined. There was no way to utter what had happened in words that would not be hollow. And, as the woman beside him brushed her flesh against his, he could not help but reckon he was in with a chance.

A simple solution to a complex problem, that was how someone had defined it, he remembered, feeling the beauty of walking away, past the garden, and towards the awakening city streets.

The Pleasant Light of Day

The man had looked at a map and figured it was a simple walk from the hotel to the museum. Now he observed the alien script of the street signs and shop signs which could not even be resolved into individual letters and heard snatches of strange speech as the faces passed at speed. He was conscious of the maleness of the street, the few women scarved and overdressed in the warm weather. He held his son's hand. It was early morning and the boy's mother was still drowsing in her bed.

His son, five years old, was silent now and very serious at the task of getting down the street. The boy had never seen so many people. The noise of the car horns and the intense traffic made it difficult for them to speak. The boy was usually very talkative. He was very good with words, and when he did not understand a word he would ask what it meant.

For example, once the man had taken him to fish from the rocks at home and the boy had soon become bored. 'You don't have patience,' he told him.

'What's patience?'

He had thought for a moment and then replied: 'Patience is giving to each thing the time you need to do it well. So, to fish, you need patience, until the fish comes to you.'

Later that day he asked the boy what patience was, and the boy replied immediately: 'Waiting.'

Or, when they had been collecting bait, using stones to whack limpets off rocks, the boy, who loved animals, asked, 'Doesn't it hurt them?'

'Fish bait. They're history.'

'What's history?'

He thought about this. He liked the process of taking a word apart in order to explain an idea simply. It helped him notice the natural connection between ideas. And, like holding the boy's hand, explaining words gave him a place in the world. He delivered simple blocks of meaning and watched the boy play with them, turning them around as he would solid objects, examining them for use. He observed the boy's world growing, branching out in fresh directions, as he gathered words.

'History is something that has happened, and you tell a story about it.'

'So. It's a story. That's real.'

'Yes, but when I say they're history, I just mean, that's it, the story is over for them, the end.'

The boy, sitting on his hunkers on the wet sand, pondering history by the tide pool, nodded, his mouth a little open.

Later, the boy shouted across the waves 'You're history!' as the man cast a hook baited with a struggling worm. The father laughed, the wind and the sun in his face. In such moments he felt that children were geniuses in a bright new world, one that only later grew dim. He wanted to hold the boy's hand a little longer, while he still belonged to such a world. Growing older, people found dull ways to make life bearable. Or perhaps did not find any way.

And now they were walking down a strange street, with the traffic screaming, and the traffic cop at the intersection whistling, to the Egyptian Museum of Antiquities.

They reached a 'square', a vast open space where vehicles converged from a number of busy streets, and they stopped and stood there together, looking across, holding hands, as if they had reached the shore of a sea. There was no place to cross.

Cars swarmed about each other like ants on an anthill, somehow avoiding collision. It was very loud. The sounds of the horns rose above the sound of the engines. They watched and the boy waited for the next thing his father would do. The father could see people crossing, passing between moving lanes of traffic as if protected by magic charms. But he did not have the nerve for such a trick, and certainly not with a child. Then he saw the sign for the metro station and the people going down into the ground.

The man and the boy descended into the tunnels beneath the square. The tunnels branched and turned many times. They went up and down stairs. The man saw signs in Arabic that he could not read and signs in Latin script indicating streets he did not know.

'Dad, do you know the way?'

'Approximately.'

'What's approximately?'

'Kind of.'

When they came up again to the sky and the square, they were closer to the museum and there were no more big roads to cross.

'They have a really lot of cars in Cairo, Dad.'

'They do.'

'How many do they have, would you say?'

'A lot a lot.'

'But how many really, Dad?'

'Oh, millions.'

'That's a really lot! Why don't they crash?'

'I don't know. I think they do. Sometimes.'

The museum was located in a street that was blocked off to general traffic. Only police and military vehicles and tour buses were admitted. There were ordinary police, soldiers and riot police with shields. Soldiers stood guard behind blast shields.

'Why are there soldiers, Dad?'

It was a police state, for one thing. It had made peace with Israel and received American money in return, and had developed a tourist industry, the only real industry there was, and this investment had to be protected against bombers, and their deadly shrapnel.

'To keep an eye on things.'

'What things, like?'

'Crazy runaway crocodiles, from the River Nile.'

The boy smiled. They were away from the traffic now, with the tourists and the soldiers, and it was easier to speak.

'Have their guns got bullets, Dad? Real ones?'

'I'd say so.'

They entered the main gates in front of the museum, and he bought tickets and declined the services of several guides. They had a brief rest, sitting outside talking, about crocodiles and hippopotamuses, mainly, and then they entered one of the greatest museums on earth.

The Egyptian Museum of Antiquities fairly represented the country, the man felt. A musty deposit of wonders, a coffin shop, a sarcophagus warehouse. The exhibits were crowded and jumbled. Those in cases were described in Arabic and English by small cards bearing the clunky font of an old typewriter, the English a mess of stylistic, grammatical and typographical errors, comically slapdash in a museum with a grand name implying respect for the sciences.

The chaos of the city had pervaded the museum.

They wandered from case to case, stopping when an exhibit held the boy's attention and gave them something to discuss, and he explained what he could. But the boy was interested in ordinary household objects, things that he could easily recognize. Objects so banal that it seemed strange that they should be exhibited at all. Looking at such things with his son, the man felt that the world of the past was as real as that in which he lived, though glimpsed through the odd distorting glass of a museum display case. It was not the world of the dead that seemed strange to him, but the dead analytical impulse that had removed the objects from the living hands that had held and used them, from rooms where families had lived and children grown up, and put them in display cases as if they were extraordinary. They were not extraordinary. It was just that the people who had used them had been gone a long time.

As he walked the corridors of the dead he could not shake the mad hum of the city outside. He had a sudden vertiginous sensation that the living city was just one more layer superimposed upon all the dead layers. All the motion, joy, excitement going on outside – a fly buzzing blind against a windowpane.

He looked at simple functional objects such as pots and knives and sandals, and then looked up and saw the tourists performing their stations, and it was the tourists who made the least sense. What strange species of people needed to look at such things as though they were hard to understand? There was even a chunk of ancient bread on display. Preserved in the dry air of a tomb, it now resembled a rock. But what was bread when it was no longer for eating? And what kind of a human being needed to look at bread that was no longer bread, but bread for looking at in a case, and yet needed to be told 'This is bread'?

He had had a similar feeling several days before, on the plane, looking at the ancient desert through gaps in the unreal-looking clouds, thinking what an improbable thing it was to fly, to sail above the earth in a metal bird, ignorant of how the trick worked, and completely unamazed. Sustained by faith in technology, floating through a dream.

There was a long room at the back of the museum, and he overheard a tour guide explaining the giant cases. It was a row of coffins. Each was an elaborate work of art, and the smaller slotted into the larger until the final coffin was the size of a room and was placed in the earth and sealed up for eternity. But now eternity was dug up and cracked open, the mysteries of the death cult exposed. The tourists clicked their cameras, getting their money's worth, a bit of culture. Then they boarded their air-conditioned buses and went to souks that sold junk.

He wandered through the rows of exhumed objects, objects which either from utility or beauty spoke clearly of life, and he could not shake the feeling of being in someone else's dream. Could they have dreamed forward, as we dreamed back to their lives? Could they have dreamed these people wandering heedless through their treasure?

A boy, five years old, wakes and tries to tell his father about pale ghosts drifting through the aisles of a vast temple, pointing at the pharaoh's gold. The boy, rubbing his eyes, sits before a wooden bowl and the woman brings a pot and places it before them. The father scoops mashed beans into the boy's bowl. And then, Father, says the boy, they were looking at my bowl. The father smiles and passes his hand over the boy's head. He likes to watch him eat, and grow big. They begin their breakfast, as they do each morning, the sun rising above the fields, the Nile flowing tirelessly through the days.

They stopped before a painted wooden snake, projecting from a black box. A snake temple. The drawers, or doors, opened and the snake slid in or out on a wooden base. For exhibit, the snake poked out of doors.

'It's a cobra, Dad. Why is it in a box?'

'So it doesn't bite people.'

'If it escaped it would bite people. Wouldn't it?'

'That's the thing, with cobras.'

'Snakes can cause a really lot of trouble.'

'You're definitely in trouble if a cobra bites you.'

'What's definitely?'

'For sure.'

'Definitely in trouble. The snake told her to eat the apple, didn't he, Dad? Then God took off his legs and said, Eat dust.'

They moved on, holding hands, between the glass cases. He told the boy lots of stories: myths and legends, Bible stories, invented-on-the-spot stories. Spiderman and Batman and Jesus. Curious details caught the boy's interest. The expression 'eat dust', a fragment of scripture, like something from an action film. He had read the story to retell it to the boy and had discovered that the snake had originally had legs. God makes the snake limbless in punishment for tempting the people.

He had been struck, when he read, by another detail. In the story, God lies. God tells Adam and Eve that if they eat the fruit, or even touch it, they will die. The implication is that they will die on the spot. The snake explains that this is untrue: God does not want them to eat the fruit because then they will be able, like their Creator, to tell good from evil. Eve wishes to be wise, and eats the fruit. The snake has told the truth. She becomes wise. She understands that she is mortal.

God had lied as you would lie to children who have no way to comprehend what they are being warned against.

They passed a number of jars and cups, and stopped at the next interesting exhibit, a bow and set of arrows. The boy liked these toys. He liked knights and Vikings and now he liked Egyptians too, with their chariots and weapons. The father read the card and explained to the boy that the red pigment still visible on the tips of some of the arrowheads was poison.

'Snake poison, Dad.'

'Maybe. But there are other ways to get poison.'

The boy peered into the case. His mouth was open. This happened when he was thinking hard, but it also happened when he was tired. They had been looking around for nearly an hour and it was a sign that the boy would soon be harder to amuse. An hour is a long time when you are small and the days are so long you can get lost in them. The man decided they should skip the treasures of Tutankhamun. He imagined the boy's mother, breakfasted and relaxed, smiling when they returned from their journey.

'Why is the arrow like that, Dad?'

The arrows were barbed in order to rip the flesh badly if any attempt were made at extraction.

'To hurt more.'

'Oh.'

He mussed the boy's hair. 'Will we go now?'

The boy nodded. They headed for the stairs. They passed the entrance to the Mummy Room. He was not taking the boy to look at corpses. He could do without it himself, in fact. He remembered reading that Sadat had closed the exhibition because Islamists objected to the dead being displayed. Some fundamentalists had killed Sadat. The metro station in the square outside was named in his memory.

They stepped out into the light and stood on the steps. They could hear the traffic from the square.

'How about we sit down here on the steps and have a break. Then we'll go and get some ice cream.'

The boy did a little jump and landed bent-kneed, the weight of his body pulling his father's arm. They sat down.

They were just out of reach of the city. Many millions of people were out there. Charging through the streets in cars. Kneeling to pray. Walking home from a job, catching the smell of frying fish in a side street. Hustling for money, labouring in a factory or in a taxi, being a lift attendant, a street cleaner, a maker of felafel, an accountant, a shopkeeper, a shopkeeper's sweeper and mopper. Sprinkling parsley on your dinner. Buying trinkets for your room. Screaming when your team scored. Reading in the newspaper about a war in another country, while you had your hair cut. Watching the sun go down on the concrete skyline from an apartment on the seventh floor. Remembering when your son was born. Remembering when your wife was young.

Every generation went about its business, it seemed to him, as if none of it had ever happened before.

If people really saw that all their passions were infinitely ancient, he imagined, perhaps the traffic in the square would grind to a halt, the engines and horns go silent. The taxi drivers would sit in their cars with no reason to drive any further. Fares would say, 'Here is fine,' and would reach for wallets and remove the coloured notes. But the legal tender would be meaningless and would fall to the ground, and it would lie where it fell, and the passengers would get out, dazed, and wander like sleep-walkers through the stilled sea of vehicles. The drivers would fold their arms over the tops of the steering wheels, rest their chins on their arms and gaze through their windshields.

He looked at his son. He was really alive, the realest thing there was. You could tell him to look both ways before he crossed the street, but about the other thing you could say nothing, because the other thing was just a story for him. The soldiers all fall down, then they get up and play another game.

He sat there for a moment with the boy, in the sunshine. It was good to enjoy the pleasant light of day.

'Let's get ice cream, Dad.'

'Let's go.'

They walked past the soldiers and police, back towards the noise of the city, the man and the boy, holding hands.

A Time for Everything

On still nights she heard the breathing of her mother beside her and the dogs lying by the door, but on this night she awoke to the sky breathing through the high leafy branches. She lay in bed seeing the wind travelling across the wide plain to the hills and swaying the dark trees around her home, and she pulled the blankets tighter and fell asleep thinking of gathering wood the next day, the dead fallen branches on the forest floor.

When she woke again it was silent. The objects in the room were becoming themselves once more and she understood that the sky was both clear and still. Now in the growing light of the spring sometimes there was no need on awakening to fumble for matches and candle. She rose and pulled her clothes around herself while her mother still dreamt. She was the youngest child, a latecomer, and this winter her mother had shown the signs of age. The bone tiredness. The need to sleep. And now the biting in her gut. As she slipped her feet into her shoes the tail of the young dog lifted and fell to the floor several times. The rest of the dog could not yet move.

She broke sticks and when they were brightly crackling in the mouth of the stove she clanked the stovedoor shut and put the pot of water on to warm.

She stepped over the dogs and they stirred, first the lean young dog, and then the older one, its mother, with more difficulty. She pulled the door, creaking, and it was as she expected – a sky blue already in a calm morning. She saw through the clearing to the road and the steeple and houses of the town below, and the lazing line of the river that drew a border between the foothills and the plain stretching far eastwards on the other side.

The wounded-animal screech of the train whistle sounded clearly from the direction of the town. The trains were irregular as a consequence of the war. It sounded loudest to her at night and in the early morning, and sometimes the drift of the wind made it louder still. She did not think the war would come any closer.

The rail line ran alongside the river. She could not see the tracks, as the line was much narrower than the river and hidden in the trees, but she could follow the smoke from the engine when the trains pulled away, carrying soldiers, or guns, or sacks of maize. They would go upstream along the river and cross the bridge, far out of sight, to the north. Then the trains turned east, towards the war.

There was a barracks on the road by the station. That was where her lover slept. She thought of his white legs covered with the bites of fleas from sleeping in the dirty barracks but hoped he would sleep safely there by the river and the train tracks until the fighting ended and their life began.

Tomorrow morning, early, he would come to speak to her mother. The mother had never seen him. But her sisters from the town had no doubt shared information which belonged to everybody there who did not block their eyes and ears. And she was certain that her mother could know that she had lain with a man from watching how she moved. That she did not need to be told was clear from her mother's alternating bursts of anger and tenderness. But tomorrow the matter would be spoken of and put right.

She walked a distance into the wood to relieve herself. Then she went to the shed and washed from the bucket, using the lumpy brown soap. She liked the water on her skin, though it was cold. She liked to wash and would have preferred to wash completely, lazily, in a tub, with scents. But in the morning she liked cold water on her face, and would have chosen that even if a big house in the city were hers. Even were she taken by a man to a fine house, she would still have cold water for her face in the morning. But she had chosen a man with nothing. She would be taking him. Because the land in the forest and the cow were hers. Because her brother was dead in the war and her sisters were married to men with good flat green land that stretched out towards the river below.

She rinsed the dust and the spider and its web from the milking pail and carried it to the byre. The smell of hay and fresh dung. She led the cow, with its heavy delicate full-udder walk, and tethered it at the milking place. The cow crunched hay and she rinsed the teats. Then the first straight lines of milk ringing off the bottom of the bucket, her strong hands pulling the milk from the placid beast, her head pressed to its warm hide. While she milked the smell of the cow's hide came to her in waves, as if she had never smelled it before. It was not a bad smell but there was something strong and new in it. And for a moment even to be milking a cow seemed strange and she wondered why she should think of it that way, a thing she did every day. It was because of Lent perhaps, the foods she could not eat, the milk she could not drink. The milk was saved and on Easter morning they would return from the midnight service in the town, carrying candles through the streets with the townspeople, and at her sister's house they would eat the fresh white curd cheese with honey.

When the flow slackened she massaged high up in the udders to bring the milk down. She milked this last part and it was done.

She carried the bucket outside, now a good weight on her arm, covered it with a cloth and put it at a height where the dogs could not drink.

She was a short way down the track to the town, the bucket of milk from morning and the bucket from the night before on each arm, when she heard the whistle and shunt of the departing locomotive. She thought of the train station and the barracks beside it where he slept and his thin white legs, spotted red from flea bites, and she smiled. She smiled when she caught herself thinking like a wife, thinking how she would cure such trouble for him when he came to live in her house, when he was no longer a soldier living in the filthy barracks. They were not the worst, those fleas that bit only the lower legs. They were not the fleas that lived on people, but fleas of animals that had got into bedding or clothing. They were never far, such fleas. Blankets and clothes had to be boiled and beaten out, and winter bedding stored carefully away. That was how it was done. It was a disorderly home where fleas multiplied in the bedding.

He rolls over and hitches his trousers up and ties them. She smiles at the whiteness of the tops of his insect-bitten legs then looks above at the clean air passing through the high leaves.

It was wrong, what we did, he says.

She is disappointed to hear him speak like this, now that it is done, the fear of other people, or God, in his voice. The thing that made him want to lie with her in the forest, though they know it is forbidden, is something true, and very simple, and they felt it at the same moment. She does not want it spoiled with fearful words. It felt right as it happened, and the good feeling of him stays with her now that they have done it. It is something that they have been waiting for and it has come on the appointed day. That is all. That was what it meant. That this is the day it was to happen. She wants to explain to him that there is a time for everything. There is a time for being born and one for dying. There is a time for planting and a time for reaping. There is a time for love also, though it may be short. The bloom is brief and then it passes on to something else, to the time for marriage, perhaps. There is even a time for war. This is evident now. But when the time of peace comes he will return. There was the land and they will manage it better together than apart. In this way, each moment will ripen and pass and all the things that people do will be accomplished in their turn, and sorrow will be tolerable.

We will make it right, she says. If from this moment on we do everything right, then it will be right.

We shouldn't do it again, he says, his conscience easing, until we are married.

She nods, knowing that soon he will wish to lie with her again. Because now it is unstoppable. And she knows that she will let him, even though if he is sent to the war and dies, the consequences will be hers alone.

The track through the woods was not very steep. It had been wide enough for a cart, but since her father had died there was no longer the cart trundling down with loads of timber towards the village, or returning with the hay for which it had been exchanged, and brambles and seedlings of oak and beech were becoming established. They had even sold the horse. There would be a horse and cart again, though, when the time came, and her husband would bring wood down to the town. She saw a cluster of mushrooms by the path, the good brown meaty ones that had the taste of the woods in them, and enough that some could be dried and stored. She noted the place in order to gather them on her return.

The path levelled out and the forest ended and there were supple young trees by the roadside and the first houses and fences, and the first man with a cart who hailed her, and dogs at gates, barking. And then the long straight road and bigger houses, and then she was on a paved street. She passed the church, where she would pray after she had left the milk.

Something strange was happening in front of the railway station, and the townspeople had come out to stare. She sought him among the dozen or so soldiers but his soldier's face showed nothing and he refused to look at her. The officer was giving orders and he was obeying. Some thirty or forty men were lined up against the wall of the station in the thin sunshine. They were being counted by one soldier while another shouted out their names and made marks in a register. They were of different ages and their clothes were dirty and they were tired and afraid and were underfed. She looked at one of the men, who had somehow kept his glasses, a pair of round lenses before his scared eyes, and for this mark of individuality he had retained she pitied him more than the others. He must have been from a town. Perhaps he had been a rich man, or a teacher. Perhaps he had a wife. Perhaps he had had a big shop in the capital. These were the Jews she had heard of. They had probably been on the train, crowded together in a wagon for a very long time. Perhaps they would board the train to cross the country again, and disembark in another country town by a river where strangers would stand in the street and stare at them.

The officer barked a harsh order and the soldiers moved in to herd the prisoners away from the station. Some of the townspeople followed the procession down the street.

She saw her lover turn his back. She heard the heavy boots of the soldiers on the road.

The remaining townspeople began to drift away, talking quietly, except for a group of young men who lingered. One of them had said something and the others were laughing loudly, in the nervous doglike way of young men, inflamed at their own noise.

Across the road, her sister's husband leaned against the doorway of his shop. He nodded to her and flicked his cigarette end away and stood up straight. The shopkeeper's freshly shaved jowls had the womanish blush of a man who lived indoors, by the stove. She picked up the buckets which she had set down on the road and walked towards the shop.

Who were they? she asked, approaching the doorway, the weight of the buckets new on her arms again.

Jidani, he replied, using the word they had that expressed a sentiment about that people.

They entered the shop. It sold dry goods and served food and drink to those who kept the fast and to those who did not. Her sister was behind the counter, leaning against it. She had grown stout and ruddy in her time in the town. A man in a railway company uniform, the signalman, sat at a low table at the wall, his hand curled around a cup of dark wine. The room was badly lit but hot from the stove. There was an unpleasant smell of cooking, of onions and other things that had been frying. She carried the pails through the shop and set them down in the cool yard behind the building.

She returned to the muggy room. The signalman was speaking in a low voice.

They send them east. Past the Prut, past the Dniester, I believe. We had two trains stop here last week, to take on water. The stink from the wagons!

The Steppes, said the shopkeeper, straightening up as though quoting a schoolbook poem, the Steppes extend forever east.

He took a cigarette from the packet and tapped it on the counter. Extend forever, he continued. Room enough for all the *jidani*, all the Gypsies. The *jidani* can cheat the *ţigani*, and the *ţigani* can steal it back.

The signalman shook his head.

The stink from the wagons. You wouldn't believe.

But these ones, she said. In our town. Where are they taking them?

The signalman looked at his wine. Wood crackled in the stove. The shopkeeper, leaning on the counter, placed the much considered cigarette in his mouth and struck a match. His big face glowed as he lit. Smoke curled from his lips.

To work, he said. For us, for a change.

Much you know of work, said his wife, occupied at the stove.

Speaking of, said the signalman, rising and draining his glass.

Health, said the shopkeeper.

Health, said the signalman. The door became a bright rectangle of light, then closed after him.

She felt unwell with the smoke and heat and the smell of food and it was worse when her sister slid the plate onto the table before her. The mound of dull yellow cornmeal was covered with fried onions and garlic, and even in the dimness it glistened.

I'm not hungry.

You ate already?

I wanted to pray before.

Her sister looked at her, and at the food, steaming.

You've got very holy. Eat it now, since it's hot.

It disgusted her but she ate, forcing each mouthful.

She had heard of the arrogance of the Jews. But there was no arrogance left in the tired and dirty prisoners she had seen. It was Lent and they were starved and she was eating food she did not want. Her lover the soldier had told her Codreanu and the Guard would uproot the corruption of the *jidani* and the communists. He described how Codreanu had come to his village. He had never seen so fine a man. Mounted on a white horse, in front of the church, a man of the land and the woods, the people gathered around him. This he told her, about Codreanu, in the forest after they had lain together. It had been beautiful to hear, because it was him telling it to her, about the church and the white horse, as they lay beneath the swaying branches as man and wife.

Finally it disgusted her too much. The smells. And her sister, and her ugly shopkeeper-husband, turning the pages of a paper spread on the counter. The cloying warmth from the stove made her want the clean air outside. Her face was hot. She pushed the plate away.

You ate nothing.

Can't.

Her sister looked at her hard and saw. She picked up the plate.

Go pray, then.

The cool air of the street was better. There was no sign of the earlier commotion. The food was curdling in her belly as she carried the empty buckets back up the main street. Her nausea tinged everything, even the thought of her love, and when she stopped before the church and looked at the icon of Christ crucified naked on the cross and bleeding from the chest and hands and feet she had to look away and did not go in, and instead hurried on past the houses that became fewer and the dogs barking at her from the gateways. She was climbing the forest path again, fast, breathing hard. She was glad she was alone.

She froze. The crows scattered, patterning the sky between the branches with their confusion. The first shots were cracking dry sticks snapping in a small room, then many gunshots ran together. Then the shots were individual events again. The guns became tired of firing. A final report echoed across the hills.

She breathed through her open mouth, looking at the tops of the trees. The crows soon began to settle in the branches again.

She hurried on, upwards. At the place where the mushrooms grew she put the buckets down and leaned against a tree and emptied her stomach.

When she reached the house the door was open but she did not see her mother. She set the buckets down and went inside. The woman was lying on the bed under blankets. Her eyes were squeezed closed as though light would kill her.

Mama, did you hear? Did you hear it in the woods?

It's biting me, said the mother. Give me the tea.

A pot on the side of the stove contained an infusion of herbs. She poured it into a cup and brought it to the woman's lips. She drank, then sank back down in the bed.

She sat with the silent still woman for a long time in the darkened room. Soon, she thought, I will be completely alone in this place, with the animals. The house had been full of people when she was a girl, the youngest. The world was becoming unrecognizable. She sat for far too long, thinking this kind of thought, about being deserted by those she loved. The fire in the stove had gone out and she considered lighting it, or sweeping the floor. There were things to do and it was daylight.

Her mother stirred, opened her eyes, turned her head to her daughter. It could not be so bad now, if she had opened her eyes.

Mama. Tomorrow he will come to speak to you. In the morning.

The woman was still, watching her. Perhaps she no longer cared about such things.

My poor child, said the mother. You don't have to. There are ways to stop it.

This she did not want to hear. She thought of things to do. It was time to do things, to get out of the dark room smelling of sickness.

Tomorrow he will come to speak to you, she said. She stood up and went outside.

He is coming, she thought, waking in the night to the dogs scratching the door, whining. But it was too soon for him to show. Moonlight through the window and pale objects. She looked at her mother sleeping, rose, pulled her long coat around her and unlatched the door. The dogs slipped out ahead of her, claws clattering on the wooden porch. She felt the cold air.

She stepped outside and saw and it froze her. The dogs too held back, silent. The man was naked beneath the milky moon in the courtyard. He was trembling. She had never seen a man so naked, not even Jesus on the cross. The bones spoke through his starved flesh. He looked at her, shivering, his armbones hanging so his hands shielded his crotch, then looked away. The dirt of the earth streaked his body and the black blood mixed with it from the wound on his shoulder.

When she could recognize what she saw she unfroze and walked towards the man and took her coat and placed it around his shivering shoulders. The dogs followed her at a small distance, tails tucked between their legs. She guided him away from the house, across the yard towards the byre. She took him slowly. She unlatched the wooden slat and opened the byre door. The cow stirred in the hay. The dogs held back.

Lie down here where it is soft, she said.

He folded his knees and with her help lay upon a pile of hay. He put his head down upon the hay.

She recrossed the yard. In the room, her mother slept. She took the matches and lamp and a blanket and went again to the byre. She lit the lamp. The cow was standing now, watching her with big long-lashed patient eyes.

She removed the cloth covering the bucket and dipped the wooden bowl into the milk. She carried the milk while the lamp trembled the shadow of the cow and the woman on the walls of the byre and then kneeled in the hay and cupped her hand behind the man's head to raise it and offered him the shallow bowl. His head was young and ancient and his eyes which had been closing now opened a little, heavy, and he sipped the milk. He drew a breath and then his lips took the milk again, drinking it down to the end of the bowl, thirstily. He let his head down upon the hay again, his eyes closing. He breathed twice sharply as though trying to yawn. Then he sighed, deeply, and the borrowed breath passed from his tortured flesh.

She looked at him, the empty bowl in her hand, feeling the relief. She pulled the blanket over the man's face.

Under the watchful eyes of the cow she covered the milk. She extinguished the lamp and latched the byre. She crossed the yard. The dogs slipped silently into the house and she closed the door. She lay down in her bed to wait.

He was coming up the track. Taking far too long. She was standing in the sunlight while her mother lay in the house, unable to rise. Some things went too fast, other times they went too slow. She watched him walking.

When he came she would tell him about the life that had ended and say nothing about the life beginning. He would know nothing about that. It concerned her alone.

She had seen a man who had risen from the dirt his killers had piled upon his body, and she had given him milk to drink, and he had lain down before her and died. There was nothing else to know.

She lost sight of him in the trees. In several minutes he would reach the clearing, his legs tired from the ascent. His white legs with the red marks from the fleas from the dirty barracks, which she had pitied him for. And she would tell him.

He would say, Is this a dream you had? And she would say, No, this is not a dream. This is the man you did not kill properly, or even bury properly, and she would lead him to the byre and pull back the blanket and show his unbelieving eyes the body of the dead Jew.

Tombstone Blues

But to avoid being heedless, it is good to consider the words of the Apostle, 'I die daily.' For if we too live as though dying daily, we shall not sin. And the meaning of that saying is, that as we rise each day we should think that we should not abide till evening: and again, when about to lie down to sleep we should think that we should not rise up. For our life is naturally uncertain, and Providence allots it to us daily . . . But thus ordering our daily life, we shall neither fall into sin, nor have a lust for anything, nor cherish wrath against any, nor shall we heap up treasure on earth. But, as though under the daily expectation of death, we shall be without wealth, and shall forgive all things of all men, nor shall we retain at all the desire for women or any other foul pleasure.

Saint Antony, as recorded by Saint
Athanasius in the *Life of Saint Antony*

I

I got out at Zafarana, late afternoon. The bus pulled away and I stood at the side of the road in the settling dust, alone. Everybody else was going down the coast. I was going inland, down a small road that ran between two barren rocky plateaus, hazy in the distance. I was going inland, but not today.

Across the baked gravel waste the words *Sahara Inn* shimmered across the gable of a building behind a petrol station. I started walking.

No sign of life from the scatter of one-storey breezeblock hovels. There would be barefoot children and chickens pecking the dirt and a problem with refuse disposal. I could not see it from where I stood, but it was surely there, if you went a little closer. Even the Red Sea glinting behind the town was not enough to make it pretty. The desert came right to the coast and the desert was not pretty either. It was just gravel.

The ground floor of the Sahara Inn was a restaurant. The only one in town. It looked like a factory canteen and was doing no business. I approached a food counter and asked about a room and was directed to a corridor leading from a rear corner of the restaurant. A man was working over a ledger there, in a windowless office. We exchanged our bits of English and Arabic. When I told him I was a pilgrim, he pulled up his sleeve, revealing the Coptic cross tattooed on the inside of his left wrist.

The room was on the upper floor. The handle came off in my hand when I closed the door. I fitted it back in place and put my bag down. The sheets had probably been washed, or the last few visitors had been fairly clean. Dead wires hung from the back of a huge old television. The bathroom waste-paper basket contained half a sandwich. The toilet clanked and rumbled when you tugged the chain, and eventually flushed. The most interesting thing was the dusting of fine sand beside every window and door. It was unstoppable. It seeped like gas through the tiniest of cracks.

I showered. The dust became mud and was washed to the Red Sea. Then I sat on the bed and opened the notebook and began to write.

Cairo, a.m. Fought through city to station. Early. Bus smoke, noise. Sat on a wooden bench, read Bible. Eccl. Boy walks up. Plastic flip-flops. Unhealthy patches of dry skin on the face. Welcome, where from?

Tea, coffee? Pepsi Fanta Sprite? Shake my head. Welcomes me again, then stands over my shoulder while I try to read. Keeps returning to repeat offer, welcoming me, while best book of the Good One says it's all worthless, winds blow north, winds blow south etc., and the buses are arriving and leaving, people on and off, same scene over and over. Ha. Bus came. Porter loads my bag says because I'm foreign, one pound. Give seventy-five ersh. Received shit-eating grin. Board bus and wait. Long time.

Bus jerks through traffic. Millions of bodies pressed together and struggling through noise and smoke, labouring at the wheel. Rowers of slave boats, pulling to the rhythm, the machines driving us. Insane. Barefoot man in workshop, oil everywhere, working a giant tyre with a crowbar, getting the rubber from the rim.

Driver puts a film on. Screen at the front of the bus, me halfway down the bus. Characters charging into funny situations, waving their arms, shouting a lot – and a fat woman in a blonde wig. Wanted to plug my ears. Someone at the back goes up to driver, complains he can't hear. They turn it up.

The actors scream, the city goes on.

City of 20 (?) m. Then desert. No transition.

Expected beauty. Not there. Construction site. Of course – they've made a road. Desert is a skin that does not heal. No rainfall, vegetation, to correct human interference. Everybody had curtains pulled, except me. The film.

Ain Sukhna, Gulf of Suez, calm waters, smaller road curving down the coast, but driver maintains speed – sea and the hills close on either side, scenery rushing by in fast-forward. Now a film about a Roman gladiator. Big dazzling thing, battle going on, slashing and hacking, horses tumbling to the ground. Sounds of slaughter blended with epic music. Signified tragedy and pain of war, nobility of the warrior. Sthing like that.

You live in junk, consume junk, and to keep yr nose above it yr

thoughts are reaction to junk, defence against junk – man walking
around, fingers in ears, humming a tune, trying to keep it out. Swearing
at the world, shut the fuck up, can't hear myself THINK!

Where's yr sense of humour, they'll say –

Excellent question. Let me turn the volume down, I'll try answering
that –

Antony was already an old man when he came here. Spent his entire
life along the Nile valley. A voice told him: ' . . . If you really wish to
be in quiet, depart now into the inner desert.'

I tried reading the Bible, but my eyes were hot and tired from
the hours of bus-window desert glare, and the writing. It had
got dark while I wrote. I went downstairs for food. I was not
hungry. It was something to do.

I chose a table in the empty room and ordered and was served
a cheese sandwich. I was the only guest in the Sahara Inn. Under
fluorescent light the restaurant looked even more like a factory
canteen, the workers now dreaming in their beds. The waiter
stood at the open door, arms crossed over his chest, gazing out
towards the coast road at the lights of a passing truck, going
north to Suez. I ate my cheese sandwich. It was not much good.
Just dry bread and slices of cheese.

I bought six litres of water and went to my room. I packed
the water, ready for morning. It was fifty kilometres to the
monastery and I had to be prepared to walk much of it. I set
the alarm for an early start.

Getting permission to stay at the monastery had required
persistence.

On two consecutive days I went to the address in Cairo and
stood in an empty waiting room while a caretaker with a bad
limp went away to find someone who could understand me,

and both times he returned, dragging his leg, alone. We were unable to communicate.

On the third visit, after again walking the hot noisy streets, there were two Coptic priests in the waiting room. One was ancient and leaning very low over a bowl of beans set on a stool before him, eating. I shook hands with the younger priest. The geriatric was down in his bowl of beans, did not know what was happening, except beans. I explained that I wanted a week in the monastery, if possible, to study in the library. I was a student, I said, of the ascetic life. The priest pulled his beard. Was I attached to a university? I was not. Had I written books? No, I admitted, I was still taking notes. He did not think a week was possible, but perhaps a night could be managed. He instructed me to return the following afternoon. The old priest slowly wiped the bottom of the plate with bread.

On the fourth visit I was conducted down hallways, up stairways, to an old priest in an office. Icons on the wall, and two framed black and white photographs: Pope Shenouda III of Alexandria and Bishop Yostos of Saint Antony's. The pendulum of an ancient wall clock ticked heavily, turning individual seconds into big clunky objects, like bricks. The conversation of the previous day was repeated. Why, exactly, did I want a week in the Monastery of Saint Antony?

Because it was the world's oldest Christian monastery. Because I wanted to see where it had begun and to have time to study. I was taking notes, I told the priest, for a work that would make the teachings of Antony, and the philosophy of asceticism generally, intelligible to the modern world.

The priest caressed his whiskers. I felt I was doing well and dropped the first letters in the ascetic alphabet – *anachoresis, apatheia, apostasis*. And then, I added, there was Athanasius's *Life of Antony*, the prototypical hagiography.

He nodded gently and reached for a sheet of paper. I stopped speaking. He uncapped an ink pen and began to write. I listened to the clock dividing out huge resonant seconds and watched the words take shape. Writing in Arabic is more like drawing, especially if you are right-handed and using ink; writing from right to left requires that you hold the pen further from the nib to avoid smudging. Finally, it was stamped. The priest blew on the ink and then folded the page and put it in an envelope and handed it to me. I shook his hand and left.

I walked through the bright hectic streets. I walked through them holding this envelope, hardly seeing the world around me.

The sun was hot at seven a.m. A minibus waited at the junction to the road inland, towards the monastery. The road was an old caravan route that crossed the desert to Beni Suef, on the Nile. I sat on the kerb and read the Bible. We waited two hours, maybe more, and no more passengers came. We set off, me in the front with the driver. He put on a tape. It was what I call *habibi* music. Every song contains the word *habibi*, repeated many times. *Habibi* means 'my friend' or 'my lover', depending on the context. *Habibi* music is usually bad and usually loud and in minibuses full of men it is usually played on a very old cassette recorder while driving fast. I told myself it would be quiet soon enough and watched the land. The road disappeared into the haze between the plateaus that rose steeply to the south and north. The wind was whipping up dust.

I got out at the turn. I shook the driver's hand and we *salaam*ed.

And then I was walking down a very straight road south, into the sun. It was fifteen kilometres to the monastery.

The desert was even less pretty up close. It was a bad place for a human being to be. The sun was hot and blinding. Gusts whipped the land, lifting dust, and you knew that it could get much worse. I swatted away the flies that landed on my face – on my nose, lips, ears and the corners of my eyes – but they soon came back. I took a cotton shirt from my rucksack and tied it around my head, leaving it open at the eyes only.

Distance was hard to discern on that flat straight road. The featurelessness of the landscape made the walking tiring and dispiriting. A gradient would have made it easier. You would have seen what there was to fight against and you could have taken it on.

After I felt I had walked several kilometres I looked back and I had come no distance at all. The long straight road still stretched ahead, endlessly. I lost track of time. I had a small clock in my pocket which I consulted to reassure myself something was happening, so it is untrue that I lost track of time. I lost track of space. I lost track of the events by which time is measured. Funny expression, to lose track of time. To lose track of your track. Because that is how we measure our progress on this earth. Enough landmarks at the right speed to feel we are getting somewhere and all is well. A road that gives an appreciable sense of events, and therefore of ourselves. My feet moved but I felt I was walking through glue. The escarpment ahead was as far away and hazy as ever. All I knew was I was on the road, the endless road, and my motion forward contained the grain of a panic to get somewhere. Know what Jack Kerouac said about the endless road, having been down it? 'I see myself as just doomed, pitiful – the awful realization that I have been fooling myself all my life thinking there was a next thing to do.' That's what he said. But what about kicks, Jack, and all that jazz? No vehicles moved down my desert road and I kept looking at the clock to reassure myself that I was moving. I was in a daze of walking, abstracted even from my reason for walking, when I perceived a swerve in the road ahead. This helped me to return to myself and I walked faster and more purposefully. It was true; space was happening again, and with it time. The road was rising a little too. And then I could see it ahead, clinging to the base of the escarpment, the walls of the monastery, like a painting of the legendary castle on a hill in a book of stories they read to children.

II

And when Antony said, 'Who will show me the way for I know it not?' immediately the voice pointed out to him Saracens about to go that way . . . And having journeyed with them for three days and three nights, he came to a very lofty mountain, and at the foot of the mountain ran a clear spring, whose waters were sweet and very cold; outside was a plain and a few uncared for palm trees.

That's what it says in Athanasius's *Life of Antony*. And the spring has not failed since. It is a very reliable spring. It is a strange and joyful thing to see trees in the desert, and vegetables growing, and the holy colour green.

I presented my letter of introduction and was shown my lodgings by a young monk called Father Shishoy. It was a simple room with whitewashed walls. There was a bathroom in the hallway. Then old Father Rewis showed me around the monastery. The wind swallowed his words and lashed sand at our faces. He took me to the library and introduced me to Father Isaac. Isaac was a little younger than Rewis, but it was going to be hard to tell the monks apart. They were all bearded and dressed identically and wore black cowls that covered their ears. Rewis left and Isaac, speaking halting English, showed me where I would spend the next week writing and reading. There were ancient illuminated manuscripts wild with decoration and geometric patterns, written in Coptic. There were later psalters written in Arabic. The room smelled of leather and musty parchment. And there were modern books, including some in English, referring primarily to Saint Antony and to the monastery. I would be free to examine any book, except that I was to ask for his help with the older ones, some of which were fragile.

Then I was left alone, and I had enough daylight for the final part of the journey.

Antony was followed by those who wished to learn from him, and a community grew up around the spring. So he removed himself to a cave in the mountainside, where he lived for the final decades of his life.

It was a steep rocky walk up the slopes of Mount Colzim to Antony's cave. I could see the monastery below when I paused for breath and looked back, and the hazy desert beneath me, still disturbed by the wind, in the dimming evening light. Forty-five minutes of zigzagging track terminated at a ledge on the mountainside. Coming over the lip, I discovered that I was not alone at this shrine of isolation. A teenage boy, dressed in a poor *jalabaya*, was sitting on a rock. We exchanged greetings, then I entered the cave, having to crouch to do so. It was a very narrow crevice, and very straight, like those ancient passage tombs penetrated by the sun only at a certain moment of a certain day. I took tiny steps in deep darkness. A dank smell. I took my claustrophobia as deep as it wanted to go and crouched down. I would spend a few minutes there in silence and that would be it. The boy was outside, sitting at the entrance. I saw him rise and enter the cave. He squeezed past me, then beckoned me deeper in. No thank you, I said. Then I perceived that the cave opened up a little further on. I felt my way along steps that corkscrewed down. There was some kind of mat on the ground, and that was the origin of the stale odour. I knelt beside the boy and he prayed. My eyes adjusted a little and I could perceive a carving of the face of Saint Antony in the rock. It was enough. I rose and the boy said something like, Leaving so soon?

It was very hard to be alone in that country.

I woke on the first morning in my room, within the inner walls, well rested. Whatever the good Father in Cairo had written, it had served to get me preferential treatment relative to the other pilgrims, who were housed in more elaborate apartments between the inner and outer walls. I had a small stove and vegetables and dried food to do my own cooking. My balcony overlooked the courtyard and the lower garden, where date palms grew. Rows of vegetables grew between the palms. To my right was a cluster of monks' cells, with their domed roofs. Past a row of buildings was another palm grove.

The life of the monastery began with the ringing of the bells at five a.m. The monks would rise and by six a.m. were attending service in the chapel. I would wake at around seven, and by around nine I would be in the library, where I would spend several hours. Mostly you would not see the monks. Each had his particular duties – the librarian, the pharmacist, the gardeners and so on. There would be a service at noon, after which the monks would break their fast. The final service was at six. I was allowed to attend this service. The small chapel contained no seating, which is the Orthodox tradition. You removed your shoes at the entrance and the floor was carpeted. I would sit at the back, reading the Bible, breaking off at times to listen to the monks singing. I began to feel as though I, like the other men in that room, had had a life once, somewhere else, and that it had been left behind.

On the second day, I was sitting out in the courtyard, by the date palms, with Father Shishoy, and I asked him where he was from. He had just guided a small group of tourists around the keep, the chapel, the mill, the spring, the refectory and so on – and I had gone along. The wind of the previous day had stilled and the air was clear, and I had been able to hear much that had been lost the previous day in grit-laden gusts and Father Rewis's beard. I had made us some tea and we were drinking it in the courtyard below my balcony.

– I am from here, said Shishoy.

With a little encouragement he told me he was from Alexandria. I asked him how he had chosen the monastery.

– It is like when you want to marry. Maybe you like a girl, she is more polite than the others, or has something special for you. For each person it is different. When you think about the life of a monk, you spend time at more monasteries, then you choose the one that is for you.

– And are you happy here?

– Yes, I am happy.

This was not a question I would have expected to ask. I had thought of a monastery as a place of silence, exile, self-punishment, denial. But Shishoy's simplicity and frankness, his smile, were not from suffering.

– Are you happy all the time?

– Yes. Well. This life is not perfect. Only heaven is perfect. There is no life without problems. Even here, in this place, problems. But as in a family.

We finished our tea. At the sound of an engine outside the gate, Shishoy went out to see who had arrived. I took the glasses back to my room, then returned to the library. Father Isaac was there. He was not reading. He rarely did, apart from correspondence necessary for his duties. He was sitting absolutely still.

Apatheia is the alpha of the ascetic life. It is a word that in the context of the Christian monastic tradition implies stillness. A holy stillness. An emptying of the mind of all perturbation, the achievement of serenity.

Isaac did not speak unless spoken to, and did not move without cause. I tried several times to speak with him about books, and he was helpful and sometimes he showed interest in the problem at hand. He did not read, as I did, out of hunger.

One day I asked him, 'Father Isaac, do you not like to read?'

He looked around at the books. I had become used to long pauses, in my conversations with Shishoy and Rewis. A conversation might appear to be over and then restart, and there would be no hurry to answer a question. This had made me uncomfortable at first, and I had compensated by becoming talkative. Then I learned to hear the nervous sound of such speech and began to slow down and let things move naturally.

'I used to,' he replied. 'It's been a long time.'

There is a passage in the *Life of Saint Antony*:

And again others such as these met him in the outer mountain and thought to mock him because he had not learned letters. And Antony said to them, 'What say ye? Which is first, mind or letters? And which is the cause of which – mind of letters or letters of mind?' And when they answered mind is first and the inventor of letters, Antony said, 'Whoever, therefore, hath a sound mind hath not need of letters.'

Father Shishoy taught me how to deal with flies. They came into my room and buzzed around and settled on my face and I would swish them away. Two seconds later they would be back. It was a gusty day and Shishoy had joined me for tea in my room and was asking about what was happening in the world. He wanted my explanation for some things that had occurred. I told him about the War on Terror.

– That is what they call it?

I nodded. He thought for a moment, then said:

– Terror is in the mind.

A fly landed on his hand. He looked at it. Then he rose slowly and escorted the fly out the door and shook it loose.

– The ones who are most strong in the world, they are the most afraid.

I asked him how he did the trick with the fly and he explained that they only responded to rapid movements.

After he left I waited for the flies to settle on me and I conducted them one by one out of my room.

I learned also that something similar works with mosquitoes. Time is of another order for these creatures. We swipe as fast as we can and they watch it coming for hours and leave at the final moment. But if one is settled on a wall you can move the flat of your palm against it very slowly. To them it is a glacier. They don't see it getting closer because they don't remember it being further away.

On my last full day in the monastery, two unexpected things happened. The first was that I found a bottle of Irish whiskey in my room. Bushmills, two thirds full. There was a cabinet below the sink and I was looking for things to use to clean the room before I left, and I found it there. I had not touched alcohol in nearly a week, and that I and that bottle should meet in such circumstances seemed a big gesture on the part of Providence and I just sat on the floor with the bottle for several minutes, holding it in my hands and admiring it. Admiring the strangeness of the event. I unscrewed the cap and sniffed, and took a little swig. The bottle made a little musical gurgle when I tipped it.

I left the library early that afternoon, put a bottle of water in my bag and climbed the trail past Antony's cave to Mount Colzim.

The last section was a steep ascent, and my feet dislodged rocks that trickled down the slope, and some I would hear falling against other rocks very far below. When I crested the jagged ridge, the plateau spread out before me, a truly desolate world extending far into the distance. Other more distant ridges caught the declining sun, glowing redly. I had entered a world of rock. Below me, the desert stretched out until it became a distant haze on the horizon, a cloud resting on the land, and I guessed this to be the Red Sea, some thirty kilometres east. On this mountain Antony had lived for the last fifty years of his life. This was the same land he had looked upon nearly one thousand and seven hundred years before.

It was nearly dark when the second strange thing happened. I heard voices and looked over my balcony. Rewis was speaking to Shishoy and a tall foreign woman was with them. Sometimes women came as part of Coptic Church groups. But this long-limbed blonde woman was not part of a church group. Rewis walked away. Shishoy gestured for her to follow him. I slipped downstairs and followed them out under the arch of the main gate. She followed Shishoy across the yard to the guest lodges. The evening star shone bright and clear. They reached a door. I withdrew.

I sat in my room and worked on some notes for an hour or so until I lost interest. I tried to read the Bible but was distracted by other thoughts. I poured a glass of the miraculous whiskey. I turned out the light and sat at the open window, drinking slowly. The stars had all come out and the monks in their cells were saying their prayers and bedding down. I went quietly downstairs, the half-bottle of whiskey under my coat, and crossed the wide dark yard to the guest accommodation. The light was on.

It was different from my room. Like a living room in a city. But lots of icons and holy statues. And a clock that said ten thirty, which meant the electricity would soon be off. We sat in armchairs with the whiskey open on the coffee table. I had explained about the miracle of the whiskey, and she seemed glad of the company. There was no television and the silence was a little too thick. She was American, she was educated, she had money, she had lived thirty-six years. Her name was Nadine. She had thought there was a hotel, or something, and only realized where she had ended up when her driver had been paid and had driven off and a rather ruffled Father Rewis was standing before her. She did not think the monks very friendly. I pointed out that they had not made her sleep in the desert.

– They hardly could, could they now? That funny little monk hardly said a word, the one who brought me here.

– Shishoy.

– What?

– That's his name. Shishoy.

– He looked at the ground the whole time.

– Well, monastery. The idea being.

That long body was well cared for, but close-up she was not as attractive as I had first imagined. Sometimes you saw the younger woman, sometimes the woman she would become, and it was a little unsettling, the flickering between the two. We smoked her cigarettes and drank the whiskey. The talk was scatty and zigzag. I had begun to forget how it was to talk to people who always had to be explaining themselves, putting themselves across. People met and wound each other up like springs, created a tension that was released mechanically. I was there for novelty and we would wind each other up. I would do this even though I had no real interest in her, whoever she was, and even though you should stay away from those who you do not care about.

Her personality was a bubble she lived inside and brought on tour. She wanted to experience Egypt, she said, but I could not imagine it happening.

She wondered why I had come to such a dead place deliberately. I told her about my note-taking.

– A writer?

– I can't type, even. I do that thing with the two fingers.

– Published?

I shook my head, but she did not seem disappointed by my lack of success. Everybody has to be something. So I was a writer. She could engage with that more happily than if I had said I was a welder. She told me I should go to some oasis in Sinai where she thought I would have more inspiration. Inspiration being associated with the picturesque. Imagine telling a welder that he should visit the Grand Canyon, because it would improve his productivity and accuracy. I slurped some whiskey.

– You should write something to make people happy, free them from suffering. Make them love each other.

– Dostoievsky did that. A very long book, full of Russian names. It's very good. But people are busy. Nobody reads it.

– What's your favourite book?

– Ecclesiastes.

– You think you're funny. I've read the Bible too, you know.

She talked about herself. Her two ex-husbands. Her boozy

parents who lived in Mexico. Her beautiful father and his lovers. Her mother, getting liposuction, breast implants, who'd asked her over a joint, Nadine, how many of your father's affairs have you known about? Oh, Mother, she said, your relationship is none of my business. She showed me pictures of the two children. From her first husband.

She smoked as she talked. She wasn't boring. We got to talking about the monks. She was very interested in spirituality, she said, but hiding out in the desert was a con.

There followed a classic polemic, over cigarettes and whiskey, between a man and a woman, alone with each other. A hundred thousand such discussions were occurring all over the planet. None would ever be resolved definitively, but in the meantime many of the participants would go to bed with each other. Because that activity, at least, involves a conclusion.

Nadine's argument was that life was for living. Every moment of it. Not for running away from.

Of course, I said. If you are alive, you are living your life.

She clarified that she meant it should be lived *to the full*.

I asked her if by this she meant that it should be exploited with maximum efficiency, like a limited resource, in order to extract the full range of sensations.

She said she did not like my choice of words and did not exclude knowledge of suffering from the life experience. She told me I was cynical and solitary because I had no children. She mentioned her own children. She said the monks had turned their backs on experience out of fear of life.

I asked her to consider that there was room on the planet for those of God's creatures who wished to turn down the volume. That, while the mind hungers for experience, one that functions correctly is busy limiting incoming stimuli. The human mind could only take so much, and it was noisy out there. If you registered everything it would overwhelm you. So you filter out what is irrelevant, take what you need, and you decide that this is the world. People who can't do this are called autistic. They end up memorizing phone books in an effort to relax, that kind of thing. Little strategies for imposing order. Some people's sense of the futility of activity is so acute that they look at the world and see people performing the socially well-adapted equivalent of memorizing phone books. At which point it is a good thing to tiptoe away to somewhere very quiet.

– It's not very brave, she said, to lock yourself up in your own head. Of course life is difficult, sometimes. But it's a big lie to say that when it's all over we're all going up to heaven, to get our reward then. This life is enough. Here and now. Anybody who runs away from it is a coward.

I was quiet for a bit. She had got unusually agitated. Maybe it was the drink.

– But that is the idea, I said, feeling for the idea as I went. I knew it was there.

– What's the idea?

– The monks. The idea is now. Not heaven later. But about every single moment being exactly the same. That the difference between them is an illusion.

– So?

The lights went out. It was eleven. I was ready with the matches. I lit the candles.

– So, what you were saying is true. There's a passage in Athanasius's *Life of Antony*. He says that we must die daily. What he means is that there is only one moment that matters, and the attitude of the soul in that moment. The plans of our lives are lies and we should not expect to live until the end of the day, or even care that it is so. *For our life is naturally uncertain, and Providence allots it to us daily . . . But thus ordering our daily life, we shall neither fall into sin, nor have a lust for anything, nor cherish wrath against any, nor shall we heap up treasure on earth. But, as though under the daily expectation of death, we shall be without wealth, and shall forgive all things of all men . . .*

I thought it was quite a good speech. I never could have managed it under a hundred-watt bulb. She looked at me for a moment and exhaled some smoke. I continued:

– The monks are artists of a fundamental kind, cutting all that is superfluous from their lives, the noise and clutter and distraction we use to deceive ourselves, in order to see what is left.

– And what is left?

– Of the personality, nothing.

– And so.

– And so, all impediments removed, the soul is again as simple as God made it, and beholds Creation.

She stubbed out her cigarette.

– You've got it all figured out.

She said it to sound exactly like, You don't know shit.

– It sounds a lot to me like suicide, she continued. Which is an option I sometimes consider.

She was going to tell me something that I really did not want to hear and I grabbed her chin and kissed her lips and tasted her mouth, her cigarettes and warm alcohol.

I do not want to go into unnecessary detail about what went on next, except to state that I licked her and sucked her and fucked her among the icons and statuettes and crucifixes and saints, I slammed her beneath the Blessed Virgin and baby Jesus, and gave it to her backways and frontways and sideways and other ways beneath Christ on the cross. I banged her till the bells rang and the birds sang. She kept coming, and I kept going.

Because she offered so many possibilities to my rising greed and it seemed wrong that it should all end in a sort of sneeze. I was lying on my back, taking a break, when I said to her:

– Nadine, I don't know what way to finish up. There are so many options, but I have to choose, and no single choice in itself can do justice to the evening. In your pussy or in your mouth, or over your face, or up your ass, or between your . . .

– Ooh, yes! Up my ass!

I wasn't so sure I really wanted to do that.

– Yes! Up my ass!

She turned over and stuck it in the air.

I had always believed that women behaved this way only in a certain style of film. Just as I thought I had it all figured out. So many men in the suburbs begging their fat wives and girl-friends vainly over years for a bit of bunghole, whacking off in front of screens. I would do it for them. So much cunt-juice having sloshed about the vicinity, it slid straight in and I got a rhythm going and she tickled her clit and chewed the pillow and made gurgling noises and I rammed it in and as sea levels rose and the world's atmosphere heated and global oil production peaked the Virgin smiled beatifically and Christ, as his body was pulled downward to the earth, raised his eyes past his thorny crown and strained to the sky to be taken home again and she came and I came beneath a full moon in the desert night where the monks in their cells dreamed of the paradise that is ours when we depart this corruptible suffering life.

I flushed the condom and went back. She stretched her long limbs and yawned and told me it was a matter of relaxing a single muscle, her yoga instructor had initiated her, and that the orgasm was much more intense.

The fruit of the meeting of the civilizations of East and West.

Maybe, I thought, as I put on my foolish garments, a woman should have seven fuckable orifices, and a man seven organs of penetration, which would mean forty-nine possible modes of intercourse, involving graded levels of taboo, disgust and physical ecstasy, and humans could devote their entire lives to ascending the ladder, pushing the boundaries. There would be no end to the doing of it, the talking about it, the philosophizing of it. The porn industry would propel the global economy into the upper stratosphere of productive excess. Everything had to be attempted, because life was for living. To the full. We were the race that had felt obliged to go up and give the moon a feel. Though now even that seemed old-fashioned, somehow.

– Well, I'd better go now. Thanks for the perverted sex.

– Don't get struck by a bolt of lightning on your way home. She lit a cigarette. I sat on the bed and put on a boot.

– Nothing in the Good Book proscribing what we just did, I said.

– Go read about Sodom and Gomorrah.

– That was because men were fucking each other. The men of Sodom surrounded Lot's house. They demanded that Lot hand over his guests, who were in fact visiting angels sent by the Lord to see if there were any decent people left in town. Lot even offered the mob his virgin daughters instead, but they weren't interested, pussy wasn't good enough for them. It's in Genesis.

– I'm sure there's *something* in the Bible . . .

I completed the lacing of the second boot and sat up.

– Go read it, then. Read Leviticus. No animals, relatives, men on men and so on. The list is very explicit. No mention anywhere of alternative female orifices.

– You certainly know your scripture.

I took her cigarette, got a good drag, handed it back.

– Sad how many young people these days don't.

I slipped out the door and she closed it behind me. I stood foolish and guilty under the silent starry sky, the courtyard stretching dark and empty to the inner walls of the monastery. I went as quietly as I could across the courtyard, under the arch, and up the stone stairs to my doorway. I let myself in and lit a candle. I lay down to sleep and got buzzed by mosquitoes. I slapped my ear. They got a few bites in and buzzed me some more and I sat up angrily and lit the candle again. I killed them one by one. I lay there for a long time but sleep did not come. And then the bells rang out across the night. It was five a.m. and the monks were rising.

The light gradually returned and filled my room again with recognizable objects. It was the day I was to leave the monastery. There was a morning to be faced and I did not feel good about the night before. It had wrecked something. My concentration, but not only. It was not the sex I regretted. It was the talking. All the clever things I had said when I should have kept my mouth shut.

Shishoy had got me a lift to Zafarana with a middle-aged German couple who were sightseeing. The Germans walked like puppets on strings. They smiled at the holiness all around them without opening their mouths.

We went out to their pick-up truck, where their driver was waiting. Shishoy smiled and said to me, I hope I will see you again. I did not know how to respond. I looked at the ground and said something awkward about life being long, who knows.

I should have said simply, And I hope I see you too, Father Shishoy. There is too much guile in the machinery of the world, and we are so used to defending ourselves at every moment that speaking from the heart, simply, is too hard. Shishoy reached

into his pocket and drew out a small cross of braided black
leather and before I could stop him he was giving it to me and
I could see he was happy to be giving it to me and now I was
deeply embarrassed. I was not a good Christian. Probably not
a Christian at all. Some kind of dabbler. A jotter of notes. A
skull full of junk.

    – Father Shishoy, I can't.

    – You have to take a present. I made it for you. I made it
well.

    – Yes. You made it well. Thank you, Father Shishoy. I'll keep
it. I'll think of you.

The freaky wooden Germans got into the cab. The driver
gave me a piece of cardboard to sit on and I settled on the bed
of the truck, facing backwards, and he started up the engine.
We pulled away across the courtyard in the bright sunshine and
I enjoyed the wind and the bright light and the walls of the
monastery, and Shishoy and I waved at each other and I felt like
a child, going away from the house of relatives who live far
away, when you are very young and one summer to another is
a long and mysterious time and you feel your world undone by
such farewells. Shishoy became a very small figure and I waved
a last time and he waved back, and I was still smiling and I was
very sad to think I might never see him again.

And then we were moving through the desert fast, it was
running away from me as I faced backwards in the truck. My
journey was in its second part now, that of return to the city,
when the things I had noted would move into the distance and
attain perspective. I felt the wind and I could see my legs out-
stretched and crossed at the ankle, my old battered boots, and
I thought, this is the way to see the country, and I felt like I was
making a film, the land unscrolling behind me, my boots central
in the frame. I imagined being shown this shot of me riding

through a strange landscape, at some earlier stage of my life, and I wondered what I would have made of it.

III

She could not have been glad to see me either, in the daylight, at the Sahara Inn.

I was having a good dead hour staring dazed to the Red Sea and to the hazy heights of Sinai beyond, when a car pulled up and she got out. The driver, an old Bedouin in a *jalabaya*, unloaded her bags from the boot. Then he took the final case from the back seat of the car. The baggage made a small mountain. She paid the man and he drove away.

I walked out into the sunlight to help her bring her bags inside. She looked up at me. Her eyes were extremely blue in the daylight. Mine were too, I suppose.

– Hey, said she.

– Hey, said I. You're following me around.

Her bags were a set, all different shapes and sizes but each piece covered in the same stylish patterned material, with little golden clasps and locks. We carried them inside in two relays each, me with the heavier ones. We sat down at my table in the corner, with the view. We ordered tea, food. It was no fun. I was tired, but for her it was more than that. Her burden was evident in her every movement, and I knew even before we began to talk that her talk would be of troubles, and complaints against the country. The time until my bus would come now stretched far ahead of me. There were only two directions, south to Hurghada or north for Suez or Cairo, and it might be the same bus. I was going to Cairo. I asked which way was hers.

She looked miserably across the gravel and the water.

– It makes no difference which way I go.

I heard about her string of bad luck. A job in Sharm al-Sheikh as a restaurant manager had not worked out. The boss had expected to sleep with her. Perhaps she should go home, she thought. Or should stay, give it another chance. There was another job possibility in Hurghada. But she did not trust Egyptian men.

I felt sorry for her, not knowing where she was going. I suggested she come to Cairo. She could study or work there for a while before heading home. It was a real place, not a resort like Hurghada. She shrugged.

More about jobs, lies, men, and about being sick but not feeling sick. The first time she mentioned being sick I reckoned it was her business to tell me if she wished. At the second reference to being sick I understood that I was supposed to ask. This made me not want to. She paused and looked out the window at the desolate coast. It was her chance to just say it, if she really wanted, or to move on if she did not. It was a long pause.

– What's wrong with you?
– What do I have?
– Yes.
– A brain tumour.

The waiter brought the pizzas. They were bad pizzas. Burned cheese and a few other things. They lacked tomato sauce, though we had a couple of plastic sachets of Heinz tomato ketchup on the side, if we wanted. They were not a variety of pizza, they were just bad. The place was bad, selling bad overpriced food to the tourists because it was the only place to stop on the road from the resort town to Cairo, and it made no difference if everybody was ripped off and disappointed with what they had to put into their mouths, because they would not be passing through again. It depended on different individuals making the same mistake, eternally, and getting back in their vehicles and driving away. And the plate had a raised rim, so the pizza sagged in the middle and in addition was difficult to cut.

Some things repeat themselves. At another time I had been in another city on another continent, in winter, in a windowless restaurant in a pedestrian underpass under an intersection, trying to eat a similarly bad pizza. The pizza had not been sliced so I was going at it with the plastic cutlery but it was not working, the knife was bending. I knew I had to eat, but could not understand why it had to be so dispiriting, with bad heavy-metal music over a bad sound system. It made no sense, a room underground, the knife that would not cut, the unforgiving noise, and I was ready for the clock on the wall to melt like a Dalí clock, and a man dressed as a giant rabbit to approach me and announce that we were running out of time. The show was getting faster and louder and if you found it hard to swallow you got convicted of having no sense of humour. I was looking through big plate-glass windows at the people, at the girls, and some of them were sexy but none of them were beautiful. And I was thinking, this is what happens when we do not care. My mouth ground the food and it did not care. This is what happens when the soul goes out of all we do, when life moves too fast and too carelessly, when we are heedless to ourselves, when we speak and give no thought to our words, when there is never silence enough to hear and all we produce is plastic junk, cans, needles, broken glass, smoke, electrical components, phones to carry the chatter and plastic bags to fly in the wind and rip and tatter on the wires.

And in the same way I sat where the Sahara Desert met the Red Sea, and the desert was a waste of gravel and the trucks picked up speed as they accelerated away from the police

233

checkpoint. In an office at the back were two young accountants and the owner, an old man with a moustache who took pills for his health. This business was for the old man's benefit, I supposed, but it did not appear to do him any good. Perhaps there was a boss above him who never appeared, because he was down in Hurghada, busy with his investments. Or perhaps it was the chief of police that had to be paid off. All these checkpoints were to protect business, so the discontented, the passionate, the insane, did not bomb the tourists and all the things that had been constructed so that they could have a nice time in a vile country.

– If it gets bigger there's a chance it can be removed. But I went from doctor to doctor and it was just bad news after bad news and then I didn't want to hear any more.

A bus pulled up in the car park, and then a second bus. You knew they were full of foreigners because they were new buses and did not look as though they might break down.

– The worst is when I look at my children and I know how much I'm going to miss out.

The tourists started getting out of the bus. They were the rich, relatively, coming to be served, but shabby and lumpy in their obscene holiday clothes. In their shorts and t-shirts and casual this-and-that they looked as if they were walking into another person's house in their underwear, without caring. But that was it exactly. They did not care. They were in that place and not another because it was cheap and the sun shone every day and there were famous hills of bricks called the pyramids.

– Everybody gives me advice. They think they know how it feels.

The tourists were surging in, finding tables, the waiters were rushing, pizzas were appearing. The event was foretold. An arrangement between the tour company and the owner of the establishment. Another little trick, another little rip-off, which was all the tourists deserved, which is all those who do not care ever deserve.

They were from the countries situated to the north and west, and their clothes and haircuts and manners and weight problems said they were what was once called the working class. Now they had their social democracy, state pensions, electronic appliances, sick leave, mobile telephony, cars, dentistry and holidays in resorts where they took for granted that they would be served to their satisfaction and that those who served them would smile while they did it. The hard and dangerous work had moved elsewhere in the world, to the plantations in the tropics, to factories in China, to sweatshops in Indonesia, and now each of them had a faith that history really was progress in the right direction, as the prophets of the cold countries had foretold.

– But nobody knows how it feels.

The level of noise was rising around us. We ate our food. I said nothing. I did not want to be another one giving advice, imagining I knew how it felt. The moment demanded a surge of pity, but I did not feel it. I could only think that she was the same as all of us.

It stared her in the face, and still she had three giant bags which she could not carry without assistance, that required men and machines and the handing over of money, so that she could think about what clothes to wear before striding into the morning, and one of the smaller bags contained creams and ointments and had to be kept out of the sun, and all these bags were coordinated, bought in the same shop, and looked good stacked in a pile, different sizes and shapes put together, to say, this is a woman who is organized and knows what she is doing, when she packs and goes out to see the world.

I had no right to say anything to her. I too would have my

moment of horror, the day when all the contradictions came home and settled like crows on a roof. It was getting too noisy in any case to say anything and the whole room was sawing at their bad pizzas. Keep travelling, good people. See all you can, eat all you can, grab all you can. There is still time.

What we need in these hard moments is a little more novelty and sensation, and faith in the ability of the foreign and exotic to entertain.

– I came here to get away from people fussing over me. To get away from a lot of things. Always I've been working, doing things for other people. I wanted to do something for myself. I wanted to climb Mount Sinai. While there's still time.

We did not like what was on our plates, but we ate it. And then I said:

– Let's get out. I have to move.

We paid and the waiter said he would watch the bags.

We walked across the gravel and down to the water, the shore of a wilderness that stretched from the Atlantic to the Red Sea, and it was scattered with junk that had washed up. Plastic bottles mainly. The freighters and oil tankers hung in the distance. Beyond, past the oilfields, the armies of the righteous were on the march, to save it, to keep the earth's black blood pumping.

I picked up a little plastic medicine bottle. Greek script. Some sailor catching the clap in Piraeus, tossing the bottle overboard. We were drowning in junk. Producing junk, eating junk, watching junk, speaking junk. Nothing made by the human hand. Everything getting far away and complicated. We've poisoned the water, said Nadine, and now we have to drink from plastic. I nodded in agreement, but all I wanted in the world was for her to get on the bus to Hurghada. I wanted to get off my bus in Cairo, alone. The hands of taxi drivers would reach out and grab my sleeve and I would shake them off, disappear down a dim street, walking fast. That was the main thing; to move, unhindered. And I saw her pile of luggage and it would be impossible. A big soft stupid bag of blood in a hungry foreign city and every hustler and taxi driver smelling the chance and moving in. And I would be her keeper, and sleep by her side.

The one sure way to keep ahead of it, while your heart still beats. To move. Keep walking, while the heart pumps the blood.

– Let's go down the pier, I said.

It was better down the pier. Wooden planks, some of them rotten. You were away from everything the world had washed up, and then the sea was coloured and beautiful and the sand clean at the bottom, through the water, the way God meant it. Shoals of tiny fish darted about. I felt myself breathing easier.

The Hurghada bus came first. She looked at it in fear as it approached, because she was being cut loose again. And I was scared she would change her mind and want to go with me. But had she decided to go to Cairo, she would have had the same fear when that bus came. The fear of where she was heading, and the opposite way being lost to her. A man got out and she loaded her bags into the luggage compartment. She tipped him. The bus revved and she was going to embrace me and kiss me, and I said, Don't, it's not done here, in public, even were you my wife. So we shook hands. She boarded. The door closed and she took her seat and the bus shuddered and pulled away.

The relief was immense. I waited for a bus to Suez, walking back and forth. It was hard to keep still.

I fell asleep on the bus to Suez and woke as we were drawing in to the bus station, and then had to run, disoriented and nauseous in the diesel smoke, to catch a bus pulling out. As the bus moved between the apartment blocks of a city that had grown too fast, I fell asleep again.

I woke, much later, and could not remember what I was dreaming. I did not know where I was or where I was going. I was in a bus moving through the desert, and it seemed part of a dream itself, with no definite context, and in a few seconds the scenery could change and a curtain lift and it would be an entirely different situation. It had happened to me before, waking in strange beds, strange rooms, not knowing what country I was in. You do not in such moments agitate your mind for explanations. You feel that it is as true as anything, to be a ghost, disconnected from any idea of yourself, the vain ideas and the very ordinary ones. And in any case you know the world will come back to you soon enough.

Once I had woken like that in a strange country in a strange bed, but with my eyes closed, listening to rain hitting the window in what was surely a cool colourless dawn. And what I remembered as I lay there was coming down the stairs at night when I was a child, perhaps three years old, when I was supposed to be sleeping. Sitting on the stairs and looking through the stairway bars, through the open living-room door, at my parents watching the screen flickering silvery images in a darkened room. I suppose I did not want to be sent back to my bed, so I pretended I was invisible. Watching my parents, I imagined I did not exist. At some point my father turned his head and looked up, I don't know why, and saw me. He called me down. He told me men were walking on the moon again. Strange shapes moved across the screen. Afterwards I sat on the bottom step of the stairs and he put on my shoes. We walked around the suburban neighbourhood. The night was special. We looked at stars. This is my earliest memory of my father.

These things I remembered about myself, lying in that bed,

in a strange country after a war, listening to the rain gurgling in the gutter, before I had even remembered where I was.

And now in the bus it quickly came to me. I knew where I was and what I had been doing. But something else felt wrong and I watched gravel and rocks, country unfortunate enough to never be rained on, and I knew something bad had happened but I had forgotten what and was waiting for the details to come again to trouble me. I remembered about the monastery. And then I noticed that the sun was in the wrong place in the sky. It was mid-afternoon and it should have been on my left. But the passengers on the right side of the bus had their curtains drawn against the glare. I rubbed my eyes and tried to explain it away as the road ran obstinately east, into endless desert. It was the wrong bus, and if we were heading east this had to be the Sinai, the land of Exodus. The Israelites wandered for forty years in this place, being tested by God. It did not seem possible that they could have survived.

And Exodus was the first bad book full of lies written in the history of the world. A book written by victors after the war, about the hard road to conquering fertile land, with God on your side, and slaughtering the natives. That, and Numbers.

I got out at a police checkpoint. The police always look the same, and the army, as if recruited from the same village, the same family even. They all have little moustaches, grin if you speak to them, showing bad teeth. They are slow-moving, or seem so from standing about uselessly all day in uniforms which, if you look closely, have been patched and sewn many times. Occasionally they will ask you for cigarettes, or a little money. I stood around with these boys and when their boss in civilian clothes, who looked like he was from another village and another family, stopped a bus to demand documents, I got on. The passengers were few and listless from the heat. I sat behind the driver, a very fat man who was eating sunflower seeds. He leaned forward to spit the husks out the window to the left. It was an inaccurate business and the closed half of the window was flecked with seeds, glued there by spit and desert wind.

My new bus went well enough for a while. Then it started dying. At first it was sluggish on the hills, then it struggled so much we feared it would not make it, and were glad when it did. We managed to be glad a couple of times before the bus stopped and the driver got out. He played with the engine for several minutes, then started it up again, and it took the hill and was doing well and we were all glad again. But there were more hills and every couple of kilometres he stopped and got out with his bag of spanners and fucked about a bit, and then got back in the bus, sweating and wiping his hands on a rag, and started it up again. He had given up on the sunflower seeds; willing the bus over the next hump took all he had. We spluttered to our final halt a very long way from anywhere. Somebody said that the company had another bus coming through four hours later, that they would have to take us. The driver got back in the bus, opened the compartment where I had kept a litre of water I was saving, opened the cap with his oily hands, drank and disappeared with my bottle. Now I had no water.

We were standing outside the bus, waiting for a sign, when a minibus pulled up, four Bedouin inside. The two sitting up front looked like killers, the two in the back looked like cretins. They were going to Cairo. I grabbed my bag and jumped in with them, left the rest of the passengers standing there. The Bedouin cranked up the *habibi* music and we took off at speed. A fifth man was stretched out asleep on the back seat behind me. It was satisfying to be moving very fast across the desert in the right direction. A sign said 340k to Cairo. There was a chance that they would try to rip me off when we got there. I would manage.

We were passed by another minibus and there was some waving. The boys seemed to know each other and it was time for a game of desert chicken. We went a lot faster and tried to overtake. It was hilly and there were no very long straight stretches and the driver ahead would swerve out to cut us off, then swerve back in lane just as he judged it was too close to the curve for us to overtake, or when a truck grew big in the windscreen. The low evening sun cast a nice light, very lucid, and I could clearly see the lower half of the other driver's face in his side mirror. He had a well-trimmed moustache and good teeth and a handsome jaw and was grinning steadily at the game. I think I was the only person in either of the two buses who did not think it fun. In the village in the rocks where these men came from there was little excitement. It is a great country for camels and queers but far too dry for the rest of us. As we screeched around a curve, the bus leaning like it might flip, I thought, well, that's all it will take, a blow-out, and we cartwheel down the rocky hill. It has to happen somewhere and here is as good as anywhere, with a fool's fixed grin in the side mirror in the desert sun.

It was night in Cairo and it had slowed a little but it had not stopped, because Cairo never stops.

They would pound you into the concrete with their Welcome My Friend and all that fake cheer. The only way to stay above it was to be a step ahead.

I was for the first one. He was sitting on a car as I crossed a street diagonally and I saw him calculate my trajectory and slide off to make the interception. The car was at the junction of a street I was aiming for, so in the moment he turned his back,

stepping off the corner kerb, I veered between two parked cars
and onto the pavement behind him. He stepped into the street
to deliver his greeting but drew a blank, then wheeled round
to see me disappearing into the side street. I'd spun him, in a
two-heartbeat piece of ballet. Welcome! he called. It was the
sound of a missed cue. But he had not been that good, resting
his fat cheeks on a car, waiting for it to come to him.

The next one was sharper, younger, marching in step with
me as if by coincidence, grinning.

– Welcome in Egypt! Where from?

– China.

I had checked his face in the first instant and was now just
looking immediately ahead, to a future free of his presence.

– Hey, why you angry? Why sad?

This was something they said to make you ashamed. Of
being cold, rich, European. Of whatever it was prevented you
communicating with people who were poor but had soul.

– My dog died.

The next one was right in front of the hotel and came up
close like he owned me.

– Welcome! What you looking for?

– The truth.

I said this without irony, looking him in the eye. He backed
off.

I took the lift to the Samba Hotel. It was on the ninth floor of
a giant building near Tahrir Square. I had stayed there before.
It was cheap. A lot of tattoos and piercings among the clientele.
Backpackers, they called themselves. They all complained about
globalization, in a globalized sort of a way. New Age zeros,
their talk of spirituality a lot of lazy farting. The gas built up
and they let it go. Take away their decorations, there was not

a lot left. And they were entirely dependent on electricity.

The receptionist remembered me. He looked like he had been smoking in the toilets again. His name was Jimmy but that was not his real name. I did not know his real name. He had cousins in America and had seen a few hip-hop videos. A baseball cap, backwards, and facial hair shaved into long thin geometric lines, and a baggy sweatshirt with a picture of Donald Duck smoking a joint. He liked working there with the back-packers.

– Monastery, huh? Did you find God?

– No. I fucked a woman with a tumour in the ass.

He was holding my key. His mouth had fallen a little open.

– She had a tumour in the ass?

I looked at all the baggy clothing and Donald Duck and reached out and took the key.

The room was a box. The window was a joke because it looked onto the concrete walls of an interior courtyard, a ventilation shaft, really. The shaft carried the noise from the square. I took off my boots. My tired body begged to wind down, go slower, but the mechanical carnival outside of engines and carhorns and the whistles of the traffic police was relentless. In my nervous exhaustion, its tempo seemed to be accelerating into madness. It was the sound of a planet at war, all the time, and it was telling me my request for a decent pause, a little respite, had been rejected by the authorities. The people of the world were en-casing themselves in metal and hurtling against each other, screaming, laughing, making it through, being replaced by others. Occasionally you did not make it through, and they had special machines to cut you out, and they lifted your squashed vehicle onto a flatbed truck, swept up and carried on.

And then it was the last song of the evening, the loudspeakers from the mosques fighting above the rest of the noise of the world, a crackling brokendown song of praise to faraway God. Holy words in a polluted sky. God most great. God that is One. Over the hill where the grass is green.

I had beside my bed a bottle with a plain orange and white label. I unscrewed the raspy cap and took a pull of aniseed heat and set it back on the bedside table, the good clunky weight of the almost full bottle. I picked up my battered Bible which had lost its covers in the land of Exodus and opened to the words of the King of Jerusalem, the words I was always coming back to, which my own words are footnotes to, of the transient melody of our striving:

It is good to be able to enjoy the pleasant light of day. Be grateful for every year that you live. No matter how long you live, remember that you will be dead much longer. There is nothing at all to look forward to.

Young people, enjoy your youth. Be happy while you are still young. Do what you want to do, and follow your heart's desire . . .

We are going to our final resting place, and then there will be mourning in the streets. The silver chain will snap, and the golden lamp will fall and break; the rope at the well will break, and the water jar will be shattered. Our bodies will return to the dust of the earth, and the breath of life will go back to God, who gave it to us . . .

I took another hit of the bottle. I knew those words before I read them, and their formulation was beautiful and I enjoyed reading them, and drinking, with my boots off and my feet up and the city back a little. I took from my pocket the cross that Shishoy had given me, and thought of Nadine telling me I should put something down for the salvation of the human race; as if the nailed-up Jew had not already done the ultimate acrobatics.

The lights went out. It must have happened in the entire hotel, because I could hear a commotion in the hallway. With my only window facing the narrow shaft, I did not even have the light from the city, or the moon, if there was a moon. I waited for my eyes to adjust but the darkness was total and I lay there with my Bible in my lap, a crucifix in my left hand, staring at nothing, listening to the traffic in the distance. There was no point moving. The problem would be resolved in due course. I extended my fingers and probed the blackness to the right of my bed, seeking the bottle. I would do it correctly. It would be foolish for a man with time on his hands to overturn his objective through too much desire.

I located it and drank and set it back down where it would be at hand.

This is fine, I thought. There is nothing I need right now and I am as well in the dark as with the light on. I am as well here as anywhere else.

When the light came back on it happened too fast. The fluorescent tube showed only imperfections – a boxy room with no view, stains on the walls, grey net curtains – and I had to think again about what to do next.

High Country

A huddle of three stocky women gripping bags and packages were pressing through the crowd and he stood aside to let them pass. Their nervous constricted steps recalled for him cattle on the brink of panic. A bus engine shuddered and seconds later he tasted diesel smoke. He eased the rucksack from his back, set it against the wall and drew from it a tattered book of maps. He checked from the map to the bus windshields, looking for a destination.

He chose a bus and bought a ticket from the driver. It was almost empty. He took a seat towards the back. Somebody had put their face against the window, leaving a mess of grease on the glass. He wiped it clean with his sleeve so he could see out clearly.

The bus struggled out of the station and into the streets of the provincial city and he was glad to be moving, glad he would soon be in open country. But first there was the choking evening traffic. Halts were made for shop and factory workers. They filed aboard and slumped into their seats and most said nothing. A small group, among the men, were voluble in their hour of release. He did not understand what was being discussed but he was not curious. He was sure he had heard it before.

A man took the seat next to him. He wore a clean white shirt but his trousers were filthy. The dirt was deep in the fibres. But perhaps the strong stale smell came also from his skin. He had seen the man advancing down the aisle, and had been wondering what it was that he found unattractive in his face. He realized too late just what it was; he was the kind who sat next to you if you made eye contact.

The aisle was now packed with people and the man invited someone there to share his place. He insisted. He would not take refusal. So the three of them crammed into the two seats.

Pressed against the window by the bad-smelling man, he looked out at advertising hoardings and construction sites and neglected fields – a landscape that was neither city nor country. A young man in the seat in front of him – baseball cap, gold chain – began to play a tune on his mobile phone, holding it aloft to hear it better over the music from the bus speakers. He was exercising his democratic right. The digital age belonged to everybody. You did not have to be clever or educated or rich or beautiful to participate. You just had to remember to recharge the battery.

They had left the city now and were approaching an outlying town. These were the first obstacles to overcome in getting to the high country. To clear the cities and towns of the plain, to leave behind their clutter and failure.

The bus emptied out as they passed through a string of villages and then the seat next to him was free and he relaxed as the narrow road curved with the valley of a fast-flowing river, climbing through wooded hills. The houses and fields were scattered now, appearing only where the terrain permitted. The banks of the river rose abrupt and rocky. Finally, treeless swathes of open country stretching under a vast sky.

The bus slowed and stopped. He was one of three remaining passengers. The engine went dead.

It was strange, in those first moments, to listen to silence.

He was stiff and lazy after the journey. He stepped down from the bus, his heavy boots crunching gravel. He dragged his rucksack from the compartment beneath the bus and stood still for a moment in the sounds of the late evening. He heard invisible things in the distance. A river was flowing somewhere, past the trees. He hoisted the rucksack onto his shoulders. A couple of hours of daylight remained.

Outside a village shop, two men sat drinking bottles of beer. He approached them and said good evening and asked about a place to sleep. They shook their heads. The village received no visitors, said the elder of the two. He opened his mouth to speak again and then closed it as a truck loaded with timber passed by. The noise of the truck receded and the cloud of dust drifted and slowly dispersed. The man resumed speaking. The nearest *cabana*, he said, was far away, in the next valley. And anyway, it was probably abandoned.

He walked uphill, past houses set back from the road behind high wooden fences. He crossed a river bridge, seeing that the small dirt road on the far bank curved up into wooded country, where perhaps there would be a good place to camp. Two village women were crossing the bridge towards him and they nodded in response to his greeting but did not look at him. He passed more houses hidden behind high gates and fences. A dog came out onto the roadway, snarling.

After several minutes he turned back. He felt like a trespasser. Camping near the village felt wrong. He had tried to overcome the feeling but could not. If you had to sleep in the vicinity of people, the best thing was to present yourself, to be accepted among them and pay money.

He again approached villagers and asked if anybody took guests, and each time they looked at him and shook their heads. The sun dipped behind the hill. The sky was deep blue and darkening. He went to the shop. The shopkeeper, a fat slow man, stood behind the counter. At a table was a smartly dressed man with a neat moustache, drinking wine.

He bought a can of beer and sat down. He was thirsty and enjoyed the cold beer going down his throat. He told them he was going to the high country, and named the peak. The shopkeeper and the customer agreed that he had very far to walk. He asked again about a place to sleep. The drinker told him of the woman in the house next to the police station.

He finished his beer and left his pack in the shop and walked uphill and found her, across the road from her house, at the door of her woodshed. She shook her head. There had been one time, friends of her nephew, that was all. There was no room. She had nowhere to put him. She was emphatic about this.

He went back to the shop and hoisted the rucksack onto his shoulders. The customer asked where he was going, told him to sit down. He paused in the doorway, thinking the man had something to add. But nothing followed. The man was just drunk.

He walked back down the valley. From the bus he had noted a guest house in a village below. Perhaps an hour of walking, perhaps three. It was hard to estimate. But it was downhill and he was moving purposefully. He would sleep in a bed and rise early, the day before him.

It was a good feeling, knowing that, and he did not mind the walking. All this, beforehand, with the people, was a test. To reach where he wanted to be, many tiny tasks needed to be resolved, one by one. He had been doing it since morning, all in order to end the day in a place where he knew nobody and had to trust in luck. Just things to be done, meaningless in themselves, like the tasks of daily life. What mattered was the reason you performed these tasks. If you did not have a purpose you lost yourself in the detail of daily existence. Got buried by it. Life was not flesh and bone, but the spirit that moved it.

If you judged the journey by setting the stretches of trouble and discomfort against those times when you could state you were happy, it would not make sense to have done any of it. But the journey could not be understood that way, any more than life could. It was not like placing two comparable things upon a scales and weighing one against the other. Getting to the high country was not something that could be done quickly or carelessly. The time patiently taken was what you offered up, trusting that the moment would come.

He woke in grey dawn in the musty room.

The night before he had tried to watch the television but the sound and image were too distorted so, to do something, he had gone out to drink a beer. The bar was a shop with a few tables. The men at the other tables took turns exclaiming at each other. Their conversation had this single register. By day they shouted over the noise of machines; in the evenings they drank and shouted above the noise of the television. They felled and transported timber and worked the sawmills. Their talk was of trucks and machinery. Workdays of diesel and grease and old motors that broke and had to be fixed. Their hands were always on machines. Each day they wrestled timber down from the hills, fighting to get it done before darkness fell.

Several times in the night he had woken to the roar of trucks passing on the road.

He rose and used the bathroom off the hall. It was cramped and cold. Then he went back to his room and assembled his belongings and clicked shut the clasps on the rucksack and hoisted it onto his shoulders and was glad to go down the steps and walk away. A place where timber workers fell into beds when too drunk to get home.

The sun had risen. It looked to be a good day. He cast a long shadow ahead on the morning road.

In two hours he had reached the village where the bus had left him the day before. The sun was warm now. He had a good rhythm and was moving strongly uphill into new country. He knew what had to be done next. A little further upstream there would be a right turn for a road or track that would take him over the rise and into the next valley.

At the turn, he met a boy on a young horse, riding bareback. For a time they kept pace together on the steep track while they talked, then he pulled ahead of the boy and the horse. After twenty minutes he had slackened enough that the horse, with its languid but steady pace, drew level again for a while. By the time he reached the crest of the hill, where there was a scatter of houses along the track, he was trailing the horse. After the houses, the road broke into two smaller tracks through the woods. He did not know which track was better but it mattered little; it was the watershed of the two valleys and all he had to do was to descend into the new valley. When he reached the river he would follow it upstream.

Further on, from a clearing, the new valley came into view below, broad and inviting in the bright sunlight, the river broken into silver veins threading through a wide stony floodplain.

He descended the wooded hillside. From the houses on the lower slopes came music from a radio and the voices of people he could not see. He felt furtive, as always, slipping invisibly through such places. He followed well-worn pathways down to the river. In the distance, on the other side, a car moved along the roadway, the sun reflecting on its rooftop, the small sound carrying clearly across the open space. Then the car disappeared among trees and the sound changed.

He was eager to be across the river and travelling up the new valley, making progress towards the high country. He had wasted time among the villages and wanted to put them behind him, and if he walked well there would be enough daylight to find a good place to camp. He would pitch the tent and gather wood for a fire and when the fire was burning he would eat. He would wake very early the next morning and be within a day of the peak. He would get above the tree line and look back and all the country he had walked would be stretched out below. Reaching the peak next day was possible, but in unfamiliar country you could not be sure. It was not a very high or well-known peak and no detailed map was available. Crossing rivers was a difficulty in unvisited places. Where there were no tracks you had to struggle through undergrowth and brambles, consulting a compass. And then there was the descent on the far side of the peak, through more unknown terrain.

The sun was high as he walked upstream, over the baked stones of the bright riverbed. He crossed the rough log bridges that spanned the wider streams. Coming up from the riverbed to the wide level stretch of good land on the other side was like entering another country. Here people could work the soil. He liked this valley. He liked the spaciousness, after the cramped feeling of the previous valley. He walked slowly through the silent deserted fields and came to a broad gravel roadway.

After nearly an hour the road brought him to a village. He walked straight on through. The sun was at its height and he wanted to rest in the shade of the forest. But the village stretched into another long straggling village and he had to persevere through the intense dizzying heat. The houses were smaller and scattered further apart along the roadside, and all around was the evidence of the hauling and the working of wood – sawmills, tractors, trucks, piles of logs and stacks of processed timber.

Trucks and horse-drawn carts passed him in both directions; empty going upriver, loaded on the return.

He crossed the river again and finally left behind the inhabited part of the valley. Now he could rest. He walked into the forest, out of sight of anyone passing on the road. He drank water and ate. Then he lay back and closed his eyes and listened to the insects and let his thoughts drift.

When it was time to move again, the sun was still high and very hot. He felt lazy. His legs were stiff as he stood up. He pulled his map from the rucksack to assess his progress.

He was on a forestry road. The map showed it pointing straight towards the peak. For the rest of the day the walking would be simple. All he had to do was follow that dirt road, along the river.

He had not been walking long when two boys with a horse and cart invited him to climb on. The cart was a metal frame for transporting logs. He stood on the bar above the rear axle, bending his knees to absorb the jolts and gripping the frame tightly to keep from being shaken off as they hurried downhill on the bumpy road. On the uphill he would jump off and walk briskly, keeping pace with the horse, climbing back on for the level stretches. He covered several kilometres quickly this way, but it was hard work. Then the boys took a side track into the woods, and he was glad to be walking again.

The sun had passed its peak by several hours but it was still hot. He walked heavily now and sometimes stumbled. He flagged down the timber truck on impulse, the moment he observed that the driver was alone. He opened the door, shouting his thanks above the noise of the engine. He threw his rucksack up and the driver leaned over and hauled it in. The driver was a thin young man, hardly out of his teens, naked to the waist and dark skinned. The heavy truck roared with effort and the driver steered vigorously to take the gentlest route on the jolting cratered road and the gears rasped and shuddered when he switched and his body rocked and swayed in the bouncing seat as he gripped the wheel and worked the pedals. It was thrilling, such noise and motion, sitting high in the air with the forest rushing past, and he shouted above the noise to speak to the driver, and the driver said yes, there was a *cabana* on the road, and when they reached that point he pulled over and pointed out the track through the woods.

He clambered down from the cab and the truck drove off. It was fortunate that the driver had shown him the track. He would have walked past and noticed nothing. It was sudden good luck. He would sleep at the *cabana* and need not worry about the weather turning bad. He would not have to pitch the tent or strike camp in the morning. There would be cooked food and perhaps beer to buy and running water for washing. The simple things he had forsworn that were now great pleasures.

A solid two-storey house appeared through the woods, growing larger as he approached, but with every step it became more evident that it was unoccupied. He unlatched the gate and entered the enclosure, watching and listening for any sign of life. It was not completely abandoned; the windows were intact and clean and the grass in front of the house had been cut. Only behind the house had the weeds been allowed to flourish.

He eased his rucksack down upon the grass. He had noted the heavy clouds gathering over the hills to the north, changing the smell and the feel of the air. It would be several hours before any rain came, and perhaps it would pass over entirely, but he was tired and it was fortunate he had found this bright clearing in the forest. On one side of the grassy area in front of the house was a raised wooden deck with a timber frame that supported a roof. Inside were wooden benches and a wooden picnic table. It would be better shelter than a tent in heavy rain.

He tried the front door. It was locked. Then he circled the house, assessing his new territory. An old barn and outhouses stood at a small distance from the house and he explored these next. Refuse had been dumped in the barn on top of the remains of some hay. It was dirty and no good as a place to sleep. Behind the barn, nettles flourished and the grass was long. He then walked the inside of the perimeter fence. The enclosed area, about half a hectare, was thinly wooded compared to the dense forest beyond.

There could no longer be any doubt about the weather. The clouds were thick and black. They were the kind that moved in a dense bank with well-defined edges and when they got close you would see their surfaces boiling. He could only hope it would pass quickly.

He opened his rucksack and took out his water bottle, a bar of soap wrapped in paper and a clean t-shirt. He drank what was left of the water. He went through the gate, down through the wood, across the forestry road and down a logging track towards the river.

At a section of the river where the water ran swiftly and cleanly over rocks he dipped the water bottle in the current. The water was cloudy and pale. He waited until it settled, then drank. It tasted different from the water he had been drinking before. He took off his t-shirt, still damp from the walking, and crouched over the stream and splashed the cold water on his body and soaped his neck and shoulders and arms and under his arms, then rinsed himself off. He washed his face and, leaning over, poured water from the bottle over his head and rubbed the cold water into his hot scalp. He stayed there a moment by the river, looking at it, dripping with the clean water as the sun glinted brightly on the moving stream and on the trees of the hillside on the far bank. There was only the sound of the birds and the moving water. Then he was nearly dry, the water dripping from his hair, and he put on the clean t-shirt. He refilled the water bottle. He had time to do this while the sun lasted. To the north, the clouds had grown higher and thicker. Soon they would block out the sun.

He walked quickly back to the house. He sat at the wooden table and opened his book of maps. It was a very old book. The scale was poor and the information unreliable. But it indicated peaks and rivers and roads and villages, and it was all he had. It showed the *cabana* and the forking of the road a little further on, where he needed to cross the river and veer towards the high country. He had a good chance of reaching it next day, leaving behind the forestry roads and the trucks and the people. The peak would come into sight and that would guide him. The turn in the road could not be far and it was necessary that he confirm his location, and not suffer doubt until the morning. That way he would have the satisfaction of knowing he was on the right path when he fell asleep and when he woke. He was hungry, but that could wait.

He went down again to the logging road, walking fast, to get it done before the rain came. Walking without the pack he felt very light and agile. Choosing his footfalls, he danced the uneven road, almost running.

After ten minutes the road forked. There was a bridge and the left fork crossed the river and veered into the hills. That was his road. He regarded it with satisfaction. He then heard the first thunder to the north, a cracking followed by a long dull rumbling. He turned back towards the *cabana*. The air had darkened and he hoped it would hold off a little longer. Then

big raindrops were striking the dust and leaping with it, painting dark splashes on the pale road, hitting it with rising intensity,
and the thrum of the raindrops on the leaves became a loud
undifferentiated hum and then a roar. He ran through the warm
rain to the *cabana*.

He sat in the shelter, panting, and the rain fell.

He took out his food and laid it out on the wooden table.
He had salt pork fat and cheese and a loaf of bread and some
onions and a small container of salt. He ate very simply when
he was walking. On the first day he would finish any fruit or
tomatoes, then he would move on to the cheese and meat. By
the third day he might eat only dry bread and onion sprinkled
with salt. It was enough.

He cut the bread in thick slices and made a sandwich of fat
and cheese and onion. The bread was dry but he was very
hungry and he swallowed the first bite quickly. Then he chewed
more slowly, enjoying the food and watching the rain. It continued falling heavily. The road would be turning to mud.

Of course, it could continue into the next day. If it rained
hard and persistently he could try to sit it out, but at a certain
point he might have to return in the direction he had come,
through the rain. He accepted that. Many times it ended with
a final day of walking through rain. He watched the rain, and
ate, recalling other journeys.

He remembered one long and difficult day, when he had no
desire for anything but to be apart from people. He had taken
the cheapest, slowest kind of train and pulling out of one village
it had braked to a halt and a woman screamed the name of her
boy and for a few minutes it seemed a child had been killed.
The passengers crowded around the windows and a boy was
carried away and the tension passed. Whatever had happened,

nobody had died, and the passengers took their seats again and the train moved on to its destination, a provincial town where the wind lashed dust in your face. At a traffic roundabout on the outskirts, he hitched a lift. A van stopped and the driver was friendly but only talked about how he could not earn enough money. Nobody ever could earn enough and the things that were free were not worth discussing. Then he was walking again, through a village that stretched for kilometres along a road to the mountains, now set starkly against the sky. Evening was coming on and the *cabana* was far away. He hailed a taxi returning through the village, back towards the town, and negotiated a price with the driver, a young man who paid attention to his clothes and had a little pouch attached to his belt for his mobile phone. The ridge of mountains grew bigger and darker on their left as they drove towards the *cabana* and he asked the driver if he had ever walked them. The driver laughed at the idea, and when they arrived at the *cabana* he demanded much more money than had been agreed. He told the driver to go to hell. A fine misting rain was now falling and he walked through the rain and into the forest. He sat in the forest and after a few minutes he heard the taxi drive away. The *cabana* was locked up. When the rain passed, he pitched his tent on the wet grass but was unable to make a fire.

Having finally achieved solitude, he felt a terrible desolation. He had been in that place a year before, happy, with other people. Now he was regretful of his life. He thought about a quarrel with a friend that was unhealed. He thought also of the girl he had left in the city, and how difficult it was, being together. He lay on his side, tired, looking out the end of the tent at the light passing from the sky. In the morning he woke shivering and when the sun crested the hill its warmth was kept from him by a single wisp of cloud curling like smoke and he begged it aloud to move away and for the sun to warm him. The sun answered his prayer then and burned off the cloud. As the morning warmed he climbed through the woods and past the tree line and within a couple of hours was walking the crest, the whole country laid out around him. The sun hit the steep western face of Piatra Craiului in the distance and the bright rock gleamed white as ice.

There were other times too. The time he chose the stretch of country not because it had a high peak but because the map showed it as roadless and desolate. He discovered a forgotten world of thickly forested hills that rose and fell abruptly, cut with steep valleys and laced with the remains of railroads left from when they had tried to exploit the timber. The experiment had failed. The narrow valleys flooded each spring and many of the bridges had been swept away. He travelled by the sun on the first day and the peak he had wanted came into view. On the second day mist descended. He had failed to bring a compass and when the sun appeared briefly at midday he knew he had veered off course. The sun disappeared again and without it he was lost. He descended to a river and followed it downstream. You were never really lost when you had a river. It would always return you to the world. Not until the next evening did he reach a populated area. He had gone for most of three days without seeing a sign of human life – not a house or a field or a domestic animal. Then it began to rain. It rained on him for hours until his boots were soaked and he walked then through puddles, because it no longer made any difference. It was nearly dark when the rain stopped but he had reached a paved road and got a series of lucky lifts that took him to a town. And there was the usual walk through the dreary town – they were always dreary in much the same way – to a railway station. He took a night train, sleeping in a seat, and got into the city at dawn, his boots still wet, unable to say where he had been, because the name of the place meant nothing to anybody.

The rain had been falling heavily for some time and was coursing across the ground in streams and rivulets. He wished he had gathered some dry kindling when he had arrived first. It was good to have a fire, to watch the flames as night came on, feeding them until you were too sleepy to tend them any longer. And as well as the light and the heat the fire was beautiful. It was alive and it was something you could watch. When there was no fire you could do nothing but watch the sky. You watched it darken. You watched the light ebb from the world. In the end you watched the part of the sky that had the most light left in it. The fire gave you something to do. You were not at the mercy of the sky. You still had power when you had a fire. The light could not be taken away from you completely. A fire burning at night was a spark of the sun. Without a fire you were a child again, fearing the dark. You remembered fear and your own thoughts became your enemy. They became your enemy not only because you imagined wild animals and magnified sounds in the forest. They became your enemy because you were finally afraid of nothingness. You were alone with yourself and you knew again the truth about yourself, that you were a coward. That you lied to yourself and the rest of the world every moment that you lived and spoke and whenever you looked in the eyes of someone else and gave them something to look back at. And now you had nothing to do except watch the part of the sky that still had some light in it. There were no buttons to press to make noise, nothing to distract you. You became conscious of time. That this state would endure for many long hours. You lay there wishing that the night was over, the light returning. You loved the light of day. This was it, this was how the world understood good and evil, life and death, from this simple turning of the planet. From the light being given and taken away. Your power counted for nothing in it. It was written already and you did not matter.

The rain fell in the darkening air and he pushed back the table and benches to make an open space and he laid out his sleeping bag on the boards and bunched together clothes to make a pillow. He was lucky not to be on the hillside, struggling to keep dry. And still, he was uneasy now that there was nothing to do but await the morning.

For two days he had striven forward, preoccupied from moment to moment with the next step to be taken on the road before him, and now finally he was alone with himself. Immobile, without even the comfort of satisfying the restless desire to be doing, to be moving always ahead, the question came to him, inevitably. About why. Why he was doing it.

It was useless, finally. He had been driving himself on uselessly. He had worked himself into a sweat, exhausted his muscles, all to find himself anxious and alone and self-doubting as he gazed at that part of the sky which still held most light.

The rain eased off finally and the wooded hills became visible in the weakening light. The general grey became again clouds that showed the movement of the air as they rolled thickly in from the north. Paler clouds appeared against the general dark mass. He watched this motion, attracted always to the brightness. There was nothing else to do.

The rain stopped. Slowly, very slowly, it became night. The clouds sealed the sky. It was completely black.

He lay on his back, attentive, staring out for something. But the sky was smothered.

From the forest came sounds. Rustlings and creaking. He lay in his sleeping bag and it was warm in the night.

He imagined the world turning.

He imagined the part he lay upon turning away to the blackness of space, away from the warmth of the sun.

It was summer and so the night would be shorter than the day.

He calculated that the night would be only eight hours long. Less if you included the hours of twilight. He wished for unconsciousness to take him away, to deliver him to morning.

He awoke. He saw the stars. The sky was no longer nothing. It was speaking to him.

His eyes fell closed.

That's good, he thought. The clouds have passed.

He walked with her on the ramparts of the castle under the sky at night. He looked over the walls, down at his chances of escaping the castle. There were none. The walls were high, the countryside beyond lost in darkness. The verdict they had delivered was final. It would never be day again for him. He pitied himself terribly and wanted to embrace her, and to weep. But she did not seem to understand. She was happy to be strolling with him, her arm linked in his. She tilted her head skywards, squeezing his arm and leaning into his body.

Look at the stars! she exclaimed.

He looked up and opened his eyes.

He blinked in the daylight.

He was lying on his back. A weight laid on his chest had just been removed, and his ribcage shuddered with the slow inhalation. Each of the breaths that followed were like this, the tide rushing across a wide beach, trembling at fullness for a moment, ebbing across an expanse of sandflats, leaving them naked to the sky. Then the water rushing in again.

He sat up slowly and looked around.

The sunlight was hitting the front of the abandoned house and the tops of the trees and a patch of glistening wet grass.

I'll take my time, he thought, get a fire going, have some coffee.

He got out of the sleeping bag and stood up. He moved very slowly, looking all around. He put on his trousers and t-shirt. From the rucksack he removed a jar in which the ground coffee and the sugar were already mixed. He would boil it together in a little pot he had. The sugar would dissolve and the grounds would sink to the bottom while it cooled and he would drink straight from the pot.

He put on his boots and laced them up. There was no rush about anything. He took from the rucksack a plastic bag containing old newspaper. He would use it to dry out some damp kindling and get a fire going. First he would take a walk down to the river and wash his face, wash the sleep from his eyes. Then he would walk back and make the fire. He would sit around for a while and enjoy the fire he had missed the night before. It would be a good cup of coffee. He could afford to sit around for a while, feeling lucky. He thought about her, down in the city. It was very early and even the birds sounded astonished how early it was. The sun was coming through the trees, lighting grass freshly washed by rain. He would drink the coffee, slowly, tasting it. And then he had the day ahead of him, to reach the high country. But it did not matter any more. At this point he knew he could turn back, descend the forestry road towards the villages, towards the city, and be satisfied.

He picked up the water bottle and began walking towards the river. The ground was soft and damp and depressions in the forestry road were pools of water, and water filled the ruts worn by the wheels of heavy vehicles along the logging track that went down to the river. He had to choose his steps in the sodden earth.

At the riverside his view opened out. He stood for a moment on the stony bank, looking downstream, where the sun had crested the low hill and was shining up the river valley, glinting on the water and catching the leaves of the trees around him. Upstream, the folds of the earth were textured in light and shade and the depressions between the hills were pale with mist.

At the river's edge, he knelt at a flat rock where the water was deeper than in other places and he could see the clean stones on the riverbed. He filled the water bottle. Then, still kneeling, he leaned forward and put his left arm into the river until his hand touched the stones on the bottom. The cold water came to above his elbow. Dipping his other hand in the water, he slowly washed his eyes, rinsing each one several times. Then, with both arms in the water, to support himself as he leaned forward, he touched his mouth to the water and drank.

He paused a moment after drinking, his face above the water, and then he closed his eyes and put his face in the river. He lowered his head under the water and stayed like that in the quiet and darkness, feeling the water flowing about him.

He raised himself out of the water and gasped, beads of light falling from his head.

Straightening, he withdrew his arms from the water. He remained kneeling at the edge of the river, water dripping from him, feeling the gentle warmth of the sun on the side of his face. He tilted his head slowly to one side and then the other to unblock his ears. The sound of flowing water and birdsong came to him clearly again.